Gift of the Bambino

Gift of the Bambino

Jerry Amernic

Thomas Dunne Books ✺ New York
St. Martin's Press

For my father

THOMAS DUNNE BOOKS.
An imprint of St. Martin's Press.

www.stmartins.com

Library of Congress Cataloging-in-Publication Data

Amernic, Jerry
    Gift of the bambino / Jerry Amernic.—1st U.S. ed.
    p. cm.
    ISBN 0-312-31759-X
    1, Grandparent and child—Fiction. 2. Ruth, Babe, 1895-1948—Influence—Fiction. 3.
Baseball players—Fiction. 4. Baseball fans—Fiction. 5. Grandfathers—Fiction. I. Title.

PR9199.4.M47G54 2004
813'.6—dc22

                                                                                    2003058790

First published in Canada by Boheme Press

First U.S. Edition: April 2004

10 9 8 7 6 5 4 3 2 1

Prologue

A hundred years from now it will not matter what my bank account was, the sort of house I lived in, or the kind of car I drove. But the world may be different because I was important in the life of a boy.
— Forest Witcraft, Boy Scouts of America

It all began with the ball. And Grandpa. That ball is the stuff of miracles. With it you can hold a dream right in your hands and its magic is so great that it knows not only where you've been, but what you want to be. It's the thread that weaves myth to reality. So much of Grandpa was in it that he was incomplete without it. It was a piece of him that tied his heart to his soul and now it's a piece of me too. Maybe it's in all of us.

It was more than a baseball. Much more. Sure, it started out that way, but it was more like a time capsule with incredible powers that transcend days, months, and years. Its powers transcend all time and space and it was just sitting there waiting for the right person to come along and fetch it. Exactly how far it traveled no one really knows, but four hundred feet is a pretty good estimate. Maybe it went even farther. Unfortunately, no accurate record of the distance exists, but by all accounts it was a blast of gargantuan proportions.

We know it landed in the lake, or in the bay rather. It was

1914, just when the Great War was breaking out and it had been sitting there on the bottom for more than three-quarters of a century. What ravages water wreaks on a baseball over that length of time I didn't know. The only thing I knew was that it was there – all that time. Waiting.

It happened so long ago that things were a lot different than now. The shoreline wasn't the same. The islands at the foot of the city weren't nearly as large as today and the game, of course, was better. It was more honest back then. They played for the sheer love of it. They played for the feel of the bat, for the sudden smack when contact is made and for the sight of the ball sailing through the sky. They played for the smell in the air.

It was almost too late for me when I found out about the ball. If only he had told me earlier, I would have known that dreams can exist with reality. He should have told me right at the beginning. When I was a child. I wouldn't have understood how important it was to him or how it could direct the course of a man's life, but at least I would have known about the potency of its powers.

I guess I was always destined to retrieve it. It had to be destiny. But still, who could have known after all those years? A lifetime. He had never mentioned it to me and it was almost by accident that I even found out in the first place. Time didn't matter for that baseball. It just didn't. What is a mere three-quarters of a century in the greater scheme of things?

"If you find that ball you can be anything you want to be," he told me. "It has a magnetism and it's reaching out to you. You must find it. You have to find it."

If anyone else had told me such a story I would have thought he was crazy, but it was Grandpa who was telling me, my Grandpa, and because it was him I believed. Because it was him I had faith. Now there isn't a day that goes by when I don't think about him. And the baseball. They serve as my crutch. They give me hope and the will to do what I want to do. They allow me to dream and that's important because without dreams we are nothing.

I think about them whenever I'm faced with a new obstacle. I think about them when I venture to that special place where we used to go, gaze over the water and see nothing but the horizon joining sea and sky and going off in both directions forever.

I can see them so clearly now.

And it's all because of a baseball. A simple sphere of cork, stitching, and skin. But it isn't of this earth. It is something celestial that belongs in the heavens with the stars, planets, and myriad unknowns that make us gnaw away at our brains in the search for discovery. Maybe it's known to God.

I'm thankful he explained its strength when there was still time to do something about it and savor even a morsel of its infinite capacity for making fantasy come alive. Because of the bond between Grandpa and that ball, I have come to learn the true meaning and essence of life; not only his life, but anyone's. Anyone who believes, that is.

He had never told a soul about it. All those years he hid it from me just as he hid it from everyone – his parents, his wife, his children, even his teammates when he played the game himself. No one ever knew. No one. Only Grandpa, me and *him,* of course. The big guy. Just the three of us. It was our little secret.

One

When I was a boy Grandpa took me for long walks where the sparkling glass waters of the lake meet the sharp edges of the cliffs that tower over the shoreline, but it wasn't just any shoreline. It was a place, a special place, where time, all time, comes together. It was where the mastodons walked and where primordial creatures of ages long past once inhabited a much simpler world, dwelling in the great seas that were many times larger than today. This was where history was made. These were the glacial beds where the past five hundred million years had slept. How much life and death has transpired in that time.

But what did I know of life and death? Life was breathing the fresh scent of the morning air that hung in mists over the pavement of my street and relishing the vibrant colors of fall when the trees relieved themselves of another season. It was going for a long walk in the cold of winter, the beautifully carved snowflakes dropping on my eyelashes, the howling wind rolling off my face, my boots sinking into the immaculate virgin whiteness until they disappeared and all that were left were my knees. That was life and it made my senses come alive.

But death? I knew less of death. I was only a boy and "dead" was a concept – not even a concept, it was a thing – that was just

there and it wasn't deep, but shallow, without substance or reason. It happened to an ant when you stepped on it in the driveway. It was dead. Crushed. It happened to a spider when you
grabbed it off the bathroom wall and squeezed it into a Kleenex.
"Dead" even happened to birds who would mistake the reflection in our living room window for a wide open space. I had a
problem when I saw them lying still until someone explained it
as an unfortunate accident due to clear skies.

I was six the first time he took me there and I remember it
vividly. My mother and father were at work and the sitter was
sick, so no one came to get me at school. I waited and waited
and then he showed up. I had a key just in case. It was a
symbol of freedom and responsibility that sat in the bottom of
my pocket, tucked into a corner where only fingertips dared ex-
plore the dark world of bubble gum packages and elastic bands.
It was a sizzling summer day and the key was attached to a thick
wad of partially melted gum, probably Juicy Fruit, the wrapper
immersed in a sticky ball of rubberized sugar.

Luckily, the key wasn't needed that day because of Grandpa.
He was the most exceptional man on earth, not at all like my
parents, and for years I wondered how my own father – his son –
came from the same stock. Their shared bloodlines must have
been an accident much like the birds striking the window. They
were so different, but Grandpa was different from everyone.

I thought he was God. He wasn't as busy as everybody else.
He had time. Loads of it. Especially for me.

His jowls had enough lines, craters, and cracks worthy of
some great historical record. Back in those days I figured he was
as old as those clay and sand deposits he was always telling me
about. He had a long forehead with three or four deep lines
running across. His hair had begun to whiten, especially around
the temples, and though it wasn't thick it wasn't thin either. Suffice to say that if his hairline was receding it wasn't noticeable.
His nose was more than ample and a little off center and I attributed its lack of symmetry to the elements, to the same wind and

water erosion that was busy carving those geological monuments down by the lake.

I thought if the earth's landforms could change because of the elements, why not people? But those deposits were more than half a *billion* years old – that's what he said – and since he was also very old – the oldest person I knew – there was no reason to exempt him from the ravages of time that were forever wearing away at the two-hundred-foot-high cliffs called the Bluffs. His ears were oversized to be sure, but I respected these organs immensely because he once said that the larger your ears are, the better you hear. Grandpa, I figured, could hear a butterfly alighting on a leaf a mile away. But it was his eyes I loved the most. They weren't big – which naturally posed the question as to how well he could see – but they ran a deep blue, the bluest eyes I have ever known.

After he met me at school we went for a walk that was only two or three blocks, but it seemed like an eternity and then when I first laid eyes on the Bluffs I thought we had reached the end of the world or maybe touched the fringes of another one. I thought this must be heaven, whatever that was. My grandmother talked about heaven all the time and it seemed a nice enough place, so I asked him. He pondered the question for the longest time. I could tell because he bit his lower lip the way he always did when in deep thought and scratched his chin that was rough with white stubble, the kind of stubble I figured only God could grow.

"You know, Stephen," he said in the methodical manner that was his way, "heaven must be a peaceful place with water, trees, fresh air . . . a place like this. So maybe this is heaven."

Grandpa taught me a lot and he did it without wasting words or cramming too many of them into a single sentence. Words were a precious commodity to him and he didn't use them lightly. Sometimes he didn't talk much at all, but everything he said mattered – at least to me – and when he pointed off in the distance and described the advances and retreats of the great glaciers, I listened. The story was hard to believe, but how I wanted to believe.

Grandpa understood children. With him, everything was real so there was never any room for "pretend" in my world. It was like those frightening creatures from the old horror movies. They were "pretend" like a hole in the head. Little black bats that got stuck in your hair in the dark of castle stairwells just when Bela Lugosi was staring you down or the giant Godzilla stepping on tanks and infantry of the United States Third Army looked pretty real to me and they were, but if someone said they were just "pretend" that would ruin it. What an awful word it was. It destroyed dreams and terminated all those delicious nightmares.

This special place he always took me to was a land of dreams and fantasy too, but it *was* real. The way Grandpa told it, giant glaciers encompassing miles and miles of ice were constantly moving and carving great formations in the rock and when the climate got warm enough, which happened every hundred million years or so, they would melt and leave fossils behind. We weren't talking tens, hundreds, or even thousands of years, but hundreds of millions of years for this to happen and I couldn't begin to think how many zeros were in a number like that.

It was fantasy and that made it fun, but Grandpa said it happened and it was still happening. He told me to stare at a solitary pebble lying on the sand near the water. But we were two hundred feet high and I couldn't make out a pebble down below on the beach so he said to imagine a pebble there and I did, but it was a big pebble, a huge pebble, so huge it shouldn't have been called a pebble at all, but a boulder. He said to imagine that a great wave rolled in and washed that little pebble – he didn't know how large the pebble had grown – out to sea. Then another wave came in and took another pebble and soon there were no more pebbles on the beach at all. That allowed the next waves to roll in closer to the base of the cliffs and gradually wear them away. A few inches a year.

It was hard to think of a few inches a year. I couldn't place a year along the edge of a ruler and determine where it began and ended, but I knew it was a long time. But something happening at the rate of a few inches a day, never mind a year, was hard to fathom. Even a turtle moved faster than that and he talked about turtles, giant sea turtles with shells five feet across that lived in this very spot a long time ago. Soon it became clear he was talking about a phenomenon that was older than he was, and since he was the measuring stick by which I regarded all time, I was impressed.

Grandpa often got carried away when discussing the ages. He was immersed in the story and took me with him on the journey even when I didn't know what he was talking about. It wasn't words he got carried away with – he was pretty economical with those – but the general vision of what he was trying to explain. He'd make grand sweeping gestures with his arms, his voice would drop an octave to a mysterious whisper and his eyes would light up in exclamation. Naturally, I was captivated.

Forgetting that my ability to comprehend plate tectonics and the earth's geology was limited to primary school, he would lapse into great descriptions of ancient trilobites and one-celled organisms of the Paleozoic era. Later when I knew what such words meant, I figured Grandpa had a secret ambition to be an archeologist or something like that, but no, he was a philosopher and these were mere ingredients of his philosophy. Nevertheless, I would nod my head as if I understood, satisfied to hear about the huge glaciers, giant sea turtles, and other creatures whose remains lay beneath my feet.

He said the last ice age ended only twelve thousand years ago when the climate warmed and the ice melted. This passage of time merited an "only" because he was talking thousands, whereas before he was into millions. I figured if something that happened twelve thousand years ago was a recent development and not in the same league as ancient sea turtles and trilobites, then Grandpa must have been a boy at the time and probably saw it with his own eyes.

"How old were you?" I asked him and the question caught

him by surprise. "Were you little? What did it look like?"

"What?"

"The ice. The glay-see . . . glay-see . . . what was that word you said?"

"Glacier."

"Yeah. Did you see it move?"

I probably asked him a question for every one of those two hundred million years, but he never tired of explaining the story or listening to my unending curiosity. He made it sound simple and it seemed logical enough. These continents of ice moved forward and backward and a few million years later, they moved forward and backward again. In between these advances the world got warm, the ice melted, and gushing rivers carved deep valleys in the earth. He said the top half of what is now North America was buried in ice *two miles thick*. He said the glaciers surged forward across the great forests, rounding out peaks of mountains and chiseling valleys like a wonderful artist at work. I remember his exact words because his metaphors have stayed with me to this day.

The Bluffs had their roots some time between the ice invasions. For thousands of years a great river – Grandpa called all the rivers, lakes, and mountains of the ages "great" – carried clay and sand to the lake and a huge delta was formed. But the delta soon dried and rivers began to cut valleys in its beds. After one of the glaciers melted and retreated to the north twenty-five thousand years ago, the forerunners of the Great Lakes were formed. One of these lakes was Lake Iroquois and this is where the Bluffs come in. Grandpa said the cliffs receded thousands of feet over thousands of years.

I thought this was a magnificent story and it was all due to the ice, but I was little when I first heard it and the only ice I knew was the kind found in the freezer of our refrigerator and it didn't have anything to do with continents. This ice came out in neat little cubes sitting in two rows of six, a dozen cubes to a tray. For the amount of ice Grandpa was talking about – I figured it must have taken a godawful number of cubes to make this glacier business occur – I imagined a world full of so many ice cubes that ice cubes were all you could see. Right up to the sky. I told him this and he said it was possible, except there were no people around to invent ice cube trays so the ice must have been a sheet of ice like a blanket only very thick and that was what moved.

That's what I liked about Grandpa. If I didn't understand what he was trying to say he would tell it so I could. As for the sheets of ice, there was no limit how big they could be, which was perfectly fine with me. He was the trigger for whatever creative juices were within me. He would let my imagination run wild and even give it a push.

"No, I didn't see it move."

"Then how do you know it happened?"

Grandpa wasn't a man who gave up easily, especially to his only grandson.

"Stephen, we know it happened because scientists studied this rock in the Bluffs. The rock told them the story about the glaciers."

"The rock *told* them?"

"Lookit. The ice left a lot of things behind. Like little messages. These messages or clues tell us lots of things about what the world used to look like."

"I see."

But of course I didn't see at all. I said, "I see" because that's what Grandpa always said. Then he laughed and pressed his hand softly against my face the way he always did and whispered a quiet – so quiet I almost didn't hear him – "Stephen." It was his way of saying he loved me and he said it all the time. I will forever feel his hand caressing my cheek, always his left hand against my right cheek because he was a left-hander. A southpaw, he called himself. That first time he took me there I was six and he was seventy-three and despite the difference in our ages, we were best friends.

The Bluffs was the most beautiful place I had ever seen. It was where the past, present, and even the future came together, a place where I was free to think and dream whatever I wanted.

Grandpa made it the kind of place that gives credence to magic and the best part was there were no limits. I could think back any number of years I wanted. A million. Ten million. A billion. I could make the great glaciers as huge and monstrous as I dared, and for all I knew they might have covered the whole world. The trilobites might have been so small that millions of them would fit on the tip of my finger and the shells across the backs of the giant sea turtles might have been as wide as a house.

"That's enough for today, Stephen. Time to go home. Got your key?"

I stuck my hand into my pocket, wiggled my fingers around the packages of bubble gum, felt the sharp edges of the key and nodded.

"Good. Let's go. We'll come back again."

"Promise?"

"Promise."

With that he put his arms around me, and I wrapped mine around him and kissed him softly on his rough cheek and all was well with the world. It was like God himself was taking me into his bosom and filling me with love. This wasn't just a grandfather hugging me; it was God and everyone was always talking about him. My mother would say, "God, are you crazy?" or Uncle Joe would stub his toe on our coffee table and cry, "Oh God!" as loud as he could. Sometimes he'd even yell, "Jesus Christ!" which made me wonder why people screamed the names of God or Jesus when they injured themselves. I figured pain had something to do with religion.

I began saying "God" when I was very young because I heard everyone else saying it. I'd say, "God, this food is bad" or, "God, that's beautiful," but it was just an expression. I didn't think of the word in religious terms, at least not until after catching my first glimpse of the Bluffs. That was a Godlike place, and if it really was heaven, which everyone said was nice, then God must be nearby since "heaven" and "God" always went together and since Grandpa was the one who made this place real for me he had to enter the picture, too.

At first I wasn't sure where he fit in, but soon it became clear. It was on one of our trips to the Bluffs, still long before he had ever mentioned the baseball, and these great – because of Grandpa I started to use the word "great" for emphasis myself – gray clouds were rolling in off the horizon. Grandpa said we had to leave because it was going to rain. He picked me up and parked my chin on his shoulder. I was still pretty small back then and carrying me around like that was no problem for him in spite of his age. As he walked off with me I stared at the clouds and watched them move. It was the first time I had examined the skies closely enough to notice that the clouds weren't still, but alive. It was spectacular. The darkening skies about to burst open. The rough waters of the lake crashing hard against the shore. The Bluffs rising majestically two hundred feet high. And Grandpa.

I was in such awe that a warmth surged through my body. If God was old, kind and, wise – all the things Grandpa was – and he was always near when you needed him – as Grandpa was – then God must be Grandpa. It was only years later when I was older and Grandpa began to face the fact of his own mortality that I realized he was just a man. But a very special man.

◆

Grandpa's parents came from Poland and their ways were very different. Grandpa once told me how he used to help his father by pushing "hundreds of pounds of salamis" – he probably exaggerated about the weight – in a wheelbarrow a few blocks from the local meat-packing plant to the family grocery store. He said he was obligated to contribute to the family enterprise as meagre as that enterprise was. School was a lesser priority and if there were truant officers back then they didn't take their jobs seriously since, according to Grandpa, most of the kids were busy working and not much interested in school. There was little time for leisure. It was early in the century and the local community was full of immigrants so the struggle to make ends meet was a full-time affair. The notion of leisure, Grandpa used to say, only came into being in the '50s before it went into overdrive in the '60s, but in spite of it all there was one outlet for his energies.

Baseball.

He never came right out and told me and his avoidance of the subject for so many years was a mystery since I was pretty crazy about the game myself. I had to discover his fascination for baseball on my own. It happened by accident one day when I was visiting him and my grandmother. I was ten or eleven. It was fall, and we were sitting outside on the porch and my grandmother had just brought us two peanut butter and strawberry jam sandwiches. God, did he ever love her homemade strawberry jam. The air was cool and draped around her slight frame were two wool sweaters and a coat so she could avoid contracting diseases that afflict hypochondriacs. But Grandpa was perfectly content sitting there in nothing but a short-sleeved shirt.

"Stephen, go get your grandfather one of those heavy sweaters I knitted him. The blue one. It's in his drawer in our bedroom."

I didn't know which drawer to pull and tried them all. In the second one I made my discovery. Tucked away beneath a pile of wool socks was a pouch I had never seen before. It had a string tied snugly around the top. I pulled the string open and out fell a small medal. It looked like it was made of copper or bronze. It was tarnished and blackened with age, but the inscription was easy to read:

City Baseball Champions – 1920.

I was amazed. It was closer to a coin than a medal, about the size of a quarter with a pitcher throwing a ball embossed in the middle. Hastily etched across the top were the initials *L.S.* A second medal identical to the first, but a little worse for wear, was from 1919. It also had those same initials. I put them back in the pouch, tugged on the string, and returned the pouch to the drawer with his socks.

This was a great find, of the same magnitude as my first glimpse of the Bluffs and later, of the baseball itself. The only thing Grandpa had ever said about baseball was that it was a dumb sport since no one ever worked up a sweat. He said it wasn't a grinding game like football or hockey and that professional ballplayers didn't deserve the money they made because they didn't push themselves.

"You see a lot of grown men standing around in what looks like their pajamas waiting for something to happen and usually it never does. And they get paid for that?"

Baseball produced the only glimmer of a stubborn streak I ever saw in Grandpa. It would transform a man who enjoyed life and who always gave freely of himself into a withdrawn, steely curmudgeon. Whenever the World Series rolled around and we were all glued to the TV, he would sit tight-lipped in a rocker – he hated rockers – going back and forth, back and forth, looking like the bitter old man he never was.

If Grandpa had a nemesis, baseball was it and only after I started playing the game myself did he finally come around and reveal the great secret about that ball in the lake. At first I didn't believe him. The days of make-believe were long gone and this tale was so incredible it made even the Bluffs seem ordinary. But it was true. Grandpa never lied to me.

Never.

Two

Lazaros Slackowicz had never seen so many men in uniform. They were everywhere and the word on everyone's lips was "war." The soldiers were guarding railroad stations and bridges and a large group was gathered at the ferry docks, each of them with a cigarette trying to look handsome and nonchalant for the benefit of the young women passing on the way to the ferry. The ferry was the only way to get to the ballpark. This was his first time on a boat and the *Trillium* was a magnificent way to begin. It was a large ferry with three levels and Lazo, as he was called, opted for the top deck. It was wonderful. The cool fresh air of the lake was stronger there, so strong that his father, Josef, had to hang onto his hat for fear it would be whisked into the waters of the lake and be lost forever.

In 1914 a man without a hat was a man without clothes.

When the ferry was three-quarters of the way across, a tremendous blast resonated from the smokestack and Lazo felt his bones shake with the tumultuous vibrations of the floor beneath his feet. The ferry was coming in to dock at the Toronto Islands and the anxious passengers edged to the starboard side.

Baseball was becoming popular in a city whose people were suddenly faced with the outbreak of hostilities in Europe. The Archduke Franz Ferdinand, heir to the throne of Austria, had been assassinated a few weeks earlier and it wasn't long before all the great powers of Europe were at war. Now it was the fifth of September and the tensions of the times were becoming increasingly visible to eight-year-old Lazo. A seemingly abandoned railroad car sat in the middle of the street, a huge sign on its side. The cold stern face of a soldier, the biggest soldier Lazo had ever seen, had his finger pointing directly at passersby, asking for volunteers with the words: *Last Chance! Victory Loan. Lists Close December 1st.*

But that didn't matter today. Lazo was going to his first baseball game. Maple Leaf Park, also known as Hanlan's Point Stadium, was only five years old and it retained the smell and feel of a new stadium. Inside, Lazo was in awe of the large covered grandstand that stretched around the infield. It offered an excellent view of the proceedings as well as of the waters of the bay and the city back on the mainland.

It was incredible. As soon as he entered Lazo forgot all about the war. He and his father were going to see the hometown Toronto Maple Leafs play a doubleheader against the Providence Grays. The Grays were in third place in the eight-team International League while the locals were in fifth, but still a respectable team at five games over the .500 mark. Josef said this wasn't the first ballpark on the island, but the third. The first two, both of them primitive wooden affairs, had been lost in fires but the current structure was concrete and would last. Lazo thought his father knew everything.

This was an adventure and not only because of where they were, but because Lazo would spend the day with his father, a man who didn't have much time for his youngest son. Josef Slackowicz worked fourteen hours a day, six days a week, at his small grocery in a corner of the city that was home to a new wave of immigrants from Eastern Europe. It was hard work and the customers were friendly, but demanding. Today was Saturday and Josef usually worked Saturdays, but this day had been planned for some time. His two older sons were minding the store along with his wife and it was she who had urged him to take "the young one" to the game. Just this once.

"Look, Papa!"

Lazo was pointing to the stadium. It was the biggest thing he had ever seen, but small compared to major league parks in the United States like Chicago's ultramodern Comiskey Park that seated almost thirty thousand people. The tickets were fifteen cents each and Josef felt a pang of guilt as he parted with the money. For a baseball game? It didn't make sense. But when he saw the look of awe on Lazo's face as they walked into the cavernous structure he thought maybe his wife was right. But just this once.

Lazo had never seen so many people in one place. His heart pounded with excitement as he and his father climbed the rows and rows of seats before locating the numbers matching their tickets. Even Josef was excited. He had never been to a ball game either. They settled into their seats and watched the Maple Leafs shagging balls in the infield. Josef admired the slim, lithe bodies of the athletes whom he had read about in the newspaper. He wished he had known them better so he could have pointed out the best players to Lazo and given him a thrill, but for Lazo just being here was thrill enough.

The Toronto pitcher was a powerful hurler named Ellis Johnson and even to novices like Josef and Lazo it was easy to see that his fastball had what those in the game called "smoke." He wound up and delivered and the ball carried as if on a line right into the catcher's mitt. His form wasn't especially smooth, but the ball landed with such a thud that whatever Johnson was doing obviously worked well. Lazo watched him intently. After a few minutes the pitcher and his teammates finished their warm-up, and the Maple Leafs retreated into their dugout to light applause from the spattering of fans in the seats.

Then the visitors took to the field. Josef had checked the standings before they left home so he could tell Lazo that the

Grays were a good team with seventy-five wins and fifty-three losses and within striking distance of first place. They didn't look all that different from the other team. They were young men who threw the ball effortlessly and one of them, the biggest, caught Lazo's eye. He was the Grays' pitcher and a giant compared to the others. He was tall and slim and, judging by how he threw, very strong.

Lazo had no one to compare him to except the Maple Leafs' pitcher who'd strutted his stuff a moment earlier, but this pitcher threw the ball even harder. He was a young left-hander and on his wide, round face was an expression of total concentration. His delivery was a thing of beauty. This was only the warm-up so he wasn't throwing at full speed, but his artistry was evident. He would wind up and bring his arm around and over his head in a perfect arc as if drawn by a mathematician's compass. It was precision in motion. When the ball reached the plate his feet were on the ground and he was well positioned for a fielding play. He had style.

The warm-up over, the fans were now spilling into whatever empty seats remained and when the game began almost all eighteen thousand seats were filled. A boy not much older than Lazo was in the stands selling programs and when Lazo asked for one Josef hesitated, then stuck his fingers into his pocket and deposited a nickel into the boy's outstretched hand.

"Here La-zzo," he said in his heavy accent, his "r" coming out like a "d," his stress on the first syllable of his son's name. "Now you'll know the players."

Most of the pages in the program had information about the Maple Leafs, but in the middle of the program was the lineup for this game. Lazo looked at the Providence side and checked all the names. Platte, right field. Fabrique, shortstop. Shean, second base. E. Onslow, first base. Tutwiler, center field. Powell, left field. Baumann, third base. J. Onslow, catcher.

The pitcher was named Ruth.

"He's got a girl's name, Papa," Lazo said.

Josef just smiled.

"Big girl that one."

The visitors were up first and they scored a run. Then the Maple Leafs came to bat and the big, young left-hander for the Grays quickly retired them in order. The Leafs' Johnson settled down in the second inning and through the next four frames neither pitcher allowed a run, but Johnson was lucky. While Ruth was whizzing strike after strike by the Maple Leafs and didn't give up a hit, Johnson was being hit hard by the Grays, but they couldn't advance a runner past third base and the score remained 1-0. After Ruth threw his third strikeout, the man next to Josef smacked his hands together and shouted with glee.

"That kid's got what it takes!" he exclaimed, turning to Josef who gave him a smile. "You know they paid twenty-five thousand bucks for him?"

"They did?" asked Lazo.

"Yep," said the man, who had been filling in the game box score with every batter.

"Who?" said Josef. "Who paid it?"

"The Boston Red Sox. That's who. They paid twenty-five thousand bucks to Baltimore for Ruth and two other guys. Egan, a catcher, and Shore, another pitcher. But Ruth was the one they wanted. The other two were just thrown in."

The first pitch to the next batter was a fastball that caught the outside corner of the plate. *Whoosh!* It sailed in as if it had eyes. The big pitcher studied the signals from his catcher, then threw another. *Whoosh!* Strike two. The man beside Josef looked up from the program he was scribbling in, his cigarette hanging by a thread out the side of his mouth.

"Shit! Can he ever toss that ball!"

Josef shot a glance at his son whose eyes bulged open at the mention of a word not permitted in the Slackowicz household. *Whoosh!* Strike three.

"Unbelievable ain't he? And he's just nineteen. What's that? Four strikeouts? He won't be in the minors long with an arm like that. Look at him. Just look at him!"

Lazo looked. He was getting stronger as the game wore on.

While the Maple Leafs' Johnson was having trouble in every inning, Ruth didn't even let anyone on base except for a walk in
the early going and that runner never got to second. In the fifth,
the Maple Leafs got their one and only hit of the game and it
came with two outs. Their catcher stroked a soft liner to the outfield and tagged up at first base with a single. He was followed by
his pitcher, Ellis Johnson, who could only muster a foul tip to
the first baseman and the "rally" was quickly nipped in the bud
and the side retired.

In the next inning the talented left-hander showed he could
do more than pitch. With two runners on base he came to bat
and it was pitcher against pitcher. He battled Johnson to the hilt
and ran the count to three balls and two strikes. On the second
strike Lazo couldn't help but notice how hard he swung his bat
only to miss the ball. His follow-through was such that his body
twisted completely around so he was facing the stands behind
home plate. And what a beautiful swing it was. Just like his
pitching delivery when he'd been on the mound, his swing was
an exercise in fluid motion, but he had an unorthodox stance at
the plate. The biggest man on the team, he had his feet close
together in the batter's box, only eight or nine inches apart,
which was unusual since many of the smaller players had wide
shoulder-to-shoulder stances.

Lazo watched his face as the three-and-two pitch rolled off
Johnson's fingers. Ruth's eyes were riveted on the ball. He raised
his bat slowly over his left shoulder and just when the ball was re-
leased he began twisting his body so that his back was half
turned toward the pitcher. The ball came in knee-high in front
of the outside corner – right where he liked it – and he started
spinning his body into the pitch. The bat came around and up to
meet the ball, the point of impact slightly ahead of the plate.
There was a tremendous "SMACK" and the ball lifted up into
the air to deep right field.

Lazo watched it soar. That ball was alive as it conquered the
heavens with an energy that couldn't be explained. It flew like a
bird, carving a route in the sky, parting the atmosphere, sailing as

if it would go on forever. The tall graceful pitcher turned hitter dropped the bat and started racing to first base, his eyes still on the ball. It kept lifting higher and higher and by the time he rounded first it was far and away over the right field fence and then it disappeared and dropped into the waters of the bay.

A home run.

Three runs scored and now it was 4-0. Someone said it was the longest home run ever made at the ballpark. At the time, home runs were a rarity in baseball as strategy called for a series of hits mixed with deft base running in order to manufacture runs, but these three runs had come in an instant and it wasn't so much a team that had broken up a close game as the monstrous clout of one player. Just when the ball reached its apex way over the right field fence, Lazo stood up and cheered wildly, screaming and waving his arms over his head.

"A home run, Papa! He got a home run!"

Josef was cheering too. The man with the girl's name trotted around third base and then to home much to the delight of his teammates. When he arrived they kept slapping him on the back. Lazo checked the program to find his first name, but no first names were listed so he turned to the man beside his father. He seemed to know everything.

"That guy Ruth," said Lazo. "What's his first name?"

"Ruth?" said the man. "George. They paid twenty-five thousand bucks for him and he's worth every cent. Ain't he?"

Lazo agreed. In fact, he thought he was worth even more.

The rest of the game was anticlimactic. The Grays kept hitting everything Johnson threw at them, but they came up empty in the seventh inning as did the Maple Leafs naturally when Ruth returned to the pitcher's mound. But in the eighth the Grays managed to advance their runners and struck for a pair of runs to make the score 6-0. Three more came in the ninth and the final tally was 9-0. A rout.

George Ruth, a fresh-faced, nineteen-year-old rookie, had pitched a sparkling one-hitter, struck out seven batters, didn't allow anyone to reach second base, and added a three-run home run shot that turned the game around. It was his first ever professional home run, a sign of things to come.

Lazo caught a glimpse of him in the Providence dugout as he sipped water from a paper cup. There would be a short break before the bottom half of the doubleheader would begin, but Lazo wasn't interested in the next game.

"Stay here, Papa. I'll be right back."

"Lazo, where you going?"

He was already up and rushing down the aisle. Many of the spectators had left their seats for between-game snacks and it didn't take Lazo long to reach the first row and field level. The Grays were busy congratulating themselves for the win, their pitcher still the focus of attention. But Lazo wasn't the only boy who wanted a moment with the hero of the game. At least a dozen other youngsters were hovering over the railing by the Grays' dugout with more coming.

Ruth responded to the cries of the boys and stepped out from the dugout. In the true fashion of a showman he tipped his hat and all the boys cheered. He gave them a broad smile, relishing the adulation. Then he walked over to the railing and each one of the boys – now there were more than twenty – thrust a program into his face begging for a signature. Someone handed him a pen and he started signing autographs just as a newspaper reporter who was covering the game began to ask him questions.

"Where'd you learn to pitch like that, fella?"

Ruth was busy with the kids, enjoying himself immensely.

"Whatcha say?"

"I said where'd you learn to pitch like that?"

"In school."

"What school?"

"St. Mary's in Baltimore. Best damn baseball school there is." The reporter was scribbling madly, recording every word. "And you can credit Brother Matthias with teaching me how to pitch."

"How do you spell that?"

"M-A-T . . ."

It was no use. The throng of kids had grown so large it was

impossible to talk over the din that they made. There must have been thirty of them, or maybe forty or fifty, each and every one screaming and hollering as loud as he could. Ruth kept signing autographs, engaging in chatter with the boys who were smothering him in idol worship. Some were even hanging over the railing, clinging onto the bars by their fingertips. There was barely enough room to scratch his name on the backs of the programs they had brought. Then he looked up and saw a pair of bright blue eyes staring at him sadly. Lazo, his hands sunk deep inside his pockets, had been in such a mad rush to get to the dugout he'd forgotten to bring his program to get signed.

For a moment their eyes met. He looked so handsome in his uniform, Lazo thought, but any man who stood six-foot-two, had pitched a one-hitter, and knocked in a three-run homer would have looked handsome that day. He wore a white pinstriped uniform with a circled "P" for Providence over his heart and even his cap had pinstripes. He was a large man. Slim, lean, and powerful. He had a huge round face with full lips and dark eyes. His nose was wide and his nostrils big and round. He didn't look particularly happy when he was playing – such was his state of concentration – but now he was kind, gentle, and caring. Lazo could see that. All the boys could see it.

Ruth smiled and Lazo smiled back, then Ruth made a motion with his hand as if writing something. Did Lazo want an autograph? Lazo eagerly nodded his head up and down, but then laid out his open outstretched hands to show he had no pen or program. The tall lanky pitcher solved that. He finished the autograph he was signing, stuck out his neck and looked for the reporter. He spotted him a few feet away buried amongst the boys.

"Hey, keed," Ruth said to him. "Hey keed! Gimme some paper will ya!"

The reporter, his body almost hidden beneath the multitude of boys, managed to deliver a solitary slip of paper through the morass of arms and heads and then through the railing to the waiting ballplayer. Ruth still had a pen in his hand. He scribbled two words on the paper and folded it in half. They

looked at each other again. Ruth was the biggest man Lazo had
ever seen and not only that, he was a baseball player, a professional baseball player who had just won a game with nothing less
than superhuman pitching and hitting. Lazo had never seen
ballplayers before, but this one was different from all the rest and
it wasn't just that he was bigger or even better. There was something else.

It was almost as if they had met before, but where? Lazo was
a young boy who had never been away from home in his life
while Ruth was a ballplayer from Baltimore who just this year
had ventured into another country for the first time with games
against the Toronto Maple Leafs and Montreal Royals. Ruth kept
looking at him. He had been getting used to awe-struck kids staring at him like he was from another planet. One-hitters and
three-run blasts did that sort of thing. He had seen them at all
the stops in the International League, but this kid's face would
stay with him for a long time. Maybe it was just that he'd saved
his best game for Toronto and this boy happened to catch him at
the right moment. Lazo saw how Ruth looked at him. A look
that spoke almost of recognition. Still, something was connecting
them and a bond was formed. Lazo had found someone to worship, a hero, and this ballplayer had found the biggest fan he
would ever know. Ruth glanced out to the bay where his tremendous home run shot had landed. He smiled warmly.

"Here son," he said handing Lazo the autograph through the
railing.

How Lazo wanted to thank him, but he couldn't utter a
word. He was speechless. So much joy came over him that his
tongue was stuck in the back of his mouth. He couldn't even
breathe. A few seconds later and Ruth disappeared from view, his
face blocked out by all the kids who hungered for him. Lazo
opened the slip of paper and looked at the name.

Babe Ruth.

Babe? But he thought his name was George.

"Wait a minute," Lazo said, suddenly finding his voice, but it
was too late. The big hurler was busy signing other autographs.

No sooner would he sign one than a sea of program-wielding hands would be pressed against his face as more and more boys kept coming down to the dugout to receive him and pay homage. Lazo looked at the name again. Babe Ruth. But what kind of name was that?

◆

The next day the local sports pages were full of the exploits of the young Providence pitcher. Lazo clipped out the story of the game. "Only one hit made off pitcher Babe Ruth," the newspaper said. He was called a "pitching sensation" and of his towering home run the words read: "Ruth whaled the bulb over the right field fence with two runners on the bases. He had Johnson in a three-and-two hole and the Kelley twirler grooved the next ball. Crash!"

When Lazo got home after the game, he put his autograph and the program inside a folder and stuck them in his drawer. They were souvenirs he would treasure and it wouldn't be long before he'd have to get more folders for all the clippings he would collect. He jumped onto his bed and closed his eyes. All he could see was the big round face of the Providence pitcher smiling at him saying, "Here son." There were eighteen thousand people in that stadium and this wonderful man had taken the time to talk to him and give him an autograph.

Lazo went to sleep that night thinking only of Babe Ruth, rookie pitcher of the Providence Grays, who would hit no more home runs in the minor leagues, and he started to dream. He had done more than just attend a baseball game. He had embarked on the first step of a long journey that would take him far from his father's little grocery. The way he had it planned it would take him to fame and stardom and win him the admiration of fans the world over. Lazo had found his calling. He was going to be a ballplayer.

Three

There is something of the marvelous in all
things of nature.

— Aristotle

"I remember the first time I saw you," Grandpa once told me. "I
was looking through the window where all the new babies were
on display and I didn't know which one was you. They all had
name tags but they were so small it was hard to read them. The
only thing I knew was that the boys had blue tags and the girls
had pink ones so I just looked for the most beautiful baby with a
blue name tag and I knew right away it was you."

He must have fallen in love with me right then. I wasn't his
first grandchild, but I was the first boy and maybe that made a
difference. But there was more to it than that. Grandpa had three
sons and my father was the youngest and he was also the sole
"professional" of the group. A lawyer. That meant long hours. He
wasn't around a lot and my mother wasn't much better. She was
an interior decorator and that meant long hours, too. Suffice to
say that I was born into a household where work was the top priority, so Grandpa must have had an inkling that a grandfather
was going to be very important in this particular case.

The day I was born my father was away somewhere in the
States advising a client who had gotten into some trouble. It

seemed that all his clients called him only when they were in trouble and their trouble always involved money. I figured that's what being a lawyer was all about, helping people hang onto their money. Apparently, my mother had a rough time of it late in the pregnancy. She had gained a lot of weight and her ankles were all swollen, giving her what she called "the look of an old, fat Russian woman who's good for cooking and cleaning and not much else." Why she singled out the Russians I never knew, but that was what she once told me. Needless to say, she had no other children after me.

My father squeezed in a telephone call that morning to offer his congratulations as well as his condolences for not being able to attend the birth of his one and only child. But he did return at night to offer Grandpa a cigar. As with the birth of his other grandchildren – all girls – Grandpa took one puff, coughed, and promptly deposited the stogie into the nearest wastebasket.

It seemed like he was always around. All the time. I remember him constantly holding me, cuddling me, and playing with me and I even remember the first thing he ever tried explaining to me. It was called "the energy crisis" and it apparently caused a lot of trouble for President Nixon, but not nearly as much trouble as something else called "Watergate." I found out about these things after the fact, but knew they were both serious since the residue hung around for years. I was just a kid and TV reruns, movies, and Top 40 hits were more than enough for learning what was happening in the world. Still, Grandpa provided the most useful education.

As far as Watergate was concerned, he would describe Nixon as "the former president of the United States" and Watergate was the reason he was former. Some time later I saw Nixon on TV commenting on the world scene and all Grandpa could say was that "Watergate killed him" so I pictured this old man Nixon pushing himself against a small door or gate and enough water to fill the Niagara Falls gorge was quickly gathering on the other side. The force of the water kept increasing and soon the poor guy could no longer keep the gate shut. It burst open, the water carried him away, and he drowned. Why he was still alive was a problem I hadn't yet addressed, but his bout with Watergate explained why he looked the way he did.

It was a little joke Grandpa and I would share later.

I never understood the oil thing too well, but I knew oil was important. I was told the stuff even heated our house and that without it we would freeze to death in winter so I made sure to treat it with great respect. When we had salad with dinner and were served French or Thousand Islands dressing, I didn't mind if some dressing dripped over my lettuce and formed a pool at the bottom of the plate only to be poured down the sink afterward, but if we had *oil* and vinegar as the dressing I wouldn't waste a drop. Uncle Joe, my mother's brother, told me that this same oil affected the price of gasoline and he and Grandpa often spoke about the "gas wars" taking place at the local service stations. I figured a good place for a battle would be at a nearby intersection where there was a gas station on each of the four corners. I never saw a gas war happen, but could imagine the havoc unleashed when an attendant turned on his hose and aimed it across the road at his enemy – who no doubt would return fire – and when all four of them were going at once it must have been some sight.

Discussing the news was the one thing that brought our family together. My father, when he was around, buried himself in newspapers every day and if Grandpa was over when the news was on you could rest assured that talk would eventually get around to the latest government scandal, child abduction, or drug bust. My grandmother was especially fearful of child abductions. The tales she told of almost being whisked away by some shadowy character when she was a small girl were legend in the household.

Both Grandpa and my grandmother played more than supporting roles on the day of my birth. Judging from the memoirs of relatives, there was a definite theme of chac
That my father was away, my mother hated being pregr
my grandmother drove the hospital medical staff crazy a

That Grandpa did most of the running around is another given. He even purchased the very first package of that hated formula for my bottle, but since he was merely following orders and doing chores for my mother I never held it against him.

Home was a house that I shared with my father and mother, but it was never really a "home." We were a small family, just three, and when I was young I desperately wanted a little brother or sister. It would have made my early years a lot richer, but I didn't get one and that later got me wondering why my parents had bothered having me. They were both professional people, well educated and refined in the synthetic definition of the word and their careers came first. As I say, my father was a lawyer and I'm sure he was a very good one, but his work controlled him and used up every ounce of his being so there was nothing left when he got home.

Unlike my father, my mother the interior decorator had flair and creativity, but whatever spark was within her stemmed from her work, which she approached with a passion. It was a time-consuming job that occupied her fully and left little time for a child. There was always a nanny or a sitter around, but I never wanted these people since it was obvious I wasn't that important to them. It was just a job. I was first in nobody's book. Except Grandpa's, that is. He was the only one who deemed me more important than catching the daytime soap operas – one of my sitters never missed a single episode of *As the World Turns* – pressing matters of corporate litigation or deciding where Ionic columns should stand in the foyer of a bank.

I was so unimportant in my parents' books that I missed out on the one great event that bonds an infant child to its mother. I was never nursed. Not once. Circumstance was such that I didn't merit natural rights to my mother's body and that caused a few problems.

When I was little and Auntie Ellen was near – my Uncle Joe's wife who was well-endowed – I was always fascinated with her breasts. It was more than a preoccupation. I just loved to sit on her lap and feel her boobs and even remember trying to remove her clothes, but she never gave me the chance, preferring to shoo me off with a pat on the head and dismiss her nephew as a silly little boy. Her husband, my Uncle Joe who stubbed his toe on the coffee table, must have known something was amiss since he was always taking me under his arm whenever I made a beeline for my aunt, probably trying to provide some guidance suitable to a four-year-old although he never came right out and said to stay away from his wife.

My mother was to blame. For years I couldn't understand how a woman would refuse to nurse her newborn child. But eventually I discovered why. She was a person who admired herself completely and was worried that an infant suckling on her body would alter her form later. My mother was so terrified of aging that the day she hit forty she visited a plastic surgeon and had what is commonly called a "tummy tuck." Indeed, her avoidance of this most natural act had to do with sex appeal, vanity, and everything that didn't have to do with being a mother.

I could talk to Grandpa about sex. When I was about fourteen I even reasoned that if I, as a member of the male species, felt a strong yearning to touch a girl then Grandpa, as a member of the male species, probably wanted to as well. I must have been the only boy in high school who could discuss such things with his grandfather, but we could because our relationship was special. It was a relationship that transcended the great gap in our ages. It transcended everything. And so, even on matters as delicate as sex, I confided in him.

"It's perfectly normal, Stephen," he said. "There's nothing to worry about. You just have to learn to control your feelings, that's all. Sometimes you see a girl and you feel like you're on fire. Right? Sure. But one day you'll meet someone you really like and everything will be fine. You'll just click."

And he snapped his fingers as if all was well with the world.

◆

As I got older my parents thought something was wrong with me. They never for a moment considered that perhaps something was wrong with *them*. When I was in second grade my mother even took me to a child psychiatrist. I recall the session vividly. The woman's office was in an old building. A number of Corinthian columns – I knew about columns from my mother's work – dominated the facade and ran all the way to the top. The building was square and solid and its shape made a definite statement that all that transpired inside was full of righteousness and wisdom. It was downtown, not far from the lake, and it stood all by itself. The other buildings nearby were bleak aluminum skyscrapers whose architecture didn't make much of a statement at all except for the fact they were very ugly. The woman was a "top" family counselor – all medical practitioners and other professionals were always referred to as the "top" in our household.

I remember she was a pretty woman with stunning blond hair. I didn't know the word "platinum" at the time, but if I did I would have called her hair that. It was so perfect and full of sheen that it seemed to reflect light. Most of it was swept over to one side of her face as if a monsoon wind pushed the entire mass up and to the side, but left every hair intact.

My mother thought I had a behavior disorder, that I had problems relating to her and my father and that I kept to myself too much so this doctor started talking to me and when she called me "dear" I knew it was trouble.

For as long as I can remember, whenever people, especially people I didn't know, called me "dear" they were up to no good. A few questions later and the prognosis was in. I had low self-esteem. Then the conversation turned to Grandpa. My mother said something about Grandpa and me spending so much time together. She talked about our long walks and how we often went away for hours at a time down to the Bluffs.

"The Bluffs? Down by the lake?"

"Yes. That's right."

"Tell me. Have you ever considered the possibility that Stephen's grandfather might be a pedophile?"

I distinctly remember my mother giving rise to the loudest "What!" I'd ever heard at that point in my life. She said something about that being the dumbest thing anyone had ever said to her. But the doctor insisted, and then she asked me if Grandpa ever touched me. I wasn't sure what she meant.

"You know. Has he ever put his hands in places where he shouldn't?" she said.

So I told her about the time he stuck his hand in a hornet's nest by mistake and got all stung, but that wasn't the answer she was looking for. Finally, my mother interrupted.

"Doctor," she said, "I assure you my father-in-law is no . . ." She almost spit out the word . . . "*pedophile.*"

Naturally I wanted to know what that was and so I asked, but the question was quickly dismissed. After awhile the talk turned to "love" and how much of that commodity was found in our household, which brought up the subject of Grandpa again. The doctor asked me what was the worst thing I could imagine and I said something about Grandpa slipping and falling over the Bluffs.

"It's a long way down," I remember saying. "There's lots of rocks at the bottom. He'd get hurt."

"I see. Do you love him? Your Grandpa?"

I told her I loved him more than anyone and I guess that made my mother uneasy. The doctor must have sensed the awkwardness of the moment and I remember she offered me some gum. I remember because it was sugarless. I was only seven years old but it was obvious to me this woman didn't have any children of her own. Once or twice I again asked about that long word I couldn't pronounce – the thing the doctor thought Grandpa might be but that my mother insisted he wasn't – and was told to keep quiet. Finally, we were about to leave. Well, surprise, surprise, but all of a sudden this doctor lady got real friendly and told me to sit on her lap. Then she told me to give her a hug. She called it "hands-on therapy" and so I gave her a hug, a little harmless one, the kind you give an aunt you see maybe once a year. But that wasn't good enough. She wanted a bigger hug. A *much* bigger hug. So I put my arms around her and felt her chest against my neck and it felt good so I grabbed one of her breasts and squeezed it as hard as I could. Hands-on. That was what she said. It was the only time my mother ever slapped me like that and it was also the last time she ever took me to a woman doctor.

◆

We were fortunate to live in a house on a ravine and if you went not far into the woods you'd find a long meandering brook that provided countless hours of adventure and exploring. I often went down to the brook or creek with my friends, but if my grandmother ever got wind of my being near a waterway, even one as innocent as this, all hell would break loose. She would rant and rave about her little grandson dying a horrible death by drowning or being kidnapped by some recently escaped child molester who was lurking in the woods waiting for little children. But I went there many times with Grandpa. It was there that he introduced me to the wondrous world of the tadpole. We studied tadpoles in school, of course, but filling in coloring books and labeling body parts – head, tail, fins, gills – isn't like seeing the little creatures in person.

"Look at them, Stephen. See them? They're all over the place. Tadpoles. Lots of them. They're going upstream."

I thought they were funny and cute since they were small, wiggly, and always on the move. They swam the way people drove on the freeway, going straight in one direction for a bit, then suddenly swerving to one side and heading off that way before cutting to the other side. The remarkable thing about the tadpole was that it had two lives – and not two lives in the way that a cat has nine – but two separate and distinct lives. Its first life was as a tadpole and its second was as a frog or toad. Grandpa called this phenomenon *metamorphosis*. It was the first really long word I learned to pronounce.

"The tadpole changes from a small thing that lives in the water, with fins and a tail, sort of like a fish, to a land animal with four legs. It's amazing. What took millions of years for nature – to have fish evolve to land animals – takes just a few weeks for a tadpole. It's like the whole history of the earth happens overnight. And growing up is like that too. Look at you, Stephen. Just yesterday you were a little baby and now you're so big. By tomorrow you'll probably be six feet tall."

"You think so?"

"Sure."

I knew that waking up the next morning and explaining such sudden growth to my parents would be a problem. I would need a new bed, new room and new clothes. My bicycle would be useless and so would my desk at school. I wondered what I would tell all my friends.

"Look at that little tadpole in the water. You can't tell, but at this very minute he's growing a tail. It's the tail he'll use when he becomes a frog. And his gills . . . you know what gills are?"

"Yup. He uses them to breathe."

"That's right. Right now his gills are on the outside of his body, but soon they'll be inside and when he becomes a frog he won't need those gills at all because they help him breathe when he's in the water, but when he's a frog he'll be living on the land. It's like leaving home when you grow up. That's metamorphosis. It happens when he changes and grows into an adult. It's happening to you too and it happens so fast it's scary."

The metamorphosis of the tadpole was of particular fascination to me, but the way Grandpa told it this phenomenon went far beyond life in the creek. A tear fell from his eye and I didn't know why. I knew Grandpa wanted me to grow up, but at the same time he seemed to be afraid of it. My parents were always rushing my metamorphosis with talk of increased responsibility and all that, but Grandpa wanted it to slow down. It made me wonder if Grandpa wasn't involved in metamorphosis himself.

"What about you, Grandpa? Are you changing, too?"

"Of course." He bent over and showed me the top of his head. "See all those gray hairs? It wasn't long ago that they were brown. And look at my skin. It's not as soft as it used to be." He straightened up. "I'm getting older. Every day I get a little older."

"No you're not. You're always the same."

I really believed that. As long as I could remember Grandpa had looked exactly as he did just then. He'd always had some gray hair, especially around the temples just above his ears, but I'd never noticed any of it on top of his head. Until that day.

"No, Stephen. I'm getting older. Everybody is. Someday – "

"Someday what?"

He looked at me and smiled. "Someday I won't be here."

I couldn't imagine life without Grandpa. He was everything to me. The thought was frightening and I refused to accept it. Maybe he was talking like this so I would get a little more inde-pendent since I was in the process of replacing my external gills with internal ones and it was time I did more things for myself.

"Grandpa, where will you go if you're not here with us?"

"Heaven I hope."

The Bluffs. It was my favorite place and spending eternity there wouldn't be so bad. Equating heaven with the Bluffs was one of our little secrets – Grandpa and me – and no one else knew about it. But not having him around was still unthinkable.

"Will I be able to see you when you go to the Bluffs?"

Grandpa chuckled to himself. He touched my face with his hand, his left hand, and it was a touch unlike anyone else's. His hand just naturally belonged there on my cheek. It fit so well.

"You're darn tootin."

It was one of his expressions. What "you're darn tootin" actu-ally meant I didn't really know. It didn't make any sense unless you were a train – of the steam engine variety – and got a sudden urge to let loose with a whistle. But Grandpa said it all the time. You're darn tootin. Another thing he always said was "Yehudi," which referred to some distant mysterious person who was re-sponsible for the things no one else took credit for. Nobody else ever said this. Only Grandpa.

So he was destined to wind up at the Bluffs or in the Bluffs or beneath the Bluffs. I wondered if the birds that crashed into our window or the spiders that were captured off the wall wound up there too. I wondered if the tadpoles – or frogs, rather, after the tadpoles had grown up – would go there and then it all began to make sense. The Bluffs were the oldest place in the world. They went back to the great ice age. For millions and billions of years every form of life had died and somehow been deposited at the Bluffs or maybe in the rock at the Bluffs. There were the clues – the fossils that Grandpa had talked about. The trilobites were there. The great sea turtles were there. Everything was there. No wonder the Bluffs were so high.

I figured people must also go there after they die and now Grandpa had virtually assured me this was true. But was it? I once had a hamster – it was the only pet I ever had – and when it died it didn't wind up at the Bluffs. I know because I was there when it happened. Grandpa was the one who found it lying still, its legs straight up in the air in the little cage where it lived on my night table. I was overcome with grief in this, my first real sense of loss. We, Grandpa and me, put it in a shoebox and buried it in the ravine behind the house and that was where it wound up. Not at the Bluffs. Then there was the time I actually saw a dead person. He was my mother's great uncle – he was eighty-two – and I realized then that all the earth's creatures are mortal, that they don't live forever and people don't live forever either. Grandpa had said so.

Dead started with the ants in the driveway and the spiders on the bathroom wall. Dead happened to the birds and dead happened to my hamster. Now it happened to a man. I didn't know him well myself, but I saw him there lying in a coffin, his body still, not even a hint of breathing on his chest. He was a man and he was dead. Everyone was saying how old he was and that his time had finally come, but he was only a little older than Grandpa.

Before we left the funeral home I began to imagine Grandpa in that coffin and the vision wouldn't let go and that night I had a horrible dream. I dreamed Grandpa died and all the relatives came to pay their last respects. Everyone was saying how old he was and that his time had come. It was one of those dreams that felt so real I woke up trembling. I was trembling with fear and grief. I woke up thinking he was really gone. I sat up in bed and looked around the room. It was empty and still. There wasn't a sign of life anywhere. Everything seemed to be dead. Including me.

That was when I finally realized Grandpa couldn't be God because God lived forever. He survived us all. Maybe, hopefully, he lived within us and perhaps even watched over us protectively, but he was immortal and we weren't. He was God and we were only human. Grandpa was one of us. He was just a man.

My metamorphosis had begun.

Four

On January 5, 1920, the Boston Red Sox sold Babe Ruth to the New York Yankees for $100 thousand, four times the amount of his earlier sale in the minor leagues. It was the most money ever paid for a baseball player. But the actual price was much higher. The Red Sox owner was Harry Frazee, a man who ran a string of theaters and produced his own shows. He had money and mixed with show-business people and big names from the sports world. Once he even promoted the Jack Johnson-Jess Willard heavyweight title fight, but history doesn't remember Frazee as a boxing promoter. History knows him best as the man who destroyed the Red Sox.

In 1918 the Red Sox won the World Series, but the next season Frazee was in a financial bind. His stage shows were losing money and his ball team, mired in sixth place, was losing games. The fans weren't coming out, gate receipts were down, and the mortgage on Fenway Park loomed. He needed money and fast. He knew Yankees' owners Jacob Ruppert and Til Huston were businessmen who would listen to a deal. The most valuable commodity Frazee possessed was Ruth.

In 1914, his first professional season, the raw left-hander ran up a record of 23-7 in the International League. Fourteen wins came with the Baltimore Orioles who were firmly entrenched in first place with their young pitching sensation on the mound, but in mid-season Ruth was sold to the Providence Grays, the Red Sox farm team, where he won another nine games and helped win the pennant. To cap off his debut he also appeared in three major league games and won two of them. In 1915, playing with the parent Red Sox, Ruth went 18-8 and also showed what he could do with the bat. He hit .315 and smashed four home runs, tops on a team with a combined thirteen round trippers. His performance inspired a New York sportswriter to write: "His name is Babe Ruth. He is built like a bale of cotton and pitches left-handed for the Boston Red Sox. All left-handers are peculiar and Babe is no exception because he can also bat."

The next year he established himself as the best southpaw in the American League with a 23-12 record, nine shutouts, and the league-leading earned run average. In 1917, he did even better, winning twenty-four games and hitting .325, the fourth best batting average in the league behind only Detroit Tiger superstar Ty Cobb, Tris Speaker, and George Sisler.

Not bad for a pitcher, but a pitcher only played every third or fourth game and it wasn't long before the Red Sox brass began experimenting with Ruth in the outfield. In 1918, he started fifty-nine games in the outfield, hit .300 and got eleven home runs, which tied him for the league lead even though he'd spent most of the season pitching, carving up a 13-7 record. By the next season he was a regular outfielder and promptly broke the major league record with twenty-nine home runs.

He was the Babe, the "home run king," the most exciting player in baseball.

The deal that sent him to the Yankees took place eleven days after Prohibition began, so Boston's baseball fans, who liked to mix baseball with alcohol, were dealt a double blow. But Frazee was happy. Jacob Ruppert, the man who called the shots for the Yankees, not only paid him $100 thousand, but guaranteed the mortgage on Fenway Park for $350 thousand. Frazee's immediate financial needs were over and if he was to be hanged in effigy by the Boston fans, so be it.

◆

Lazo Slackowicz was called Lipsy because of his full mouth. His friends taunted him with "Niggerlips," the same moniker pro ballplayers teased the Babe with early in his career, but Lazo didn't mind. The school records listed his name as Larry Slackowicz and there would come a time when he'd be known simply as Larry Slack, but he was still Lazo at home. At fourteen he was of average height and build with a thick mass of curly blond hair on his head. The boys kidded him for his big ears and the girls fell for his deep blue eyes and everyone knew he was a good ballplayer. He had a smooth natural swing and others tried to copy it, but couldn't.

Lazo played the outfield for the local bantam team, the Lizzies, so called after the community playground on Elizabeth Street, and he wore number three, which would soon correspond to the Babe's number in the Yankees' lineup. Lazo would attribute this to fate. His swing, of course, had come from the man himself. The Babe was everything to him and the most valuable item Lazo possessed was an authentic autograph given him that memorable day six years earlier. No one thought it was real until his father told the boys how Lazo had worked his way down to the dugout and met the Babe.

Lazo's scrapbook quickly grew from one folder to two to three and would have gone to four if one of his older brothers hadn't told him to put all the newspaper clippings and photographs into a sturdy binder that could hold more. He could recite every statistic from the Babe's record by memory. Pitching and hitting. Shorty, or Stanley Hooper, the Lizzies' second baseman – at five-one he was the shortest player on the team – was his best friend and would test him on how many extra-base hits the Babe got for the Red Sox in 1918 or how many runs batted in he'd produced in the season just past.

If anyone asked Lazo about the wisdom of removing the American League's foremost southpaw from the mound and putting him in the outfield, he was armed with numbers and quotes from baseball people in the know, eager to defend the switch from pitcher to everyday player. The baseball world was stunned with the dramatic sale to the Yankees and so were all the Lizzies except for their starting pitcher, Hoodlum, who only laughed.

His real name was Leonard Dixon and he was called Hoodlum for good reason. He was the local tough who relished in the recognition. It brought him respect, but so did his fastball. He didn't have a great variety of pitches, but his fastball was as good as anyone's in high school baseball. He was tall and lanky and used his long legs to advantage when wheeling around on his delivery to get maximum velocity on the ball. He always wore a smart-aleck smirk on his face. The story was keep him mad and he'd fire that old pill down the pipe with amazing regularity.

Airbrain was the catcher and the two boys hated each other, but while Hoodlum's hate was forthright and aggressive, Airbrain's was restrained. Eddie Parrish was quiet and not too quick at school – hence his nickname – but he managed to scrape by with a C minus, the minimum grade allowed for playing on the baseball team. Roll along with at least a C minus and you were out there every spring when the team began practicing. His teachers always felt that if the minimum had been a C, young Eddie would have achieved that as well. He was four or five inches shorter than Hoodlum, his nose wide and squashed-like, his ears sticking out from his head. Hoodlum mocked him unmercifully and said he wanted to throw such a sizzling fastball that Airbrain's hand would be crushed into a bloody pulp. Airbrain would counter by catching Hoodlum's best smoke and urge him to throw even harder, which was good for the Lizzies.

Only Airbrain could bring out the best of Hoodlum's fastball, so they were kept together despite their mutual hatred or maybe because of it. Besides, Airbrain was the slowest runner and weakest hitter on the team and could do the least damage from the catcher's position. He hit in the number nine slot. He liked catching because a catcher could hide behind a mask. Sometimes Hoodlum threw the ball so hard – not hard enough to render Airbrain's hand into a bloody pulp, but enough to sting the bottom fleshy part of the hand – that his face would show pain, but if it was covered, no one, especially Hoodlum, would know.

"Take this you moron," said Hoodlum stepping into his windup.

Thump.

"C'mon, gimme a fastball," replied Airbrain. "I wanna see some speed."

Thump!

"Is that the best you can do?"

"Okay, you asshole. Take this."

THUMP!

Airbrain's hand would go numb, but the slightest pause and Hoodlum would unleash such a verbal barrage about his nose or ears or other body parts – nothing was spared – that the fragile catcher couldn't continue. That's why Jackson Wallace, the vice-principal who doubled as coach of the Lizzies, didn't mind if Airbrain got only the odd hit through the season as long as he kept catching for Hoodlum.

"You sure ain't no Babe Ruth, that's for sure," said Airbrain as he returned the ball, wincing in agony.

"Ah, who's he? He's just a bum."

If there was one way to get under Lazo's skin, it was knocking the Babe.

"He's a bum," Hoodlum told Lazo. "The Red Sox got rid of him 'cuz he couldn't make up his mind what he wanted to do – pitch or hit. They finally got sick of all his whinin'. He wasn't that great a pitcher anyway."

"Then how come he never had a losing season?" Lazo said. "How come he had the best earned run average in the league in only his second year? Trouble was every time he came to bat he got a double, triple, or home run and they couldn't play that kind of power every fourth day so they had to make him a full-time hitter and he's a great hitter. Cobb himself said that him, Joe Jackson, and Ruth were the three best hitters in the league."

"If he was such a good pitcher they woulda kept 'im there. He ain't no Walter Johnson."

"Then how come he beat Johnson every time he pitched against him?"

Lazo didn't hang around with Hoodlum, choosing to spend his time with Shorty. The two endured Wallace for history class on Tuesday and Thursday afternoons and eyed the same girls, though they were too shy to do much about it. There was speculation that Hoodlum had "done it," but most of the evidence was Hoodlum's own long-winded tales of conquest.

Every member of the Lizzies had a nickname. Pancake was the class clown and next to Hoodlum was the first to smoke. The standing joke in the locker room was that Pancake was short – he towered a scant inch and a half over Shorty – since the weed stunted his growth. His real name was John Rutledge and he was called Pancake because his face was full, round, and flat. He was the all-purpose utility man who could play anywhere, and his pranks knew no bounds. The easiest target was Airbrain. Once in practice, after Airbrain removed his catcher's mitt and was shaking his head in pain from a Hoodlum fastball, Pancake offered to help. He said he had something that a lot of big-league catchers were using.

"Just put it on your hand and rub it in real good," he said. "Make sure it gets right into the skin." He held out a small package and told Airbrain to apply the concoction. "The only trouble is it really stinks so keep it away from your nose, rub it in fast and the smell will go away. But be careful. It can leak out so don't open the bag up. Just stick your fingers in and rub it all over your hand."

Airbrain's hand was all red and anything to deaden the pain was worth a try. He took the bag from Pancake and inserted his fingers.

"Rub it in quick," Pancake advised, "or it won't work." Airbrain did and when his hand was full of it Pancake burst into laughter and was immediately joined by all the other players. "IT'S DOG SHIT, YOU JERK!" screamed Hoodlum, who was doubled up on the pitcher's mound, gasping for breath.

Airbrain dropped the package and stared at them, his mouth agape, and ran into the school in search of soap. He threatened to quit the team, but the next day he was back. Hoodlum refused to throw to him until he could sniff the ball to make sure it wasn't "infected." Rumor had it that Airbrain had washed his hands in every brand of soap known to man, then tried rubbing alcohol, the strongest dish detergents, clothes cleaners, and finally tomato juice before convincing himself that his hand was all right.

Noser – Charlie Waxberg – played the outfield with Lazo. A Polish Jew, he could exchange a few words of the mother tongue with Lazo, but was more accustomed to Yiddish. He had a long, skinny nose that grew into a big bulb at the end and if he wasn't self-conscious about the size of his nose when he tried out for the team, he was when he became a regular and, notwithstanding his religion, was immediately christened.

The other Jewish boy on the team, Jack Gershwin – alias Bananas – was the third outfielder and the most nimble. He was quick with his hands and feet and could scoop up a bouncing ball on the fly, transfer it from his glove to his throwing hand, and fire to the cutoff man with split-second accuracy. The best athlete on the team, Bananas had a wide mouth and always looked like he was smiling. Why he was called Bananas was a mystery since he had always been Bananas. There was a story from first grade that had him squeezing a banana through a crack in the peel during lunch; maybe that was it, but nobody really knew. Still, he was highly regarded for his prowess in center field and he could hit.

The coach, Jackson Wallace, had a nickname too, but no one ever said it to his face. He was "The Iceman" because of the cold steely look carved into his features, probably from birth according to those boys in his history class and on his baseball team. He was a big man, six-feet-two and over two hundred and twenty pounds, and would use his bulk to intimidate rabble-rousers. He regarded his students as good kids of solid, working-class stock, which gave them a common fabric that was thicker than any racial lines. Wallace expected commitment. That was the big word for him and it had to be there – in great heaps – in class and on the field. But he was a better baseball coach than history teacher since his own knowledge of the subject was questionable. Lazo's pal Shorty was the local history buff who wouldn't hesitate to question Wallace, like the time Wallace said Napoleon was in exile on the Mediterranean island of "Alba" when Shorty knew there was no such place.

"The island is called Elba, sir. It's between Corsica and the Italian mainland," said Shorty to the amusement of his fellow students.

"Thank you for correcting me, Stanley," said Wallace, who would make a mental note of how many times Shorty had interrupted class and be sure to offer a similar number of tips on playing second base at practice after school.

If Wallace was anything he was fair. Get on his wrong side and you might as well stay away from school for good he'd make your life so miserable, but come to class every day with your homework done and play hard at practice – it didn't matter if you weren't talented as long as you played hard – and he'd give you all the support in the world. His Lizzies were precious to him. They gave him a chance to work with boys and help them develop self-esteem. He thought of them as his own personal mission. Building a team from individuals meant that he had to spot some ability, then combine the wide range of it with other ingredients. Where does the boy want to play? Where does he play best? How does he get along with the other kids? And more than anything, how much does he really *want* to play ball? Next to "commitment," "character" was the most weighty word in his vocabulary and to play for him you had to have both.

The biggest problem on the team was Hoodlum. His father was an alcoholic and his older brothers beat him. He would come to school with a black eye or bruised cheek and word would get around that he'd been in a scrap. Once he arrived looking real bad and asked Wallace to keep mum about his brothers. Hoodlum didn't want people to think someone got the better of him. Besides, black eyes, scrapes, and bruises were all befitting the tough guy image he desperately cherished. He grew up thinking he had to prove himself and that meant being a man. Wallace knew he would never develop self-respect academically, but he sure could pitch. No one had to tell him how to plant his feet and shift his weight to get the proper motion and power behind the ball. He just did it, but he had no discipline. His mind would wander and he could be thrown off his game in a second, which was suicide for a pitcher and sometimes for the whole team.

The previous season, Wallace had tried four different catchers with Hoodlum and none worked out until Airbrain arrived. The day of his first tryout was a memorable affair as Hoodlum wasted no time offering his views on Airbrain's ears, nose, mouth, hair, and build until there was nothing left to attack. But when Airbrain was behind the plate Hoodlum threw with confidence and savage power. He would never like his catcher, but if he could only work with him they could be an effective combination. It had worked last year when the Lizzies upset crosstown rival Valley Playground for the city championship. Valley Playground had been the champions two years running and were heavily favored to win again, but Hoodlum and Airbrain had stopped them.

When Hoodlum tossed a two-hitter and the Lizzies won a squeaker, he wasn't apt to get into trouble. In the right frame of mind he would even apply himself to his studies, but when things weren't going well on the mound he would explode and blame everyone but himself for the number of batters he had walked. He would blame Airbrain.

Wallace was grateful there was only one Hoodlum on the team.

The other boys on the Lizzies were Johnny Black, the third baseman who was called Bronzeman because he was the biggest and most muscular; Drago Yakovski, the Yugoslavian first base-

man known as Slav; and Frankie Valentine, who was dubbed
Holler since he rarely spoke, but he played shortstop with nimble
dexterity and along with Bananas in center field could do anything and make it look good.

This was the 1920 edition of the Lizzies.

With one championship in the bag they were poised to repeat, but Valley Playground had bolstered its offense with a powerhouse Italian who got as many extra-base hits as singles. In one
game against the Lizzies he smashed a triple his first time up, a
double his next and another triple his third. He knocked in six
runs – all the runs his team had scored – in a 6-0
drubbing of the defending champs. After the game Wallace asked
about the boy's age and was shown his birth certificate, which
said he was born in 1906 like the others. Later in the locker room
Hoodlum wrestled Airbrain to the floor and would have pum-
melled the hapless catcher if Bronzeman didn't intervene.

Halfway through the season the Lizzies were in second place,
but had lost both their games against Valley Playground, who
were riding high in first. But the Lizzies almost won that second
game. In the top of the ninth inning Valley Playground was
ahead 3-2. Both teams had played well and more than two hundred spectators had shown up in the popular park known as
Christie Pits to watch them. It was Valley Playground's home
park and most of the people were the parents, relatives, and
friends of their players, but the Lizzies had a following, too, and
the fans of both teams had a great time trying to drown each
other out. Two runners were on base with one out. The Valley
Playground pitcher was tiring so there was a chance to bring in
the tying run and go ahead.

Lazo was up. More than anyone on the team, it was Lazo
who wanted to be a ballplayer. He burned for it. He'd felt this
way ever since seeing the Babe clout that ball over the fence at
Hanlan's Point. It was because of the Babe that he spent hours
every day practicing his hitting and throwing. He even modeled
his swing after him, and though it wasn't as crisp or fluid and
didn't possess anywhere near the power, it was a good easy swing

for a boy in high school. Lazo had mastered the technique to the point that whenever Wallace needed to demonstrate what a good swing was all about he chose him.

He was a left-hander like the Babe and that was no handicap in baseball. It was an advantage. It meant he had a split-second lead over a right-handed hitter after connecting with the ball. He would swing at a pitch and immediately start turning his body toward first base, already thinking of running down the base line. It was also an advantage since right-handers were bewildered by lefties. They regarded them as a curiosity because they were different. A left-handed pitcher was harder to figure out. Anyone in baseball knew that. It was the same for left-handed hitters. Just put a leftie on the mound and another at the plate and what might happen was anyone's guess.

But in school being left-handed was a liability. You were supposed to write with your right hand so the authorities tried to teach these oddballs how to function. As early as grade two Lazo had his left hand tied to his chair so he would learn to write with his right hand and he did, but not nearly as well as with his left. So he wrote with his right hand in school and did the rest of his work at home with his left. Anyone could see that Lazo's handwriting for the completion of his work had a different tilt than the beginning part. Lazo wondered if the Babe had that problem at St. Mary's Catholic School in Baltimore, the place where he had learned to play baseball. It was there, Lazo discovered, that the young Ruth first came under the tutelage of Brother Matthias, whom he would later call "the greatest man I've ever known." Officially, it was called St. Mary's Industrial School, which was a nice way of saying that it harbored wayward boys.

The Babe had a reputation as a troublemaker, but he was awfully good at baseball and often played on teams with older boys. The best players of the school's eight hundred aspiring major leaguers were placed in an elite group and their teams adopted the nicknames of professional clubs. Once George Ruth was the catcher for the Red Sox. In his final year at St. Mary's he turned a lot of heads by setting a record for home runs and winning every game he pitched. He spent his spare time playing ball with amateur and semiprofessional teams and held his own.

In the majors he revolutionized the game and there was no single year that it changed more than 1920. The war over, many good ballplayers were returning from Europe, and there was a popular theory that even the ball was different. This was the "lively ball" theory and while it was never proved, rumor had it that once big league owners saw how fans flocked to see the new wave of home runs, they changed the baseball. Nobody really knew. But there was no arguing about the Babe's accomplishments. He was changing the game all by himself. Before he had burst upon the scene as a full-time outfielder and started terrorizing pitchers with the long ball, "inside" baseball was the order of the day. It meant playing for a run, one run at a time, with a concoction of single-base hits, steals, and sacrifice flies, but now brute power was taking over.

On July 19, in his first season with the Yankees, he set a new major league mark with his thirtieth home run. By the end of the month he had thirty-seven and there was a lot more baseball to go. Lazo was so confident Ruth would hit sixty that he bet Hoodlum a dollar, not an insignificant sum for a teenager in 1920.

But hitting a home run at the age of fourteen was something else. Few boys that age had enough strength to hit a ball over the fence at Christie Pits, never mind the Polo Grounds in New York. The fence was almost three hundred feet away and it took just the right combination of strength and timing to smack one out for a home run. Lazo had hit only one all season and the Lizzies had but six with Bronzeman contributing half of them. Four-baggers aside, Lazo was a good hitter whose .377 average was second best on the team, next only to Bananas. Lazo's average was hovering close to the Babe's and if he couldn't match his idol in the home run derby – who could? – at least he could strive to equal his batting average.

But Lazo had a weakness and a good pitcher could spot it. He couldn't hit a low inside fastball. It caused him unending agony because no matter how hard he worked on his hitting, he just couldn't get good wood on that pitch. Wallace pointed out that Lazo had long arms and unless he changed his style he didn't have enough room to get a good arc on his swing when the ball came in low and inside. If a strong pitcher threw nothing but strikes to the low inside corner, Lazo would be gone in three pitches every time.

The Valley Playground pitcher knew about Lazo's sore spot, but tossing the ball to the low inside corner every time wasn't easy, especially with two runners on base. And this time the two runners were Bananas and Bronzeman, and Bananas in particular was a whippet on the bases, always a danger to steal. He made life miserable for opposing pitchers. He would take long leadoffs, taunt them by sticking out his tongue and hurling obscenities, then challenge them to try and throw him out. They rarely did because when they were rushed the throw to first was off target and Bananas would steal. This time he was on second, in scoring position.

"C'mon, Lipsy! Hit me home!" Bananas screamed as he lined up ten feet off the bag.

"C'mon, Lipsy! Let's do it!" cried Bronzeman from first.

Wallace was clapping his hands, revving up the bench, getting everyone going. He wanted to keep the rally alive. The Valley Playground pitcher glanced over his right shoulder and caught a glimpse of Bananas out the corner of his eye, looked over his left shoulder and checked Bronzeman at first. He wound up and threw. Strike one. Low inside. Lazo cursed under his breath. The catcher called for time and walked to the mound. He was stalling, giving his pitcher a few extra moments to rest his weary arm.

"Keep throwing 'em low'n inside and he's outta there," he said.

The next pitch came in low again, but was way inside and Lazo didn't move. Ball. The pitcher took a deep breath, collected himself, and wound up again. Lazo saw it coming and took his arms back, just the way the Babe did, then brought them around and swung as hard as he could, but missed. The ball caught the corner of the plate, low and inside. Strike two.

Lazo looked at Wallace, who wanted him to step back from the plate and get more of a swing, but Lazo didn't budge. He had worked hard to develop this stance and had it down to a science. He could have closed his eyes and stepped right into position at the plate just by the feel of the ground on his feet that were exactly eight inches apart. Like the Babe's. The next two pitches were way off. The first was high and outside and Lazo let it go to even the count to 2-2. The one after that was well inside and now the count was full.

"Way to watch 'em, Lipsy!" shouted Bananas from second base.

The pitcher took another deep breath. If he threw a bad pitch and walked Lazo the bases would be loaded with only one out and then three good hitters would be up – Shorty, Pancake, and Hoodlum – before Airbrain who was a sure out. His eyes focusing on an invisible spot low and inside over home plate, the pitcher wound up and threw. Lazo swung with all his might, but only caught a piece of the ball. It was a grounder to the shortstop, who easily tagged Bananas at second base for the first out and then rifled the ball to first to end the game. A double play.

Later in the locker room Bananas said Lazo should follow Wallace's advice and change his stance to get more of a swing.

"You should listen to The Iceman," he whispered. "If you don't they'll get you with that pitch every time."

"I'm hittin' .377 so I ain't changin' a thing," Lazo replied sharply.

"The only reason you're hittin' .377 is that most of the pitchers in this league can't throw a low inside fastball."

"Break it up, fellas," said Wallace, when he joined the team. "The game could have gone either way. We'll get 'em next time."

◆

Valley Playground was two games up on the Lizzies and the teams wouldn't play again until the last weekend of the season. Both clubs consistently beat the rest of the league except for a surprising win by the last-place team over Valley Playground, which reduced their margin over the Lizzies to a single game. The season-ending, head-to-head contests would take place over the Labor Day weekend and the players from both teams wanted to return to school as champions. One year earlier all the Lizzies had received a small bronze medallion, emblematic of the city's bantam baseball championship. With a small metal ring at the top, it could be attached to a chain and worn around the neck. It impressed the girls, but two medallions would impress them more.

Everyone wanted to play the final two games on the best field, which was Christie Pits. None of the Lizzies cared that Valley Playground knew the park better since the turf was thicker and better maintained than at the schoolyard where the Lizzies played so Christie Pits it was.

It had been an exciting season for the team and for baseball. Everyone was paying close attention to the frenzied incidents that took place with the Yankees that summer. In the middle of the season, Babe Ruth was reportedly killed in a car accident along with his wife Helen and three Yankee teammates. They were driving from Washington back to New York after a game and crashed. When Lazo heard the news he burst into tears. It was in the locker room after practice and only Shorty was there. But later that day reports said no one was hurt and the Yankee star was all right, which made Lazo feel like a fool. He learned then not to take what he read or heard at face value. The Babe was so much alive that he didn't miss a single game and the day after his alleged "death" he even slugged a triple.

Ray Chapman of the Cleveland Indians wasn't so lucky. As the second half of the season got under way Yankee pitcher Carl Mays, once a Providence teammate of the Babe's, hit Chapman in the head with a pitch. The Cleveland hitter crumpled in a heap at the plate, struggled to his feet and fell again. He died in hospital the next morning. The Indians and Yankees were in the midst of a pennant race and Mays was removed from the lineup as fans cried for his scalp, but he returned a week later. The day after Chapman died, the Lizzies had a game. Before throwing his first pitch Hoodlum called Airbrain to the mound and said he was going to throw the ball so hard that the Lizzies' catcher would be joining Chapman in the cemetery.

"I've already booked a plot for you," Hoodlum said.

"Asshole," whispered Airbrain under his breath.

◆

At first it was a story no one believed and if you loved baseball you didn't want to believe it. The Chicago White Sox were the defending World Series champions. On the eve of the first game of the 1919 Series Chicago second baseman Eddie Collins said there never was a better ball club than the White Sox. "We've got everything," he told reporters. "Cicotte and Williams are two of the greatest pitchers that ever planted a foot on the slab and our gang can field and hit. We ought to win."

But in the first game star pitcher Eddie Cicotte allowed five runs in one inning and even gave up a triple to the opposing pitcher. He had lost his stuff and it was a sign of things to come. The nine-game series ended five games to three for the underdog Cincinnati Reds of the National League. Cicotte and fellow hurler Claude Williams performed like rank amateurs.

The next season a grand jury began investigating reports that the Sox had thrown the Series and on September 28, eight White Sox players were indicted. They were pitchers Cicotte and Williams, center fielder Happy Felsch, shortstop Swede Risberg, pinch hitter Fred McMullin, third baseman Buck Weaver, first baseman Chick Gandil, and the one that hurt most of all – Shoeless Joe Jackson – the hitter the Babe modeled his swing after.

The team was forever known as the Black Sox. It was said that underworld gambler Arnold Rothstein was involved, but he was never indicted and though the eight players were acquitted the next year the man brought in as baseball's high commissioner – Judge Kenesaw Mountain Landis, as strong a name as America had ever produced – kicked them out of baseball for life. The Black Sox Scandal was the most humiliating escapade in the history of the game and it would have been worse if not for the Babe.

Just when the public's fascination for baseball was most vulnerable, he began his assault on home run fences and wound up the season with the unheard-of total of fifty-four – almost twice the record he had set a year earlier. The fans poured through the turnstiles to see him. He hit .376, scored 158 runs, and batted in another 137. He even had fourteen steals. New York's vocal Italian population took him to their hearts and christened him the "Bambino," a name that stuck throughout his career along with the "Sultan of Swat."

On July 9 – he'd been with the Yankees only half a season – it was Babe Ruth Day at the Polo Grounds. Gifts came from fans all over America, from young and old, rich and poor, black and white. In 1920, the major leagues were still an all-white affair with the best black players confined to the Negro leagues, but that didn't stop wide circulation of a story that he had black blood. Everyone wanted a piece of the Babe. It was the greatest year anyone ever had, but the Yankees finished no better than third. Cleveland won the pennant, the newly decimated White Sox were second, and New York was next. The team destined to be the best in history was still in its formative stages.

◆

On the weekend before Labor Day, when it still looked like Lazo would win his dollar bet with Hoodlum, the title of best bantam baseball team was up for grabs. As in the American League, the high school circuit had all the makings of a feverish touch-and-go pennant race, but this was a pennant race the locals could see, hear, and smell. The Lizzies, of course, could taste it.

Christie Pits was easily accessible by trolley – the best way to the game for people who didn't live nearby. The trolley went right to the park and if there was no room in the wooden bleachers there were always spots on the grassy slope around the back of the diamond. It was a fine place to spend a day and watch some spirited teenage boys play ball. The oddly shaped park known as "The Pits" was a popular gathering spot. If a perfectly square meteor had struck the earth with enough impact to create a depression forty feet deep at one corner and a little less at the others, the result would be Christie Pits. The big scoreboard at the northeast corner was behind home plate overlooking the park and there were usually a lot of gulls about. Spectators thought the birds added nostalgia, but they annoyed pitchers and outfielders. Then there was the wind that came in from the southwest that forced outfielders to change their alignment.

It was a good park for hitters since they could get a good fix on where they wanted to place the ball. From home plate the batter could see the small building with the showers in left center field and the top diving board of the swimming pool way out in right center. A right-handed hitter who liked to shoot for deep left field would aim for the four tall oak trees out on the street and if he could pull the ball it might land in the adjoining ballpark on the other side of the fence. But no one had ever done that.

Lazo had something to prove in these last two games. He had felt responsible for the Lizzies losing the last game with Valley Playground and wanted to atone. He had been playing well. He was hitting .386, fourth best in the league, and was easily Wallace's most improved outfielder having committed a paltry two errors all season. But it meant nothing if the Lizzies didn't take two from Valley Playground.

The first game would be held on Saturday morning and there was concern in the Lizzie's camp that Jack Gershwin – Bananas – wouldn't be able to play because his father wanted him in synagogue. When the teams agreed to play the games at Christie Pits, the coach of Valley Playground went to reserve the ballpark. Saturday afternoon would have been the most logical time for the game, but when the coach learned that Bananas never got home from synagogue until noon, ten o'clock Saturday morning suddenly seemed like a good starting time and the booking was made.

Wallace was furious. He called the city parks department and tried to change the game to the afternoon, but was too late. Two other games had already been booked and all the slots were filled. The Lizzies' coach usually didn't intrude into the boys' family affairs, but the city championship was on the line. If he couldn't change the time of the game maybe he could speak with Bananas' father so he paid a visit to the Gershwins to see if his star center fielder might miss the service. The season hung in the balance. If the Lizzies lost on Saturday they would be two games back with only one to go and confined to second place. No medallion and no championship.

Wallace knew Bananas' father was a big baseball fan who came to most of the games, but not on Saturday mornings. When he appeared at the door of the Gershwin home a few days before the game, Bananas' little sister recognized him right away.

"The Iceman!" she said, shocked to see the vice-principal of her brother's school towering over her on the doorstep.

"What did you say?" Wallace said.

"The Iceman."

"What's that?"

"That's what my brother calls you."

"The Iceman?"

The little girl nodded. A moment later and Bananas' father told Wallace to come in.

"Mr. Gershwin, Jack is a fine boy who has done you proud at school and on the ball team," Wallace said. "I only wish that I had him for more than history and baseball. But the whole school, the whole community, is rooting for us to beat Valley Playground. Jack's our best player. Without him our chances are slim."

"Jeckie is good boy. No trouble."

"Yes he is, Mr. Gershwin, and he's a heckuva ballplayer."

Bananas' father was beaming. It wasn't every day that the vice-principal and coach of the Lizzies dropped in.

"You know," Wallace said, "I think he could play pro some-day."

"Pro?"

"Yes. But he needs the experience of playing under pressure and he'll never get the kind of pressure that he'll get this weekend."

Wallace was a straightforward sort. He always felt honesty was the best policy. That was what he told his students. But repeating as city champions was important. The last thing he wanted was seeing Hoodlum throw a tantrum after losing to Valley Playground. But having them book the park for Saturday morning was a dirty trick.

"You really think he can play professional?"

Wallace swallowed hard.

"Mr. Gershwin, as the coach of the defending city champions I can guarantee you that when he has completed high school I'll do everything I can with my contacts in major league baseball to make sure he gets a tryout with one of the teams."

"You can do that?"

"Absolutely."

"I didn't realize you knew such people."

"I don't like to tell everyone about it and I'd like you to keep this between you and me. I wouldn't want Jack to get a swelled head."

Religious observation was important to Bananas' father, but the majors was something else. Still, he hesitated. Wallace tried again.

"Of course, these people pay more attention to teams that win championships. Not many pros come from losing teams. If the Lizzies put together three or four championships in a row these people might even come to us without my calling them. They'll say the Lizzies are a great team and ask who's our best player and I'll say, 'Jack Gershwin, that's who. Without him we couldn't have done it.'"

He had played his final hand and looked straight into the eyes of Bananas' father.

"Okay. He can skip the service. But don't have no more games on Saturday mornings. Baseball is important. But being a Jew is important, too."

With that they shook hands.

On the day of the game hundreds of people congregated at Christie Pits. It was the largest crowd of the season. The rivalry between the Lizzies and Valley Playground even made it to the local newspaper and a sports reporter who covered the International League Maple Leafs was on hand. During the Lizzies' pregame practice, Valley Playground's coach was surprised to see Bananas shagging balls in the infield.

"Is that Jack Gershwin out there?" he asked one of his players.

"Yep."

"I thought he was gonna be away today."

"Nope. That's him all right."

The bewildered coach shook his head and started making notes. His strategy had been built on Bananas' absence from the Lizzies' lineup. Now he would have to adapt, but he was confident. His team and his big hitter were ready to wrestle the championship back from the enemy.

The game began as a pitcher's duel. Hoodlum had his best stuff, Airbrain was calling a good mix of pitches, and for once Hoodlum wasn't quarreling with his catcher's selections. But Valley Playground's pitcher was at the top of his game too, and neither team scored a run through the first five innings. In the sixth the Playground's power hitter knocked a blazing fastball into the outfield right between Bananas and Lazo. It went for a double and a run scored. The Lizzies tied the game in the seventh when Bananas walked and then stole two consecutive bases with some nifty running before scoring on a sacrifice by Bronzeman.

The score stayed locked until the top of the ninth with the Lizzies at bat. The first batter, Shorty, blasted a line drive to deep left field and slid into second base with a double. Hoodlum was up next and he flied out so Shorty couldn't advance. Then it was Pancake's turn. As usual, he'd been brought in to pinch hit, this time for Airbrain. On the first pitch he smacked a bouncer through the legs of the shortstop and Shorty scored. The Lizzies went up 2-1. They hung on to win and found themselves tied with Valley Playground in first place.

The players erupted in celebration as if they'd just won the World Series, but Wallace calmed them down with the subtle reminder that another game was coming Sunday. And that was the big one. The team held a meeting in the locker room after the game and Wallace tried to get them thinking of the task ahead.

"It's one game and anything can happen," he said. "But we're the better team. I believe that and I want all of you to believe it too. We've all played together for two years now and we're a good unit. We've got good hitting, pitching, and fielding and enough speed to win it all. The one thing I have no way of measuring is desire."

Bananas lowered his head and prepared for the worst as The Iceman was launching into another of his famous motivational speeches. Everyone knew it was coming when the prize was referred to as "it."

"If you guys really want it then you'll win it. There are two awfully good teams in this thing and whoever wants to win it more will. Of course, Len's going to have to be at his best. But if he can pitch another game like he tossed today we'll do just fine."

The boys cheered for Hoodlum, who only smirked.

"All the bats have to be cracking. Valley Playground has good pitching too. They didn't get that earned run average by accident. And they have that big Taglietti kid who can knock the ball out of the park any time." Wallace paused and caught his breath. The day and squeaker of a win had taken its toll on him as had the Lizzies all season long. "I want everyone to go home, have a good dinner, and get a good night's sleep. And I want to see every one of you here tomorrow afternoon at one o'clock. Sharp."

Bananas looked up and met Wallace's eyes.

"That's it?"

"That's it."

Like an army troop after getting its battle assignments, the Lizzies broke rank and headed off to the showers. That night Lazo couldn't sleep. Many of the Lizzies couldn't sleep. But while Hoodlum was in bed thinking about which pitches he'd throw to whom, his right hand clutching a baseball under his pillow, and

Bronzeman was dreaming about the statuesque blonde in math class, his right hand on his crotch, Lazo was fancying himself as the big power hitter of the New York Yankees. It wasn't just a dream – it was an *obsession* – and he had been there before. But now it was the night before the seventh game of the World Series. Winner take all. Everything rested on his shoulders and forty thousand people were at the Polo Grounds cheering him on.

He was the Babe. The Bambino. The Home Run King. Businessmen would stay away from work and teachers would send their students home early so they could catch the live action on radio. But what in the world would the Babe be doing the night before such a game? Would he spend a quiet evening at home with his wife or be out on the town as he was apt to do? Lazo drifted off, his mind in the fantasy land of baseball, a land that was often a haven for his dreams.

"Lazo. Get up! You got a game today!"

It was his mother. She was always the first to rise. Lazo didn't normally start the day with a bang. He would typically roll over two or three times, bemoan his fate, and beg for another five minutes in bed. But not today. He dressed quickly, ate, and told his parents and brothers he'd see them later at the Pits. The family would be there. This was *the* game. The biggest one of his life.

The Lizzies' uniforms didn't have pinstripes, but they were adequate. The word "Lizzies" was written in black across the chest. The off-white shirts and pants were loose-fitting and comfortable and the caps said loud and clear that these boys were ballplayers. At one o'clock Wallace gathered the team together.

"Well boys, this is it. This is what we've been playing for all year. The city championship. You all know Valley Playground won it twice in a row before we beat them last year and now we have a chance to do it again. And it will be especially sweet against them. The plan today is to play them the same way we did yesterday. We've got more speed than they do. We've got better hitting. And we've got pitching that's just as good as theirs. Or better. What we don't have is the power they have in Taglietti and if we can keep him away from those extra-base hits, which means the outfield has to play a little deeper for him, we'll win it. And that's all there is to it. Do you guys want this? Do you want it?"

A modest "yeah" erupted from the mouths of the Lizzies. Wallace wasn't satisfied.

"I said, do you guys want it?" and a thundering "YEAH!" echoed loud enough for all the people in the bleachers to hear. "Okay. Let's do it. Here's the batting order. Leadoff. Jack Gershwin, center field. Number two. Frankie Valentine, shortstop. Number three. Drago Yakovski, first base. Cleanup. Johnny Black, third base. Number five. Larry Slackowicz, right field. Number six. Stanley Hooper, second base. Number seven. Len Dixon, pitcher. Number eight. Charlie Waxberg, left field. Number nine. Eddie Parrish, catcher. Alternate. John Rutledge. Let's warm up."

As soon as Wallace finished speaking, just when his lips touched to form the "p" in the word "up," Pancake let loose with an earsplitting fart. He'd been holding it in waiting for Wallace to finish. There was a momentary silence and then everyone broke up in raucous laughter. Wallace wasn't amused.

"Who did that?" he asked.

Pancake, a huge smile on his face, bit his lower lip hard.

"I did, sir. It was me."

"Well, John, what do you have to say for yourself?"

"Excuse me, sir. I mean, pardon me. Sorry."

"That was just his way of warming up," said Hoodlum and again the team erupted in laughter.

Their families were some thirty feet away and more, filling the stands that stretched from behind the batting cage out along the base paths. They could hear the boys laughing heartily.

"The coach must be settling them down," reasoned Bananas' father, who was there with his wife and daughter. "Good idea. Jeckie was very serious this morning. That Mr. Wallace knows what he's doing."

Soon the Valley Playground team arrived and quickly huddled for a strategy session. Antonio Taglietti, their star slugger, caught the eye of Hoodlum and pointed confidently to the home run fence. Hoodlum mouthed an obscenity. Today this boy was his mortal enemy.

◆

The 1920 city championship was about to be decided. At one-thirty the Lizzies took to the field and Valley Playground came to bat. Now Hoodlum would get the chance to show his stuff. The first two batters hit harmless grounders to the infield and each time the throw to first was well in advance of the runner. The third hitter was the cocky Taglietti and he didn't wait long to show his brash self. He pointed to the fence and told Hoodlum to throw. Hoodlum's first two pitches were both inside for balls. He had to respect Taglietti's power and would sooner walk him than give him a fastball out and over the plate.

The Iceman said that was a no-no.

The next pitch was a little inside, but Taglietti connected with a tremendous blast and the ball sailed out to right field where Lazo patrolled. All Lazo could do was watch it sail over his head for a home run. The Valley Playground fans went wild and Hoodlum cursed and snarled at his catcher. Airbrain shouldn't have called for another inside fastball, he thought. Hoodlum re-tired the next batter on a ground out, but now they were down 1-0.

Valley Playground's pitcher was tall and gangling. Like many pitchers he came to the game a bundle of nerves. He would chew hard on a different piece of bubble gum every inning, his front teeth gnashing against the bottom ones. It was relentless and even the Lizzies' batters could hear him grinding the gum apart. Then he would blow a huge bubble and let it pop and if it shook the Lizzies up so much the better. Around the league he was known as Fuzzy because of the peach fuzz on his cheeks. He had allowed fewer runs than any pitcher in the league and had a good mix of pitches. He had a good fastball, too – not as fast as Hoodlum's – but just as accurate and he also had a good curve and slider.

He could throw any of them with confidence and if the Lizzies did connect the Valley Playground infield was equal to the task, but the outfield didn't figure to be that busy since the Lizzies were a singles-hitting club. Good hitters like Bananas, Holler, Slav, and Lazo went for average while Bronzeman, the closest thing to a slugger on the team, was the only long-ball danger and even he didn't have the power of a Taglietti.

Bananas ambled up to the plate.

"Batter up!" the umpire called.

Fuzzy chewed like mad and Bananas took a few practice swings showing where he wanted the ball.

Pffft.

Strike one. A fastball. Right over the plate. Bananas didn't even see it. He shook his head, looked back at the umpire and dug in his heels.

Pffft.

Strike two. Fastball again and again right over the plate. Never before had Fuzzy shown such speed on his fastball. Bananas, an analytical hitter like Lazo, muttered under his breath. If the next one was a repeat he would swing and swing hard. In it came. Bananas swung and the ball landed in the catcher's mitt with a thud.

"Strike three! You're out!" cried the umpire.

Bananas walked away in disgust.

"The guy's throwin' smoke," he said passing Holler, the next victim.

Wallace shook his head. Bananas was his best hitter. He was the leadoff man and his job was to get on base, but Bananas was intimidated by the pitches. Holler didn't fare any better as Fuzzy had to whip only four fastballs over or near the plate to retire him, the last one coming with Holler standing and watching.

Two away.

If Fuzzy had come to deflate the Lizzies, he got off to a great start. The third batter was Slav, the first baseman. He hit the first two pitches, but both went foul putting him behind with a count of no balls and two strikes. The next pitch was a curve that caught the far corner of the plate and he was gone. Fuzzy had thrown but ten pitches, not one of them a ball, in mowing down the Lizzies one-two-three.

The Valley Playground fans cheered as Fuzzy came in from the mound. It was still 1-0 and the score stayed that way until the fourth when Taglietti again came up to bat with one man on base and two outs. He didn't point this time, but his eyes told the story. He stared right at Hoodlum, then looked off into the outfield. Hoodlum was seething with rage.

"Stinkin' wop," he said, channelling all his hate onto his adversary.

After four pitches the count was two balls and two strikes. The Valley Playground slugger was making Hoodlum uneasy, getting him off his game. Hoodlum inhaled, went into his windup and threw a hard fastball that almost struck Taglietti on the temple. The batter ducked and swerved, lost his balance, and fell in a heap. The Valley Playground bench exploded and a barrage of catcalls rained upon Hoodlum, who just sneered back. Wallace grimaced. His pitcher was losing his cool.

Taglietti got to his feet and dusted off his pants. Hitter and pitcher faced each other again. This time Hoodlum went for a curve, not his best pitch, and Taglietti clubbed it out to deep right field.

From the moment of impact Lazo had his eyes on the ball and started running back to the fence. Not another one, he thought. But it didn't have the height of the earlier blast. Eyes on the ball, concentration total, he checked his proximity to the fence, a wire fence six feet high. Lazo adjusted his speed so he'd be there when the ball dropped. He was still running. He checked the fence again. He was awfully close now. The ball started its descent. Lazo had to slow down or he would run right into it, but he had to be sure he could jump and make the catch if that was his only chance.

The ball was coming in and Lazo reached out with his glove high over his head, but he could tell that his legs weren't going to carry him fast enough so he took two giant strides, then dove across the grass as far as he could. The ball caught the upper webbing of his glove pocket. He fell to the ground, square on his right shoulder, not five feet from the fence, and covered the ball with his bare hand to make sure it didn't get away.

He rolled over. His shoulder stung with the burn from the ground. Then he got to his feet and held his glove aloft for everyone to see. All the Lizzies stood up and cheered. What was nearly a 3-0 game had remained 1-0 because of his tremendous catch. The side retired, Lazo came in from the outfield, clutching his shoulder. Hoodlum, thankful for his heroics, gave him a pat on the back.

"Ouch!" said Lazo.

"You all right?" asked Hoodlum.

"My shoulder feels like it's broken."

Wallace touched it and Lazo winced in pain, then he undid Lazo's buttons and slipped off his shirt. His shoulder was red and badly scraped from the tumble.

"It's very tender," Wallace said. "You may have to pack it in for today."

"What? No way. There's no way I'm not goin' back in."

"You won't be much good to us if you can't catch or hit, Larry."

"It don't hurt."

With that Lazo stopped grimacing and put the pain out of his mind. He buttoned up his shirt.

"I'm fine," he said. "Besides there's lots of time for it to hurt after the game's over."

Wallace smiled.

"C'mon boys, we're down a run," he said, clapping his hands.

Fuzzy still had his good stuff through the middle innings, but so did Hoodlum, who had recovered from the two balls Taglietti sent deep and now he too was retiring the hitters in order. Lazo came to bat in the top of the sixth, but his shoulder still ached. He couldn't get a good even swing and flied out.

In the top of the ninth, the score still 1-0 for Valley Playground, Taglietti came to bat again and again there were two

outs with no one on base. Everyone in the park was silent and
tension was high. Another run and they would be up by two and
in a game like this that would be enough.

Hoodlum couldn't afford to save himself for extra innings.
He had to give it everything he had. He dug in, spit, and adjusted his cap. He led off with a curve that fooled Taglietti completely, then unleashed a fastball that caught the inside
corner and Taglietti stood watching. The count was no balls and
two strikes. Airbrain gave him the signal calling for another
curve, but Hoodlum shook his head so Airbrain called for a
slider and Hoodlum waved that off, too. No, it was now or never
and he would go with his best pitch. A fastball.

It caught the outside corner and Taglietti swung, but too late
and Valley Playground was retired. Now the Lizzies had to score
a run or it was all over. Bottom of the ninth. Down 1-0. It was
their last chance.

Holler was up. He watched two balls come in low and outside, then swung hard on a perfect strike and the ball bounced
into the outfield for a base hit. He was on and the tying run was
at first. Now the Lizzies were back to old-style baseball, the kind
that all teams had practiced so religiously until Babe Ruth came
along. Their job was to move Holler to second, then third, and
bring him home. It didn't matter how they did it, but they had
to advance the runner.

Slav was up next. Slav liked to stroke the ball straight across
the plate to the opposite field, but Fuzzy, beginning to tire after
eight innings of hard throwing, wouldn't quit. He had allowed
only three hits, all singles. There were only three more outs to go.

Again the first two pitches were balls and Wallace clapped
his hands. A walk would be beautiful right here, he figured. Two
guys on, nobody out with Bronzeman, Lipsy, and Shorty coming
up. But then Slav went for a curveball that was far outside. It was
a sucker pitch and he lined it right to the third baseman who
made the catch without moving.

One away and Holler was still on first base.

"Damn!" said Wallace, banging his hand into his fist.

Now it was Bronzeman's turn. He walked to the plate, swung the bat in his muscular arms, and stood very still, concentrating on the pitcher.

Fuzzy was showing less power with each pitch and had to mix things up to throw the hitters off. He tossed a fastball for a ball, a slider for still another ball, then a curve for another ball. Bronzeman, up 3-0 in the count, relaxed. The next pitch was right over the plate and Bronzeman connected, knocking it to deep left field. At first it looked like it would go all the way, which would have won it for the Lizzies right there since both Holler and Bronzeman would have scored and that would have been enough. But it just hung up there and then dropped into the glove of the left fielder. But at least it was deep enough to allow Holler to move to second where he was in scoring position. Only now there were two outs. One more and the game and the Lizzies were finished.

It was up to Lazo. If he could get a hit and Holler scored, the game would be tied 1-1. If that happened and the next batter got out, the game would go into extra innings and since both Hoodlum and Fuzzy were near exhaustion, it would mean the hitters might have an advantage.

But first Lazo had to get on base. He stood in the batter's box with the game, the whole season, on the line. Everything rested in his hands. In his bat. All those hours of practicing the Babe's swing. Feet eight inches apart. Perfectly positioned so the only way to step is into the ball. His weight on his left leg. His front leg bent slightly at the knee. His hands squeezing the wood, letting go, and squeezing again.

From the age of eight, from his first glimpse of Babe Ruth, he had idolized him and copied his every move. It had been six years since that monstrous hit that the player "with the girl's name" clubbed into the bay and Lazo knew right then and there this man wouldn't toil in the minor leagues for long and he didn't. He had made his mark and only destiny stood in the way of how far he could go. But what about Lazo's destiny? Would he have the mettle to make it as a ballplayer? Would he have the character and desire The Iceman spoke of?

This was his chance.

Fuzzy wanted to end it. One more out. That was all he needed. He chewed hard on his gum, worked it into a corner of his mouth, flattened it out and popped a bubble. He sucked in some air and let it out slowly. He checked Holler at second base, wound up and threw. It was a fastball and Lazo saw it coming. He gripped the bat hard, held his breath, brought his arms back and swung.

Pffft.

"Steee-rike!" screamed the umpire.

"No," said Lazo. It was a good pitch. Fuzzy was digging deeper. He had something left. Lazo needed time. He stepped out of the batter's box and looked to the outfield. The high diving board of the swimming pool was beckoning out in right center. Lazo had never hit one that far. Nobody had. He grit his teeth.

"Help me, Babe," he said to himself. "Help me. I need you."

He stepped back in, took two easy swings, and waited for Fuzzy's next delivery. Fuzzy was adjusting his cap, scratching the back of his head, rubbing the tip of his nose, doing all those crazy things pitchers do when the game is on the line.

Then Lazo heard him.

"Keed. Your swing's all wrong. You only got a second to see if you like the pitch. If you like it start swingin' right away. Don't wait. And you're off balance. You can't hit like that."

Lazo looked around. He could see nothing, but he heard a voice.

"Your swing's all wrong."

"What's wrong with it?"

"You're too close to the plate. Step back so you can get an arc on your swing."

"That's what The Iceman said."

The umpire stuck out both his hands and called for time.

"You got a problem, son?" he asked Lazo.

"What?"

"You talkin' to yourself? The pressure gettin' to ya?"

Lazo moved his feet back two inches. He looked at Fuzzy, who had a bewildered look on his face. Batters talking to themselves always drove him nuts. It ruined his rhythm.

"C'mon fella," said the catcher to Lazo impatiently. "Get in the game. Let's end this goddamn thing."

The umpire signaled for play to resume. Fuzzy didn't waste any time. He wound up.

"Now keed you gotta be in your groove. Get your weight on your left foot. Be ready."

"Like this?"

The pitch was low and outside.

"Ball!" screamed the umpire.

"Shit," said Fuzzy.

Lazo didn't even see it. He was so preoccupied with getting his stance just right he didn't even know Fuzzy threw the ball.

"No, you're still off balance. You won't hit anything like that. Move your left foot back. You're forgettin' you're only five-six. Not six-two."

"Ball two!" screamed the umpire. Again Lazo was moving and shifting himself at the plate, paying no heed to the pitcher.

"Shit," said Fuzzy louder than before. "What's goin' on? This guy ain't even in the game."

"Hey boy," the umpire whispered to Lazo. "Are you playin' or what?"

Lazo didn't hear him. All he could hear was the Babe.

"Now on the next pitch start your backswing early. Go all the way back. When the ball's comin' in, if it's a good one, bring the bat up a bit and across. Then wallop the livin' shit outta that ball."

Lazo saw it. A fastball. Just the way he liked it. He swung with everything he had.

Pffft.

"Steee-rike two!"

"No! Not like that. You got it all wrong. Here lemme show ya."

Then it happened. The voice gave way to a vision. It was bathed in an aura and descended onto the playing field in a shadow and there was no mistake. It was him. The wide nose. The big nostrils. The round moon face. The warm smile.

God, he was big.

"Now look, Lazo . . . Larry . . . Lipsy . . . How many names you got, anyway? You're never gonna hit anything outta here with a swing like that. You gotta get a good pop on the ball and the way to do that is at the moment of impact you gotta give your wrist a little extra twist, then follow through."

Lazo could feel the bat being taken from his hands.

"Be steady. Steady now. Keep your eye on the ball. He sure as hell don't wanna walk ya. Not with a guy on second. This'll be a good one. You can bet on it. Ready. Here she comes."

The last toss of the season was a two-and-two pitch that came in knee-high just in front of the outside corner. Just where he liked it. He brought those big arms back and started to spin. The bat came in low and then up to meet the ball head-on. There was a massive *thunk!* and the ball took off for the high diving board.

Lazo wasn't sure what happened, but he could feel his body, in slow motion, drop the bat and start for first base. The ball was in slow motion too, climbing up, up, higher than any ball had ever gone at Christie Pits before. His foot hit the bag at first and he made the turn as the ball kept soaring way over the fence. He rounded second and glanced over his right shoulder and watched the ball disappear into the sky. His arms churning like well-oiled pistons, his legs eating up the dirt with the longest strides they had ever taken, he sucked in the air and kept on his journey. His right foot touched third base and he ran for home. Holler was standing just behind home plate, screaming with both hands in the air, but Lazo couldn't hear him. He couldn't hear a thing. Everyone was there. The whole team. They were jumping up and down, their mouths wide open, but there was only silence. Wallace – The Iceman – was banging his hands together and Lazo couldn't tell if he was laughing or crying.

The ball landed with a soft splash in the deep end of the swimming pool over three hundred feet away.

Plop.

Lazo stepped on home plate and the noise was deafening. His teammates mobbed him. He fell to the ground with Hoodlum's arms around him.

"Lipsy! I love you! I love you!" cried Hoodlum.

The next thing Lazo knew he was lifted onto their shoulders. It was a mob scene. Pandemonium. Jubilation. The Lizzies carried him across the infield. Spectators were standing and cheering. Wallace was shaking hands with someone, then somebody else, then somebody else.

Lazo was the hero. The Lizzies won. They repeated as city champions.

"Hey keed, that was some poke."

And just like that he was gone.

The vision. The voice. It vanished.

Lazo felt a shiver down his spine. He did the unbelievable. He hit the longest home run anyone had ever seen at the Pits. It was a shot players, coaches, and parents would talk about for years to come.

It would become legend.

◆

On the first day of school Lazo wore his new medallion around his neck with pride. All the Lizzies did. Other students even asked for his autograph. In the afternoon Wallace assembled the team in the yard and a photograph was taken and the whole school was there.

In the front row at the far left was Hoodlum, master of the fastball. The boys were told to smile, but Hoodlum could only muster a smirk. Sitting beside him was Airbrain, his hapless catcher. In the middle of the row was the dapper Wallace in a three-piece pinstripe suit, looking every bit The Iceman. On his left was Shorty, trying to be as tough as any fourteen-year-old who stands five-one can. At the end of the row was Bananas, his lips closed tight, his hair neatly combed and parted in the middle for the camera. Directly behind him in the second row was Slav, the tall immigrant who'd been accepted because of his long reach at first base. To his right was Holler, who collected that key hit in the bottom of the ninth. Next was Lazo, the hero, his thick wavy hair still ruffled from all the pats he'd received. Beside him was Noser, squinting in the sharp sunlight, then Pancake, wearing a mischievous half-grin, and finally Bronzeman, towering over the others.

The medallion wasn't very big. Maybe an inch across. On the front in the middle was a pitcher. No one made any mention of it at the time, but he was a leftie. A southpaw. Around the edge were the words:

City Baseball Champions – 1920.

When Lazo got home that night after the party at Wallace's house, he grabbed his penknife and scratched his initials – "L.S." – on the back. He wanted to keep the medallion in a safe place and put it in the blue velvet pouch his father gave him for old coins. Lazo was told that silver dollars, if kept for years, would be worth a lot of money, but no amount of money could buy that medallion. Or the one from the year before. They were priceless. He tucked them into the bottom of the pouch and pulled on the string at the top.

He would have to write the Babe and thank him, of course, but would he even see the letter? How many letters did the Babe receive every day? Still, he couldn't have done it without him. Or had he? Was it really he – Lazo – who had cracked that ball? Or was it the Babe himself, reaching out from the Polo Grounds to Christie Pits in aid of an idol-worshipping ballplayer?

A *keed.*

The home run showed Lazo that he had the power, the missing ingredient from his repertoire. Everything was just perfect. The pitch. The swing. The follow-through. He had the power. He was complete. Now there was no turning back. He was on his way.

Five

The baseball sat in my hand like it belonged there. It fit so. My hand could have been molded around it. It was cradled, nurtured, by my thumb around the outside edge, my forefinger and middle finger around the top, my last two fingers on the other side. Every finger had a purpose. Even the pinky. I absorbed the weight of the ball and caressed its smooth surface. Skin to skin. I thought of a mathematician who wants things to be exact or a draftsman who appreciates neat symmetrical lines. Both would be drawn to the perfect simplicity of a baseball. The draftsman especially would like the stitching, which is a real work of art, sewn through the skin in an easy gentle curve. When the ball is held a certain way the stitching makes a "C" and as it's turned the opening of the "C" becomes a mouth, wide at the edges and narrow in the middle, but it's an angry mouth, the one worn by cartoon characters in a moment of frenzy. The stitching never begins and never ends. It just goes on and on. It's much different from the thread of life since that has a definite beginning and end, but nothing is out of kilter here. Baseball will easily survive the mortals who play it.

When left to its own devices a baseball is inanimate, devoid of energy, but when rifled from a pitcher it suddenly assumes a new dimension. A life of its own. The game is one of precision and science and strategy and while other games involve any number of ways to affect the outcome, baseball really has only one. The batter must make contact with the ball.

I was a little nervous. Waiting for my first time up I should have been studying the pitcher's delivery, but I wasn't thinking at all. I just kept twirling that ball in my hand, enjoying what I could do with it. A baseball is such a practical time-waster because it does so many things. Propel it counterclockwise with your thumb and it spins on your palm like a top. Roll it up your arm to the elbow and back down again and you've conquered gravity. Or just toss it from one hand to the other over and over again.

I always liked playing ball at this diamond. It was in a park at the top of the Bluffs and the lake wasn't far beyond the outfield. It was a peaceful place. There was an old cemetery nearby said to contain the remains of early inhabitants of the area. Back to the 1800s even. I never gave it much thought as I only came here to toss around a baseball, but I noticed it today.

"Stephen Slack. You're up next."

I was twelve years old and my years of fooling around with a baseball had culminated in a tryout with the local Little League team. I had never played organized ball before, but some friends thought I could throw and hit pretty good. It was the first time I ever put on a baseball uniform and it felt right. Like I belonged. When I was slipping on the stockings and pants, buttoning up the shirt and lacing the shoes, I sensed a fraternity beckoning. I had seen the medallions Grandpa had won when he was a kid and that inspired me. I wanted to show him that baseball still ran in the family. I wanted to show my father, too. Both of them were sitting behind the fence watching.

It was Sunday and my father's office was closed — not that it had stopped him from working on Sundays before. At home he would hibernate in his study and there were days — Saturdays and

Sundays – when the only time I'd see him would be for lunch and then in the evening he and my mother would be off for some engagement and I wouldn't see him again until the next day. If I saw him at all.

Work hard, he always said. Make something of myself. Go to school, get good grades, and develop good habits. Read everything I could get my hands on. He told me time and again that I enjoyed the kinds of things he could only dream about when he was a kid. I always lived in a house and was never wanting for bicycles and the latest electronic gadgets, but my father grew up in a flat where, according to him, they didn't have much. Grandpa was in sales and he drifted from one selling job to another, but never made enough money to settle down to the point where he was comfortable or not even comfortable, but stable.

"If you're not smart you'll wind up like your Grandpa, retired with nothing to show for it," he said.   .

He said Grandpa had wasted his whole life going from one thing to another, never sinking his hooks into the ground. He was a drifter, that's what he said. The only thing he didn't drift away from was his family and that was his saving grace.

He told me Grandpa wasn't there when he was born. He was away on some business, just as my own father was when I was born. What exactly that business was I don't know. My father never equated Grandpa with money other than to say he never had much of it. But so what? He was still the kindest person I knew and if he didn't teach me about money he did teach me about a lot of other things. More important things. Like hamsters and tadpoles. And history and rock formations. And the way the clouds move through the sky. And the peculiarities of my grandmother, which always brought a smile to his face.

Even her homemade strawberry jam was more important than money.

The picture my father portrayed of Grandpa was so different from the one I had that I sometimes thought we were talking about two different people. And maybe we were. Grandpa was sixty-seven when I was born and how he spent those sixty-seven years I didn't know. I do know he married late in life and was over forty when he had children. But he never talked much about his past. Still, he must have lived a lot since such wisdom does not come from nothing. The irony was that my father was jealous of Grandpa, jealous because of me. My father, the consummate professional in a fifty percent tax bracket, was jealous of a ne'er-do-well who never built a nest egg.

People were always saying how successful my father was and that wasn't always the case in my friends' homes. When you're six and your father is a police officer or firefighter it's pretty heady stuff, but later you see that chasing drunks down deserted alleyways or spending all your time on false alarms at government-subsidized high-rises isn't so romantic. My mother even thought this was demeaning work since she said it didn't require brains.

"If you wear a uniform you don't have much up here," she would say, pointing to her head, as she disparaged the likes of policemen, firemen, janitors, and security guards. My grandmother was of a different bent and felt that police especially were the saviors of society. If not for them, she would say, even more children would be kidnapped from under the noses of their parents, never mind all those murders, assaults, and bank robberies.

"Never call them a cop," she said. "Call them *officer*."

When I was a kid, I thought that word was capitalized.

Baseball made for quite a quandary in our family. Baseball players wore uniforms, which put them in the same class my mother reserved for those lacking upstairs, but there was a big difference. Ballplayers made tons of money. I had lost count of how many earned over a million dollars a year and some of them multiples of that. But ballplayers, being in uniform and working with their bodies, did not deserve respect. On the other hand, they made so much money they deserved great heaps of respect.

Unfortunately, in my family circle, not even all that money could bring a shred of this precious commodity to their efforts. There was something about *baseball* that preyed on us and it did more than prey. It devoured us. Strangely enough it was Grandpa who hated it the most. Baseball was the one sure way to get on his nerves and just why he hated it so much I didn't know. But I had to find out. One doesn't hate for no reason at all.

The game had left a sour taste in my father's mouth, too, but he still let me try out for Little League. He wouldn't stop his twelve-year-old son from playing baseball as long as I understood it was just a game, that I should never think of it as anything more. It was just a game – for boys. But baseball was also a great teaser, like alcohol or sex, and maybe that's what upset my parents so much. It was fun to play, but soon the play must stop and you must get on with your life. I was told that becoming tantalized with the likes of such vices – baseball was definitely a vice in my family – could only lead to no good.

I was thinking of Grandpa's old medallions when I took the bat in my hands at the tryout, thinking what it was like to be the city champions. But why did he keep those medallions all this time? Those medallions. They were a great secret from his past. A secret best kept in a blue velvet pouch with his socks. And it was only when he told me about the baseball in the lake that everything started coming together. It happened that very day.

◆

I had to make contact. That was the key. Make contact. The pitcher was tall and tried to look intimidating, but I thought I could hit him. And I did. I hit the first pitch out of the infield and smashed the second into left field. I swung and missed on the third and fourth ones. It went on like this. I'd hit a few and miss a few. The odd one I'd get good wood on and hit deep so at least the coaches could see that I had some long-ball ability.

They were watching me closely and then the pitcher threw something different. It looked like it was going to be a good one so I swung hard, but missed the ball completely. Then he threw the same pitch again and the same thing happened, only the second time I swung wildly and the bat flew from my hands. As I went to retrieve it there was a loud banging on the fence from behind home plate.

It was Grandpa.

"You're not swinging right, Stephen," he said. "Your swing's too choppy. Straighten it out and step back a bit."

"Leave him alone," said my father. "He's doing fine."

"No he's not. You're not doing fine when you swing like that. That pitch was low and inside and he'll never hit it unless someone shows him."

My father got to his feet and went next to Grandpa.

"Don't start," he said. "Not with Stephen."

"But he won't make the team."

"So?"

Grandpa stood firm. He looked at me, then back at my father.

"No. That's not right."

The exchange caught everyone's attention and I wanted to stick my head in the ground, but Grandpa wasn't finished. He called to the coach and put his hands in the "T" position for time.

"Just gimme a second with him," he said. "I know what he's doing wrong."

The coach, dumbfounded by it all, shrugged his shoulders. Grandpa came around the fence, joined me in the batter's box, and took the bat in his hands.

"Geez Grandpa . . ."

"Lookit, Stephen. You're right-handed and I'm a leftie, so I can't show you, but I can tell you. You're way too close to the plate. Get your right foot back more and then swing on an even keel. Like this."

He swung and I shook my head.

"Go ahead," he said. "Do it."

He returned the bat and I took a swing, but he said I didn't have it. Then the coach stepped in.

"Excuse me, old fella, but I thought he was doing just fine. Nobody on the team can hit that pitch so I wouldn't worry about it."

Grandpa glared at him.

"Nobody?"

"Nope. Young Jimmy there's our best pitcher. He's got a good fastball and when he throws like that—"

"Low'n inside just over the corner of the plate?"

"Yeah that's right. When he throws like that you can't hit it."

"You mean me?"

The coach laughed.

"No, not you. I mean *no one* can hit it."

Grandpa studied the tall lanky boy on the mound for a second or two, then looked back at the coach whose practice he was disrupting.

"I bet I can hit that pitch," he said.

The coach laughed again.

"You?" he said chuckling under his breath, trying not to make Grandpa look silly.

"That's right."

The coach raised his eyebrows and smiled.

"Well, I might ask you if you were trying out for the team. But you're not."

My father was watching all this from behind the fence and Grandpa's latest challenge made him rush over and grab him by the arm.

"Sorry about this," he said to the coach, "but Stephen's grandfather is a big baseball fan and he gets very involved sometimes."

"No problem."

He started pulling Grandpa away when Grandpa turned around to face the coach.

"You really don't think I can hit it, do you? You probably think I'm just some old fart who's too old to hit that kid's fastball. Well I played a little ball in my time and I'll tell you what. I bet you five dollars I can hit that pitch."

My father took hold of his arm again and started tugging.

"Let's get out of here. I don't want you to make a fool of yourself."

"I'm not making a fool of myself. I just want to show this guy there's one person here who can hit that kid's fastball and it's me."

"It's not necessary," said the coach. "I'm sure you can hit it but I want to see what the boy can do and he was doing fine. Really he was."

With that Grandpa wrestled free from my father's grasp, took a five-dollar bill from his pocket, and pressed it into the coach's hand.

"Here. Five bucks says I can hit it."

"What're you doing?" said my father. "You haven't swung a bat in years."

I was observing the whole affair and getting absorbed by it all. Grandpa had an interest in baseball that was beyond anything I'd ever seen before. But the coach wanted to get on with things.

"Sir, we're trying to run a practice—"

"Five bucks. One pitch. It'll just take a second."

Everyone could see Grandpa meant business. That stubborn streak that only baseball could bring out was front and center. The coach muttered something under his breath and shook his head.

"Okay pop," he said. "You're on. Five bucks. Jimmy. Throw the same pitch to the older gentleman here."

Grandpa took the bat from my hands, moved into the other side of the batter's box reserved for left-handed hitters and took a few easy slices. I stepped back and watched.

He was seventy-nine years old.

"Okay son," he said. "Gimme me your best stuff. Right about here."

He was unsteady. The bat shook in his hands. Grandpa had an average build, but he looked as lean as a stick. Without a muscle on him. He was just an old man. In all my life I had never seen someone that old with a bat. His eyes weren't bad – he wore glasses – but this was baseball. If my grandmother was here all hell would have broken loose. The pitcher didn't know what to do. The coach told him to throw.

"C'mon, let's get this over with," he said.

The boy wound up and tossed the ball, but it was no fastball. He didn't put anything on it at all. It was a lob. Grandpa just watched.

"You call that a fastball?" he snapped. "Why Christy Mathewson could throw better than that when he was dead!"

"Who?" the boy said.

"Never mind. Just gimme a fastball. Right here."

The coach, arms across his chest, told him to throw again. But a good one. The next pitch was real and it was incredible, but Grandpa was into this. Really into it. There was such concentration on his face. He swung hard and I shut my eyes. I didn't want to look. All I wanted was to hear the *clunk* of the bat connecting with the ball and then catch a huge grin on his face. But he swung awkwardly and missed the ball, losing his balance on the follow-through and then falling to one knee. He had to brace himself with his hand. He must have pulled something because he grabbed his hip. He couldn't get up. The coach and I rushed to his side, each of us taking one of his arms.

"You okay there, mister?" asked the coach.

"Grandpa?"

He looked at me as he started getting up.

"Yeah I'm fine," he said grumpily dusting off his pants like a ballplayer. "It's just this arthritis in my side, that's all. Keeps me from getting a good swing. If I was a little younger . . ."

"You okay, mister?"

Grandpa looked at the coach.

"Yeah . . . you're right," he said in a drawl. "The kid's got a damn good fastball. You're darn tootin he does. You got a winner there. He reminds me a lot of Waite Hoyt the way he throws. Keep the money."

But the coach would have none of it. He held the bill for Grandpa to take. Naturally he wouldn't.

"Hell, invest it in the team, why don't you?" Grandpa said and started walking away.

Then a strange thing happened. I don't know if anyone else noticed, but Grandpa still had the bat in his left hand. He walked a few steps and I don't think he even knew it was there. Then he stopped and looked at it for the longest time. His hands moved up and down the grip and it was weird. He seemed to be caressing it. A moment later and he made like he was going to throw the bat on the ground, but he couldn't let go. It was stuck to his fingers.

Like glue.

Finally he dropped it and walked away. My father followed him and when I watched them disappear I felt about the size of an ant. I wanted to forget all about baseball. Making the team was the farthest thing from my mind. But my time at bat wasn't up yet.

"Go ahead, Jimmy," said the coach, relieved that Grandpa had finally left. "Toss him a few balls."

Maybe it was because of what happened, but I was so full of pent-up emotion that I clubbed that first pitch out over the center fielder's head. It went past the freshly cut grass of the outfield and landed somewhere in the rough and from there it just continued on its way. After that there was only the Bluffs.

"Holy cow!" the outfielder screamed racing for the ball. "Did you see where it landed?"

"Nope," someone shouted. "It's gone."

The coach clapped his hands for my colossal hit and then the whole team took to the rough to find the ball, but no one could. It was just like one of them said. It was gone.

"Forget it," said the coach. "That one's lost. Next time you boys should play Stephen a little deeper."

That blast got me on the team and the best part was I could keep the uniform. I couldn't wait to get home and tell everyone, but first the coach took me aside.

"Stephen, maybe it would be a good idea if your grandfather didn't show up again, not until we have a game. Okay?"

I was ashamed.

"All right."

"Good and another thing. Who is Waite Hoit, anyway?"

I shook my head. I didn't know.

"Just wondered. Must be some old-timer."

◆

When I got home my father and Grandpa were sitting on the porch in silence, but it was obvious that words had been spoken. My father asked what happened at the tryout and I said I made the team. I told him about my hit. He said I must get it from Grandpa, something about him being quite a hitter in his day. Then he said he had some work to do and went inside. I took his place beside Grandpa and put my bat and glove down.

"You say you got this unbelievable hit?" he asked.

"Yeah. Right after you left. The first pitch. It wasn't the same pitch I was having trouble with."

"Low 'n inside?"

"Yeah. This one was right down the middle of the plate."

"Right where you like it?"

"Guess so. It was perfect. I didn't think twice. I just walloped it. I . . . I . . . hit the living shit out of that ball."

"What?"

I don't know why I said that. I didn't talk to Grandpa like that. But it just rolled off my tongue.

"Sorry, Grandpa. I didn't mean that."

"Sure you did. You said you hit the living *shit* out of that ball. Isn't that what you said?"

Hearing him talk like that was funny. Grandpa never spoke like that to me. And then he just burst into laughter.

"You know, I remember somebody saying something like that once."

"Who?"

"Well he didn't exactly *say* it, but I heard it just the same."

I didn't know what he was talking about.

"So how far did you hit that ball, anyway?" he asked me.

"But that's just it, Grandpa. We couldn't even find it. It went over the center fielder's head and then we all went to look for it in the rough, but we couldn't find it. One of the guys said it must have rolled down the Bluffs and wound up in the lake."

"The lake?"

I nodded.

"It's in the lake?"

"Maybe. We couldn't find it."

"Well I'll be."

Then he took my baseball glove, put it on his wrong hand, and started whipping the ball into the pocket.

"I thought you were a southpaw," I said.

"I am."

"But that's for a right-hander, not a leftie. If you're a southpaw you should be throwing with your left hand. Shouldn't you?"

He was lazily tossing the ball into the glove. His hands were feeling their way around the mitt and ball and there was a look of pleasure on his face. I thought again about his failed attempt at the plate.

"I never could hit that pitch." He wasn't talking to me when he said it. He wasn't talking to anyone. "Never could. Low 'n inside over the corner. That's the one I tried to help you with. How many times I tried. But I never could hit it."

"It's no big deal."

"Oh, yes it was. It was a very big deal. It ruined me, that pitch."

"What do you mean it ruined you? A pitch can't ruin you."

Grandpa put the glove down. He touched me on the face. Softly. He hadn't shaved and there was stubble on his chin. He scratched it and tugged on his earlobe and I sensed a struggle going on inside him.

"Grandpa, I know you played baseball. I found those medals, remember? You won the city championship. And you couldn't hit that pitch when you were a kid, either?"

"Nope. I couldn't hit it then any more than I can now."

I shrugged and he inhaled and I could hear some wheezing from deep in his chest.

"So what?" I said. "It's been sixty-odd years since then. That's a long time not to play baseball."

"It hasn't been quite that long, Stephen."

"But . . ."

"I was just fourteen, then. You think I never played baseball after I was fourteen?"

"But you never liked it much. You never watched the World Series or anything like that."

"Ah, don't get me started on those overpaid prima donnas. They're not like the old guys. No comparison. Walter Johnson. Ty Cobb. Shoeless Joe. Why, those guys played because they loved the game. For the sheer love of the game."

"Don't they love the game today?"

"Are you kidding? The only thing the players love today is looking at themselves in the mirror. No comparison. The contracts they get . . . free agents . . . why . . ." His mind was off somewhere and there was a subtle smile on his face, but not quite a smile. He was a million miles away. "You know what ruined baseball, Stephen? Television. All the money the teams make from television. You know how much the Yankees must get from television?" I asked him and he just stared at me blankly. "A lot. And with free agency and all these labor problems they have just because the players want more money. They make millions and they still want more. They got no pride."

"Grandpa, who were those guys you mentioned?"

"Who? Cobb? Johnson?"

"Yeah. And the other one?"

"Shoeless Joe Jackson?"

Grandpa sat back in his chair and stretched out his arms as far as they would go. Then he yawned a tremendous yawn, one that captured all the fatigue that can be absorbed in four-fifths of a century. He caught his breath and explained.

"Shoeless Joe Jackson was probably the greatest hitter the game has ever seen. He was kicked out of baseball for gambling on the World Series in 1919. There were eight of them. The Chicago White Sox. They threw the Series because they could make more money losing than they could winning. Ballplayers didn't make much in those days. Like I say they played because they loved the game."

"But players don't gamble today. Do they?"

"No? Ever heard of Denny McLain? Won thirty-one games for the Tigers one year and then he got into trouble with gamblers. Pete Rose. Ever heard of him? Got more hits than anybody and the same thing happened to him. And there's others. Lots of them. The only difference is they make a lot of money so they don't gamble for money. They gamble . . . because they like to gamble I guess."

"If they're ballplayers they shouldn't be gambling at all."

"You're right, Stephen. You're absolutely right. They should just play the game." He leaned over and whispered into my ear. "Ever heard of Babe Ruth? Know who he was?"

"Sure. He hit lots of home runs."

"That's right. Seven hundred and fourteen. The greatest home run hitter of them all."

"No."

"What do you mean no?"

He said it defensively.

"He isn't the greatest home run hitter of them all. He's second. Hank Aaron's first."

Grandpa laughed heartily.

"Hank Aaron?" he said, then he leaned over and brought his face close to mine. "Lookit Stephen, Hank Aaron was a great ballplayer all right. You can't take anything away from him. But as good as he was he couldn't carry the Babe's shoelaces. Besides, he had, what, four thousand more at bats? That's a lot of at bats. And another thing. The Babe was a pitcher for four or five years. Think of all the home runs he would've got if he was a hitter all that time. Put it this way. In 1927 he hit sixty home runs. That was fourteen percent of all the home runs in the league that year. You know what that would mean today?"

"What?"

"It would be like a guy hitting three hundred home runs. In one year! He was great. There was nobody like him. Ever. And you know what? I saw him play."

"You did?"

Now we were getting somewhere.

"More than once. He was . . . what's that word you kids use all the time? When something is really big . . . huge . . . colossal . . . enormous . . ."

He was moving his hands around. Trying to express himself. He was searching, reaching for something of great magnitude. I thought for a moment.

"Awesome?" I said.

"That's it! He was . . . awesome!"

Then that faraway look came to his face again. He was in a dream, a trance, not completely here in mind or body. He was far away off in the past – his past – a place I had never seen. But I wanted to.

"God he was something. He could hit a baseball like nobody else. He had such power. Such grace. Such poise. Watching him swing a bat was like watching the hands of a clock come down and around. Smooth and always on time. It was that fine. But he had power. Unbelievable power. He was . . . *awesome!*"

He took in another mouthful of spring air. I had to know more.

"When did you see him play?" I asked.

"A long time ago. Very long time ago. The game was different then. Everything was different. You know, in 1927, the year he hit sixty home runs, he was earning seventy thousand bucks a year. Seventy thousand bucks a year!"

"So what? My dad makes more than that."

"But Stephen this was 1927! You know how much money that was then? In fact, he made even more than that. He made money from his World Series winnings, from newspaper columns . . ."

"He wrote newspaper columns?"

"Someone else did, but he got most of the money. And he made money for a movie. It was called *The Babe Comes Home*. Silent movie. And he made money for personal appearances. Everybody wanted to hear him. They wanted him to endorse things. People wanted him to do everything. He was the Babe. Babe Ruth. I bet he made two, maybe three hundred thousand dollars that year. Someone once said he was making more money than the president and you know what he said?"

"What?"

Grandpa had a huge smile on his face. He wiped his mouth with his hand and laughed.

"He said, 'Why not, I had a better year!'"

He laughed again, a good hearty laugh.

"You mean he was overpaid? Like the players today?"

"He wasn't overpaid. They couldn't pay him what he was worth."

"So why did you like him, Grandpa? Because he was such a great home run hitter or because he made so much money?"

"Both I guess. He was bigger than life. So big he almost wasn't real. But then again he was. Know what I mean?"

"I think so."

Grandpa idolized him. He was his hero. Finally some of the pieces were coming together. Grandpa played baseball as a kid and worshiped Babe Ruth. I didn't know much about Babe Ruth. Just that he was a star from another era and whatever I got from a movie I saw about him. Grandpa said the movie stunk.

"You know, Stephen, I never told you this before, but when I was your age baseball was like a religion to me. Lookit . . . what do you say we go for a walk?"

He suggested our favorite place, the one place where we as grandfather and grandson could be together and away from the rest of the world. The Bluffs. The three blocks to the Bluffs was a much shorter walk than it used to be. When I was little it was a long way, but in those days everything was an extreme. Things were either very big or very small. Very long or very short. But then things became more in between. I was learning that the dominant color in the world wasn't black or white, but gray and when I told Grandpa this he said that despite my tender age I already knew more than most people do in their lifetime.

"I'm proud of you, Stephen. You're going to do all right."

I always took great satisfaction in pleasing Grandpa. That day – the day we talked about baseball and Babe Ruth – was important because that was when I discovered Grandpa's hero. I used to think he didn't need a hero. He did everything for himself. But nobody is like that.

"When did you see him play?" I asked.

"The first time was September 5, 1914."

"You know the date?"

"You're darn tootin. My father took the day off work. He never took a day off work. Couldn't afford to. But he did that day so he could take me to the ball game. I'll never forget it."

"What was he like? Your father, I mean."

I knew nothing of my great-grandfather. I saw a picture of him once. One of those old pictures in an oval frame. He had a long dark moustache. Probably waxed at the ends. People used to do that.

"He was a hardworking man. Work was his whole life. That's how it was. There was no time for anything else. Not like today. But he would do anything for his family . . . even take his youngest son to a ball game when he should be minding the store."

Grandpa and I were walking side by side. His arm was around me and he didn't have to lower it to get it around me the way he once did. He just stuck it out straight. I was only two inches shorter than he was. So there we were walking down to the Bluffs and we hadn't been there in awhile. There was no time. That's how it seemed. No time. Suddenly I started thinking about Grandpa's time. He wasn't as strong as he used to be. Sometimes he needed help with his footing and that made me think how foolish he was to try and hit that pitch. It was only when I saw him then, looking more feeble and weak than I had ever seen him before, that I realized I should cherish what time I still had with him. He was seventy-nine years old and there was so much he could tell me if only he would open up a bit. I wanted to know about that ball game he went to and the city championships he won. I wanted to know about my great-grandfather and the kind of man he was. I wanted to know what the world was like in 1914.

In a few months Grandpa would be eighty. Whatever things he still wanted to accomplish in life better be done soon because it wasn't likely he was going to begin now.

"What was your dream, Grandpa?"

The question hit him right between the eyes. His calm and easy way of a moment earlier just vanished. He looked down at his feet and then out across the lake.

"Stephen . . ." he said, but there was nothing more. I sensed a million things were turning over and over in his mind, but nothing could be translated into a word. I touched a nerve I had never touched before.

"You're growing up, Stephen. You're growing up so fast and there's nothing I can do about it. Metamorphosis, remember? Lookit, there's a few things I wanted to tell you. But the time didn't seem right."

"What did you want to tell me, Grandpa?"

He looked at me with those deep blue eyes of his.

"I had a dream. It was a good dream and it took up my whole life 'til I was almost thirty."

"Well?" I said eagerly.

"I wanted to be a baseball player."

My mouth hung ajar. Grandpa? A baseball player?

"You?"

"It's true."

"I don't believe it."

"It's true, Stephen. If you don't believe me ask your father."

"He knows?"

"Sure he knows. This was before his time. But he knows. I was playing minor pro ball down in the States . . ."

"Pro?"

"For years it was my dream to make the majors. That's why I never got married or had a family 'til later. I devoted myself to baseball. To making it. I wanted to be another Babe Ruth. I thought I could. For awhile there I really thought I could."

"And you saw him play?"

"Yeah. A few times. I only told you about the time he hit his first homer. He was a minor leaguer himself back then. A pitcher. But he wasn't in the minors long. Not with an arm like that. No way. I also saw him hit his last homer. The very last one. Number seven hundred and fourteen. That was some day. I'll never forget it as long as I live."

"You mean you saw the first one and the last one?"

"Yes, I did. The first one and the last one."

"I bet nobody else did that, Grandpa."

"You're probably right, Stephen. There's probably not another person alive that saw him hit that one at Hanlan's Point in 1914 and the last one in Pittsburgh in '35. Both of them were such fantastic shots. The first time I was just eight years old and it was the most incredible thing I ever saw. I remember the ball like it was yesterday. It had eyes and it just kept going up and up and up . . . over the fence . . . over the trees . . . into the bay."

"The bay? It landed in the bay?"

"The bay. The lake."

"The lake?"

"It's still there, Stephen. That's why I was interested when you said you hit one into the lake. Just think. There may be only two baseballs out in the lake. Yours and Babe Ruth's."

"Gee."

He looked at me just then and it was a look I had never seen before. His face was that of a seventy-nine-year-old man, but his eyes were the eyes of a boy. They were the eyes of someone whose whole life was still ahead of him. They were full and twinkling like a pair of stars and though he was seventy-nine years old there was something else about him—the bursting intensity inside—that didn't belong to a man that age. No, it belonged to someone a lot younger and for a few seconds he had me thinking I wasn't in the company of my grandfather, but another kid.

"Stephen," he said, "some day I want you to get it."

"Get what?"

"The ball."

"The one I hit?"

"No. I mean, yes if you can find it great, but I mean the other ball. The one *he* hit."

"Who?"

"The Babe! Who do you think?"

"Well I don't know."

"I want you to get it, Stephen."

"Why?"

"Because it's yours. It's ours. It belongs to us."

And then just like that he wasn't a boy anymore. He was a seventy-nine-year-old man again. My Grandpa.

"What do you mean it belongs to us?"

"Stephen, lookit, *that* ball is a lot more than a baseball. You see, it holds time. It holds life. It's got me in there and it's got you too. It's got both of us. Right inside it. It's got the year 1914 in it. It's got a teenage Babe Ruth who throws smoke inside it. Why hell, it's even got an eight-year-old kid who's seeing his first ball game inside it."

He had his arms around my shoulders and started to squeeze me.

"Stephen, everything I wanted to be is wrapped up in that baseball. Everything I wanted to do. It's all in there. My dream to make something of myself. To be a ballplayer. And I need it, Stephen. I need it so much it hurts not having it. So that's why I want you to find it because it's still there. Waiting for you. Why, it's been waiting for you since 1914. All that time."

"Waiting? Waiting for what?"

"For the right person and that person is you. Lookit, I'm too old to get it. Hell, I can't even hit a baseball anymore I'm so decrepit. But you could do it. You're young and strong. You could find it."

"But how do you know it's still there?"

"It's there all right. Believe me."

"But why, Grandpa? Why? I don't understand."

"All right, Stephen. I'm going to tell you. I'm going to tell you everything. The whole story. Right from the beginning. But you've got to listen closely because I've never told anyone else about this and it's very important."

And that was how I found out.

Six

Never let the fear of striking out get in your way.
— Babe Ruth

New York was a city of late-night speakeasies – thousands of them – as young red-blooded Americans hankered for a taste of illicit rum and whiskey. Wall Street was bull-market crazy and "get rich quick" was the order of the day. It was a time of lavish unbridled capitalism and New York was the place to be. It was big and powerful and everyone could get a piece of the pie. All you had to do was reach.

Bananas' ticket was baseball. The talented center fielder had lightning speed, a keen batting eye and deft glove hand. In his last year of high-school ball he hit .465 and was Most Valuable Player. The pro scouts came for a look and liked what they saw: a smaller-than-average player with impressive raw talent that had to be refined, but top-level juvenile ball leading to "AA" and "AAA" could only be found in the States, so the Gershwin family was asked if Jack could leave home to play for a good senior club. They would even find him a job. His father told them to say hello to Jackson Wallace, but the scouts only stared blankly into his face.

"Jackson who?" they said.

They said Jack was a developing commodity who needed "seasoning," but the family said he was too young. A year later the scouts knocked on their door again and again they declined. Besides, he was working for the railway.

"I think I'd rather play ball than lay railway ties," he told his parents.

The next year he hit .527 in the best men's league in the city and it was easy. But he wanted to know how good he was. He wanted to sample those pitchers in the States, so he considered another route. His Aunt Sadie.

The Hoboken Browns were a semipro team with a loose affiliation to the New York Yankees and every spring the club held tryouts at a park on the west side of the Hudson River just across from Manhattan. It wasn't often that fresh rookies made the squad, but those with potential were sometimes pushed into the team's feeder system and a year or two year later they had a shot at a pro career. The Gershwins had a strong connection with Hoboken since it was home to Bananas' aunt.

In the spring of 1925 Bananas planned to return to his old team along with two chums from the Lizzies' days – Lazo and Stan Hooper, alias Shorty. Another former Lizzie, Len Dixon – a.k.a. Hoodlum – was pitching for a different team in the league and they were all that remained of the 1920 city champions. It was a good league, but when you were like Bananas and got a hit more than half the time, it wasn't much of a challenge. It was the same for Lazo and Hoodlum – who now insisted on being called Len – and, to a lesser degree, even Shorty.

While Bananas was easily the best player around, Lazo was a bona fide star who had become a home run hitter of some repute. At five-ten and a hundred and seventy pounds he was no behemoth, but a good size for a ballplayer. He was a competent outfielder and runner and got that way from dogged persistence. He worked on his game for hours on end as part of his daily regimen. He was driven by baseball and the urge to improve. He worked out to build muscle, he ran around city blocks to develop lung capacity, and he rose early every morning to practice throwing balls and hitting fungoes at an empty diamond. Nothing came easily for Lazo. He had to work for everything and his hitting is what improved the most. The one area where he was superior to Bananas was power.

Muscle alone doesn't make a slugger. He also needs confidence, which explains why a hitter gets into a "groove." It happens when everything is working just right, the rhythm perfect, the body and timing finely tuned. This is when hits come in bunches and the batting average soars. But baseball is one of life's great mysteries and a player can slip out of his groove as quickly as he slips into it. He can sink to great depths, lose his stance and the feel of the bat, and watch his average plummet.

Lazo had been getting into a groove often, consistently going two-for-four or two-for-five at the plate and when he learned what it takes to club a ball over the fence he began doing that with regularity too. He developed more upper body bulk, gained the confidence to believe in himself, and could be counted on for a home run every fourth game, which made him what every ballplayer wanted to be.

Feared.

But Lazo was also a team player who would trade two points in his average for a carefully placed ground ball to right field, allowing the runner on second to get to third. That runner was usually Bananas. The two played well together. There was a synergy operating between them and others could sense it. The opposition wasn't battling just one of them, but two.

Lazo was an intelligent player. He came to the park with the keen mind of one who studies the game and does his homework. Depending on the situation – the score, inning, the opponent, and a host of intangibles – he would analyze things down to the smallest detail and plan his strategy. Once in a key game against a pitcher he had never homered against, he was at bat with Bananas on third and another runner on first. It was the seventh inning and there were two outs. His team was down two runs and a home run would give them the lead. Since he'd hit two homers the previous game, Lazo was said to be "hot" and urged to go for broke. Hit for the fences, the coach said, but he didn't. He had trouble with this pitcher and knocking one out wasn't his best percentage shot. No, he figured it was better to play for one run at a time so he consulted his ample baseball subconscious where he kept a "book" on every player in the league. He knew the pitcher was a poor runner with very big feet – too big for his body – and he had a bad glove hand. Lazo decided to bunt the ball right to him. Who would expect a slugger, especially a "hot" one, to bunt?

So bunt he did. He laid down a perfect one right to the pitcher who lost the ball in his feet, picked it up only to drop it, and, when he was finally ready to throw to home, the speedy Bananas had already scored. Then the pitcher turned to throw to first, but was so rattled he threw the ball over the first baseman's head, which allowed Lazo to reach second and the runner who had started at first to score. And the game was tied. The next hitter stroked a single, scoring Lazo, and the team wound up winning the game.

Someone said Lazo should coach after that.

But still, Bananas was the better player. He could run faster, throw straighter, and get more hits even if Lazo got more home runs.

Lazo's best friend remained Stan who was still called Shorty and for good reason: his height had peaked at five feet, five and a half inches. Shorty played second base and was adept at picking off runners and not a bad hitter, but no one ever fingered him for a ringer. He was too small. He dabbled in basketball, but his lack of stature was even more of a liability there. Hockey and football were out of the question so baseball was Shorty's calling by process of elimination. If he had a hero it was Miller Huggins, the diminutive manager of the New York Yankees.

Huggins was a logical choice. He was five six and a half and weighed less than a hundred and forty pounds. He had played major league ball, but enjoyed greater success as a manager. After coming to the Yankees from the St. Louis Cardinals, he was the captain who ran the Yankee ship and was dwarfed by most of his players – especially giants like Babe Ruth and outfielder Bob Meusel – but he ran a tight ship.

Shorty was fully prepared to join Lazo and Bananas, head down to Hoboken and sample the sights of the big city. So what if the Hoboken Browns took one look at him and told him to get lost? He had never been to New York.

The fourth member of the burgeoning party was Len who was the best pitcher around. No matter if his name was Len, or Hoodlum, he could throw his fastball with more speed than anyone else in town; Valley Playground's Fuzzy had packed it in years ago. Len was young and gangling, an inch over six feet, and his arms – his right arm especially – were sinewy and lean. But he still had a problem with concentration and getting thrown off his game.

"Let's give it a shot," said Bananas. "From what I hear the Browns give everyone a good look. We've got nuthin' to lose. We can stay at my aunt's place in Hoboken, which is just a short walk from New York City. That means Broadway. Fifth Avenue. Girls!"

Shorty, eager to take in what adventures the big city could offer, didn't need any convincing and Len had nothing to keep him at home. Bananas? He wanted to see just how good a ballplayer he was so there was little reason to stay around. Except for Bananas, who toiled with the railway, they were all working at meager factory jobs and not going anywhere, but being nineteen in the middle of the '20s didn't mean life was neatly planned out. It meant working all day and having enough money to spend at night. It was the same for Lazo. He had a tedious job at a paper plant and knew it wasn't his destiny. Baseball was. A tryout with a semipro team would be the chance to see if his hard work had paid off. Besides, the Yankees were there. And so was the Babe.

◆

Babe Ruth was no longer an unknown precocious teenager mowing down hitters in the minor leagues or a rising star with the Red Sox. He was the biggest name in baseball. After his first banner season in New York he came back to do even better the next year with fifty-nine homers, 170 runs batted in, and a .378 average. In 1922 he slipped to thirty-five homers, but hit forty-one the following year and batted .393. In 1924 he won the batting title and contributed his customary league-leading home run total, this time forty-six.

The Yankees won three straight American League pennants from 1921 through 1923 and each year in the World Series they met the crosstown New York Giants, whose ignition line was a right fielder named Casey Stengel. The Giants won the first two and the Yankees the third in the game's greatest rivalry. But in 1924 the Yankees missed the pennant and finished second to Washington despite the Babe's outstanding season.

By the middle of the '20s he was earning $52,000 a year, and was held in awe as much for his salary as for his hitting. He was a star, an enigma of epic proportion, the biggest name in the sports world. He was even making movies.

Babe Ruth was bigger than the president.

"I don't just want to see him play," Lazo told his friends. "I want to meet him. I want to shake his hand."

And he would.

◆

The flat of Bananas' Aunt Sadie in Hoboken wasn't what the boys expected. Her letters mentioned the spare room she had and said it was no problem if he wanted to stay for a month or so. When he asked about bringing a friend, that was okay, too. She had a lot of room, she said, so when four of them turned up at her door one cold May afternoon she was surprised. She was a kindly woman who never had children. After her husband died she longed for guests. Her modest flat on the upper level of a duplex could squeeze in a guest or two, but no more. Still, she couldn't turn two of her nephew's friends away, especially with all the hell-raising going on in the city. It was the Roaring Twenties.

Bananas introduced the boys and she studied their faces and analyzed the texture of their surnames. Hooper didn't sound Jewish. Dixon? Definitely not. Slackowicz. Maybe. With the Yiddish accent that he knew from Bananas' parents, she asked Lazo about his family's origins. He said "Poland" and she drew closer to him.

"You Jewish, boy?" she asked hopefully.

Lazo shook his head and she looked at her nephew with disdain.

"Jeckie vatsa mattah vit you? You bring me tree boys and all Gentiles! No Jewish boys beck home?"

Bananas tried explaining. He said they all played baseball.

"Bays-a-ball?"

Lazo decided to try his luck. He mentioned the Yankees.

"Vut? Who?"

"The New York Yankees."

"Yankiss?"

He tried once more.

"Babe Ruth?"

With that there was a glimmer of recognition.

"Da big FET one?"

Bananas, Len, and Shorty laughed and so did Bananas' aunt for the first time since their arrival. The ice was broken. She told them to come in and Bananas ushered them through the door saying something about moving quickly before she changed her mind. Each of them had a bag and a baseball glove. Not much. How long they would stay they didn't know. Work? There was little thought in this area as well. She asked about money. They didn't have a hundred dollars among them.

The boys looked around the flat and the problem was clear. Where would they sleep? There was a tiny kitchen, a narrow living room with a couch and armchair, and her bedroom. Undeterred, she went to work. Like a machine. She took a load of blankets and three pillows from her closet and laid them out on the living room floor. Then she transformed the couch into a fourth bed. She said that was for "Jeckie." The others would sleep in the living room and no one was going to argue. It was spring and the temperature was forty-seven degrees. She didn't have much room, but she did have heat and wasn't about to let them starve.

That first night she prepared chicken legs and breast, potato latkes, and eggbread. The boys washed it down with steaming hot chocolate and by eight o'clock, weary from their long bus ride, they were ready for sleep. They took a liking to her, but knew the setup couldn't last. There wasn't enough room. She also knew it couldn't last, but space was the least of her worries. There was no way she could afford to feed four young men every day. They would have to find work. She made them promise to check the employment section of the *Times* in the morning and before they retired began lecturing them on the evils of New York City. She said to beware of the speakeasies and spoke about the illegal liquor and bad girls. She said police were watching these places night and day.

The speakeasies had sprung up on just about every street corner in Manhattan, Brooklyn, Staten Island, and the Bronx and while many of them were raided and closed down, they usually opened up again a few doors away. Federal agents enforcing the laws of Prohibition knew that rounding up citizens who consumed illegal alcohol was a monumental waste of time. There were six million people in the city and so many speakeasies no one could keep count so the feds usually turned the other cheek and concentrated on bootleggers who imported the stuff from Canada and Mexico or who brought it in from other sources off the east coast. One of New York's most celebrated madams said Prohibition was bound to fail: "They might as well have been trying to dry up the Atlantic with a post-office blotter," she said.

Still, the warnings of Bananas' aunt to stay clear of speakeasies had a profound effect on the four, but not the one she wanted.

"We gotta hit one of those places tomorrow night," whispered Shorty to Lazo and Len as the three were tucked elbow to elbow under woolen sheets on the living room floor. They were like sardines in a can. Bananas' loud snoring could be heard from the couch. "They got booze and broads there."

"Right," said Len, his thumb up in the air. "Tomorrow we hit Manhattan."

And make no mistake, that was Hoodlum talking.

◆

It wasn't a good year for the Babe and the Yankees. Lazo followed his exploits and antics in the press religiously. He knew his marriage was on the rocks and his life in shambles. The Babe would eat enormous amounts of food with no thought of his health and in the winter before the 1925 season he had ballooned to two hundred and sixty pounds. He liked to drink and party all night long before a game, but somehow – no one could ever figure it out – he managed to deliver when a bat was thrust into his hands.

Miller Huggins, the tiny but determined manager and taskmaster of the Yankees, had endured his star's late-hour escapades and lackadaisical approach to team curfews for years. Two hundred and thirty-five home runs over five seasons had brought a lot of success and fans to the park. Huggins and the Babe had many battles, and the usual result was Huggins letting him off the hook when he blasted another four-bagger over the fence. But this time the American League's defending batting and home run champion was forty pounds overweight and Huggins wanted to get him down to a level that wasn't embarrassing. There was a tradition to uphold. Lazo knew all about the Yankees' history.

They began in 1903 as the Highlanders and played in a makeshift wooden stadium called Hilltop Park on Broadway. They played there for ten years until the National League's New York Giants invited the team – now the Yankees – to join them in the big Harlem horseshoe called the Polo Grounds. The arrangement worked out fine until 1921 when the Yankees, with the Babe, became baseball's biggest drawing card. They set a new

major league attendance record and so the Giants, their land-
lords, asked them to go. They were told to build a park in some
out-of-the-way place, which turned out to be a large plot of land
across the Harlem River not a mile from the Polo Grounds.

Yankee Stadium opened on April 18, 1923, with all sixty
thousand seats occupied, and when the Babe hit a home run
three innings into the game the roar from the crowd dwarfed
anything the Polo Grounds had ever produced. It wasn't long before they were calling it the House That Ruth Built. But two
years later the Yankees' star was trudging around the field like a
watermelon.

His problems started at spring training. He faced a lawsuit
for debts claimed by a New York bookmaker, he broke a finger in
practice, which kept him out of the lineup, and then he
developed such a bad cold it was feared he had pneumonia. Still,
he delivered in spades. He was hitting .449 in exhibition games
and in the space of one month had even managed to contain his
eating and lose twenty-one pounds. But on April 7 he suddenly
collapsed and was said to have the grippe. The British press and
Canadian wire service were quick to report his death. He was
alive, of course, but not by much.

Lazo, who was busy making plans with his buddies for the big
trip to New York, was losing sleep over him. He saw a photograph
of the Babe and couldn't believe how bad he looked. He was pale
and weak and getting thinner by the day. Finally he was hospitalized and remained there when the season opener was held with the
Yankees losing to the Washington Senators. Lazo sent him a card.
But then the Babe got worse. He had surgery – for what nobody
knew – and the papers had a field day speculating. His ailments
were described as everything from influenza to indigestion to an
intestinal abscess. Even syphilis was mentioned.

His weight dropped to one hundred and eighty pounds and
he looked gaunt and sickly. Without him the Yankees were
playing badly and mired in seventh place, a source of great embarrassment to Huggins, who had earlier told the *Times* that this
edition of the Yankees was "the strongest team" ever. The Babe

spent seven long weeks in hospital and didn't play again until June 1. The very same day an untried rookie named Lou Gehrig started at first base. Lazo had never heard of him, but it didn't make any difference.

The Yankees lost.

◆

Finding speakeasies required some effort. The day after their arrival it didn't take long for Lazo, Shorty, Bananas, and Len to see that Hoboken was anything but the short walk to Manhattan that Bananas had claimed. After his Aunt Sadie treated them to a filling breakfast, they took a bus through Jersey City to Staten Island, caught a glimpse of the Statue of Liberty, and ferried across to Manhattan. They went north on Broadway and strolled down Wall Street before pooling their money for a cab on Fifth Avenue. But cabs were expensive and they couldn't go far so they soon returned to walking. In their excitement taking in the sights they forgot about checking the employment ads and even lunch. By six o'clock they were hungry.

"Where are all these speakeasies she was talking about?" said Shorty.

"You think they just put a sign on the door that says speakeasy?" said Len. "You wouldn't know one if you saw one. They're illegal. They gotta do it quietly."

"Okay, big shot, so how do we find one?"

"Why don't we just ask somebody?" said Bananas.

Shorty stopped a businessman and asked where to find a speakeasy. The man looked at the four of them and laughed.

"You got any money?" he asked them.

"A little," Shorty said.

"Try the east side. East Forty-first. East Forty-second. All the way up. Any street you want."

That seemed simple enough, but they still didn't know what to look for. They followed the directions to East Forty-first Street and turned east. There were no jackets and ties in this down-

and-out area and, as Len said, no one was advertising speakeasies on the front door. Then a group of local toughs rounded the corner. Marching four abreast they controlled the sidewalk or liked to think they did. When he saw them coming Shorty stepped onto the roadway to let them pass only to have Len shove him back.

"Around here you don't give up turf," he advised, lighting a cigarette. "Hold your ground."

When the boys were close Len stretched out his lanky frame and blew a mouthful of smoke in their direction. They took one look at him and edged out onto the roadway and after they passed one of them peered over his shoulder.

"See what I mean?" said Len. "Stick with me youse guys and maybe you won't get eaten alive."

A few minutes later they were stopped by a girl in a tight hip-hugging skirt that revealed legs well above her knees. Her face was matted with layers of makeup, her lips painted ruby red.

"Hi boys," she beckoned.

"We're looking for a speakeasy," said Shorty, his voice cracking.

"You wanna buy me a drink, cutie?"

"Sure. Where?"

"Number Fifty-five."

Len put his hand on Shorty's shoulder and stuck his thumb toward the street.

"Get lost honey," he said to the girl.

She shrugged and headed off and before Shorty could ask, Len said they can do better. They hurried to the address she mentioned, which was just like any other place on the street except for an imposing iron grille on the door. Two modest "5s" hung from the bars, one of them lower than the other. Shorty, who was the most eager of them, pushed the door open only to find another door beyond it. It was dark in here with shadows and cobwebs and cigarette butts all over the ground. The air was cold and stale.

Shorty pressed the doorbell. Nothing happened. He tried it again, but it wasn't working so he rapped on the door. A few seconds later and a peephole half a foot wide and a few inches high slid open. There was a face with a monstrous nose.

"Yeah?" said the hoarse voice.

Shorty cleared his throat.

"Can we get something to drink here?" he asked politely.

"Who are ya?"

Shorty cleared his throat again.

"Stanley Hooper."

"Nevah hoid o' ya" and the panel slid shut.

"Jesus," Shorty said. "Didja see that?"

Len, the biggest of the group, elbowed his way in.

"Youse guys are hopeless," he said. He rapped on the door firmly and the panel slid open.

"I want in," Len said. "I know Bugsy."

"Sure an' Capone's my bruddah-in-law."

"I know him. He's my uncle."

"Bullshit."

"I'll tell him you said that."

The nose that looked like it had been broken many times and the eyes accompanying it came close to the peephole.

"What's yer name, kid?"

"Dixon. I ain't feedin' you no line. He's my uncle and he said to drop by. So here I am."

The panel slid shut and two voices were talking inside.

"Who the hell is Bugsy?" Shorty asked Len.

"Bugsy Siegel. One of the biggest hoods in New York."

"He's your uncle?"

"Today he is."

The peephole opened.

"Who are dees guys?" said the nose.

"My friends," said Len.

"Sorry. Only you can come in."

Len nodded and a series of locks were unfastened and the door opened. The man could have been a prison guard, or a boxer after a particularly bad pummeling. The smell of liquor flowed freely from inside and there was the sound of laughing women's voices. Battered wooden tables and chairs were about and broken glass was on the floor. Len was about to step through the doorway.

"Jus' you," said the nose.

"But they're my friends."

"Sorry."

Len, easily four or five inches taller than the man, pulled out a switchblade and parked the tip of it square on the cleft of his chin.

"Look," said the nose his hands up at his sides, "we don't want no trouble. But I can't let you all in. Jus' one. We don't have much room. Da feds are aroun' all da time."

"We want sumthin' to drink," said Len, his knife at the ready.

"Look, why don't youse nice boys try anuddah place? On da wes' side. Da Mansion. One-toity-two Wes' Fifty-foist. Just say Joe sentcha."

Len stepped in closer and eyeballed his prey. He lowered his switchblade. The man breathed a sigh of relief and shut the door.

"Let's go," said Len.

They marched west to Broadway and after being accosted by four more streetwalkers soon found themselves in a better part of town. They walked a full ten blocks until they got to West Fifty-first Street. Their stomachs ached and their mouths were so dry they would have been happy to sample water, never mind alcohol.

This was midtown Manhattan and the clientele was a few notches above that of the east side. They got to 132 West Fifty-first and there was an iron grille door here too, but the stately building smacked of monied urbanity and Len's first thought was the prices. The four would-be ballplayers – now veterans of gaining entry into speakeasies – slicked back their hair, adjusted their shirts and ambled through the entranceway.

"I'll handle this," said Len pressing the doorbell.

A narrow slit opened and a face appeared, but more human than the last one. It even spoke good English. Len said that Joe sent him.

"Joe who?"

"Joe . . . Joe . . ."

"Joe Smith," volunteered Shorty.

Len wanted to grab Shorty by the collar, lift him up against the door, and hang him on a nail. The doorman scanned the group from side to side and a smile creased his lips. If these were Prohibition agents of the U.S. government, he thought, business would be good for many years to come. He was wearing a white shirt, black tie, and tails, and greeted them cordially. Inside there was a hardwood floor that looked like it was just polished. A huge chandelier was suspended from the ceiling and silk curtains hung from either side of the hallway. Again Len thought of the prices.

"Welcome to the Mansion," the doorman said. "No doubt a friend directed you?"

"Joe Smith," offered Shorty whose expression turned to pain when Len nudged him hard in the ribs.

The doorman smiled, the plain dead smile common to butlers and house servants of the upper classes.

"We do have a dress code but don't enforce it as long as our guests are . . . presentable."

"Our suits are at the cleaners," said Shorty, his arm protecting his side. "They'll be ready in an hour."

"Fine and what is your fancy tonight? The first floor? Second floor? Or third floor?"

"We'll try 'em all," Shorty said.

Len thought of the prices.

"Excellent. I hope you gentlemen have a wonderful time."

He led them down a hallway where they passed a scantily clad cigarette girl with enormous breasts. She gave Shorty a wink and a bulge formed in his pants. They came to a door.

"The bar is in here," the doorman said placing a card in Len's hand. It was a price list.

"Thank you," said Len.

Just as he thought, the prices were so steep they couldn't afford much. Hard liquor like rye was four and a half dollars for a three-pint serving. Gin was a little cheaper at two and a quarter, but a bottle of anything was out of the question. Len showed the others the list and it was clear that volume and not quality would be the route to intoxication.

There was liquor everywhere. A crap game was going on in the middle of the floor and nattily dressed high rollers in black tie were standing around like a colony of penguins. Some of the women wore sequins and one who was very drunk was dancing on top of a grand piano, tugging on her dress, pulling one side of it all the way up her leg. The skin trade was anything but subtle. Lazo had never seen such things before. He edged over to the bar where the man beside him peeled off a hundred-dollar bill from the wad of notes in his palm.

"Johnny Walker and Shirley Brown," the man told the bartender and a bottle of JW and two glasses immediately appeared.

Lazo tried to look cool – as cool as he could without a single C-note in his pocket. The man said hello.

"What's a Shirley Brown?" asked Lazo. "I never had a swig o' that stuff."

"Well, you must be the only one here who's never tried 'er. She goes down smooth I can tell you that."

He waved to the far end of the bar and a tall brunette came by. He put his arm around her and kissed her on the neck.

"This is Shirley Brown. Shirley meet . . ."

"Larry," Lazo said.

"Shirley. Larry."

Lazo started melting right away. She was stunning, completely bare at the back and sides, nothing but a thin thread holding her dress up.

"Shirley will do anything you want," the man said pouring himself a shot glass and knocking it back in one motion.

The girl smiled and touched Lazo's face. Her fingers were long and soft and cold. She slid them along his lips and when he opened his mouth she ran them by his teeth. The man took the two glasses and bottle in one hand and her in the other.

"There's lots of girls," he said. "Just take your pick."

The couple meandered along the floor and climbed a stairway at the end of the bar. Lazo looked around for his pals. When he saw them he called out and they joined him.

"What'll it be?" asked the bartender.

"Old Crow," said Len from behind Lazo. "Four shots."

The bartender placed four shot glasses on the bar directly in front of Lazo.

"That's two bits."

"That's all?" Lazo said.

"Each," said the bartender.

Lazo slapped a dollar bill on the counter and the bartender just waited.

"Aren't you gonna tip him?" said Len.

Lazo laid down a quarter that was scooped up with the bill and a nod. He had brought twenty-five dollars to New York and now had twenty-three dollars and seventy-five cents left.

"We'll each take a round," said Len knocking back the whiskey. The others followed suit. Lazo downed his with a gulp and his throat went warm. Bananas did the same and so did Shorty, but Shorty couldn't mask the effects of the drink. He gagged and choked as the hot liquor filled him.

"This ain't bad," he said coughing between words.

"I like that little blonde over there," said Bananas.

The tryout with the Hoboken Browns was a million miles away.

Only Len, the erstwhile Hoodlum, looked like he belonged. This was a place of hot liquor, small talk, and fast women, things he knew much better than his friends, but a few drinks eased them into the ebb and flow of the crowd and when they were on their third round, four girls moved in.

"Buy me a drink," the first said to Bananas and he fished around in his pocket for loose change. "Never mind," she said. "I'll just drink from your glass," and she slipped her tongue into his whiskey. "What's your name, honey?"

"Jack," he gulped, "but everyone calls me Bananas."

"I can't wait to see why."

They teased the boys unmercifully, grappling over them, one to each, bringing their bodies in close. Lazo's girl was the prettiest. At least he thought she was. But after three glasses of whiskey he would have thought any of them was the prettiest. She was younger than him and not nearly as drunk. She paid dutiful homage to the sober reality of her trade and plied it like the pro she was. Her light brown hair was ruffled and the scent of her perfume danced through his nostrils.

After his fourth shot of whiskey, Lazo was too light-headed and dizzy to stand on his own. For every person in the room he saw two. It was crowded, too crowded to move around comfortably, and he thought of an amusement park midway, but instead of a cool breeze there was sweat, and instead of barkers hawking wares there were girls. All he could see was her soft, pretty face, but it was a blur. The next thing he knew he was climbing a flight of stairs – leaning on her for support – and then they were alone in a room. She said something about twenty something and Lazo was handling money. Her perfume was everywhere and her clothes were falling like leaves from an autumn tree. Her lips were bright red and her hair hung down to her naked shoulders. Cleopatra. That was her name. Cleopatra. She was wonderful to touch. Only they and the walls were there. He felt his body on hers and dug his fingers into her skin and then everything was dark.

◆

Bananas' Aunt Sadie often sat for children when their parents were out, but not having children of her own, she had never experienced the terror that seeps into the heart when they're not where they should be. When her nephew and his three friends didn't return that night she feared the worst. It was with a sense of relief that she answered her door the next morning and found her "Jeckie" alive. She hugged him affectionately, but he fought like a madman to escape her clutches and raced to the washroom where he promptly delivered the raw contents of his stomach into the city's sewage system. Shorty, who had rolled in behind him, did likewise and while he was draped over the toilet, she asked Bananas what happened.

"Bad food," said Bananas, clutching his abdomen. "I gotta lie down."

"Haf you boys bin drinking?"

"No, it was food poisoning."

Every twenty minutes Bananas and Shorty, both of them bleary-eyed and stinking of tobacco and alcohol, took turns in the washroom before they finally drifted off to sleep only to have their snoring broken later by the ring of the doorbell. Lazo, standing on the doorstep, was in no better shape. His shoulders began to heave to and fro so Bananas' Aunt Sadie rushed him into her washroom and slammed the door shut, escaping in the nick of time.

It wasn't until late in the afternoon when they could conduct even passable conversation, sticking to their story about food poisoning; yet, she knew where they had been and a law was struck as surely as Moses carried the commandments down Mount Ararat. Should they again venture into a speakeasy and leave her to worry through the night, her door would be closed right in their kissers when they returned.

But where was Len? He didn't show all that day or that night. Aunt Sadie wanted to phone the police.

"No, don't do that," said Bananas. "You don't know Len. He'll be all right."

He appeared three days later, sporting a new jacket, new pants, and new shoes. He looked like a million bucks and even had a job working for somebody named John Barleycorn. He said the money was good. But Len's new employer didn't have any other openings. However, Bananas' aunt had a friend working in a shirt factory in Jersey and her friend had a friend who was in hiring at some warehouse in the Bronx. There was room for three strong young men packing boxes and it paid twelve and a half dollars a week.

Each.

Lazo and Shorty spent a week staying at Bananas' aunt's before renting a flat of their own in the Bronx. It was close to the shirt factory and the rent was twenty-five dollars a month, which left them with a combined seventy-five dollars a month for food and other pursuits. They wanted Bananas to move in with them, but his aunt let him stay with her for nothing and since he was penniless after his night at the Mansion, it seemed like a pretty good idea. But once Lazo and Shorty found more affordable places to hang out, it was obvious Bananas preferred staying with his friends on the east side of the Hudson than with his aunt in Hoboken. So, after a three-week stay he packed what little he had and moved in with them. But he promised to visit his Aunt Sadie at least once a week.

And for the first two weeks he did.

◆

The first tryout with the Hoboken Browns had passed, but more tryouts were scheduled for the last week in May so Bananas telephoned the team's manager and reeled off his batting average from the last three seasons.

"You say you hit .527 last year?"

"Yes sir, I did."

"And what league was that?"

"The best amateur league in Canada, sir."

"Well I don't care where you played but if you hit .527 you musta bin doin' sumthin' right so come on down."

The manager said the Browns would be glad to see the four of them, but with one condition. They had to bring their own gloves.

The semipro club played in a skeletal facility near the west bank of the Hudson River and something about it took Lazo back to Christie Pits. The bleachers, which seated no more than a thousand, looked a lot like the bleachers from the old park, but it wasn't the seats that reminded him of the old haunts. It was the uphill slope behind home plate and the foul lines. Lazo closed his eyes and imagined the old scoreboard and far off beyond deep right center field, the diving board of the swimming pool.

Most of the Browns' players were in their twenties and they

all had a lot more baseball experience than Lazo and his three friends.

The boys hadn't seen much of Len since that first night out. He was busy working for this Barleycorn fellow and living in an apartment smack in the middle of Manhattan. He didn't talk about his work and when the day came for the big tryout he wasn't around.

The manager of the Browns was a cussing cigar smoker who paid little attention to the rookies in his camp. The team regulars and collection of hopefuls who had survived the first try-out and were still in the running for jobs, had just begun their pre-practice exercises when the three newcomers took to the field and joined in. It was a good way to loosen up the muscles and it went on for fifteen minutes. When it was over, all the players clapped their hands like an army battalion and then split up into two groups. One group was for pitchers and catchers and the other was for everyone else. Lazo, Shorty, and Bananas went with the bigger group of about twenty players. They were tossing the ball around the infield and snaring fungoes hit by one of the coaches.

"And who the hell are you?" the manager said to Lazo who was parked on third base. "I din't see you here the other day."

"No sir. I'm a friend of Jack Gershwin."

"Who?"

"Jack Gershwin. You told him we could try out."

"Who the hell is Jack Gershwin? I dunno nobody by that name."

"The center fielder from Canada."

"Oh yeah. Now I remember. He hit .982 or sumthin' crazy like that. I gotta see this guy."

"He's good."

"Yeah? We'll see."

The manager was short and stout and badly bowlegged with a deep-set paunch hanging over his belt. Everyone called him Sarge. He ordered the coaches and players together and said batting practice would begin. Two coaches would handle the pitchers in the small group. As for the other group, the regulars took to their positions while the players who had made the first cut gathered around the batting cage.

The manager wanted Bananas up first since he figured a .982 average was nothing to sneeze at. At the mention of his name Bananas was hit by the butterflies.

"Okay hotshot, let's see what you can do."

Bananas grabbed a bat, walked to home plate, and took a few practice swings.

"He's kinda small," the manager said through his cigar.

The former minor league pro on the pitcher's mound was way past his prime, but he still had some stuff. After a brief warm-up he threw a slow slider that Bananas hit easily. Bananas smiled confidently. The next one was the same pitch exactly and he hit it again. Then the pitcher wound up and threw a fastball that blew by him before he could blink.

Bananas dug in only to watch a curveball sail by the end of his bat as he swung. This went on for five minutes. Whenever the ex-pro slowed his pitches to a crawl Bananas could hit them, but when he put something on them the best he could manage was a foul tip.

The manager walked over.

"Whatsa matter kid? Yer swingin' at air. I thought ya said ya could hit like Ty Cobb."

"Guess I'm a little nervous."

"Nervous? What the fuck ya nervous about? Playin' with these old geezers? Are you kiddin'? Look, settle down. You go spell Adams out there in right field."

"Right field?"

"Ain't that what I said?"

"But I play center field."

"I don't care whatcha play. Get yer ass into right field now! Move it! We'll let one o' yer friends take the heat from this forty-seven-year-old."

Bananas grabbed his glove and trotted into the outfield, then he stopped and looked at the man on the mound.

"Forty-seven?"

The manager nodded.

"You mean that guy's forty-seven years old?"

"Sure as I'm standin' here and if you don't get movin' soon he's gonna be forty-eight!"

Bananas ran into the outfield, as far from the manager as he could get. Shorty was up next. The manager took one look at him and unloaded a huge wad of spit that landed on the ground just inches from Shorty's size six feet.

"Chee-rist you're even shorter than the other guy! What're ya a team o' midgets? Don't people eat where ya come from?"

Shorty couldn't even connect with the slow easy tosses and when the old veteran on the mound began whizzing fastballs over the plate he was pathetic. He swung wildly at pitches that were far outside and watched, dumbfounded, when strikes came in right down the pipe. After his hopeless performance he was sent to second base.

"Next!" cried the manager through his cigar and it was now Lazo's turn. The man they called Sarge was bored to death. He had always referred to these kids as "hotshots," but few of them were. The ones at the last tryout were a bad batch. Not one had shown a thing he liked and now this. He suspected that his Browns, sixth-place finishers in an eight-team league the year before, would resemble the 1924 squad when the season started and that wasn't good, but tryouts were usually like this. Young hotshots who could do all kinds of great things playing sandlot ball were suddenly caught with their pants down when they tried strutting their stuff with a real team. It was a crushing blow to inflated egos. Still, the old dinosaurs who never made it to the bigs and who ran things in minor pro and semipro circuits, ordered everybody around as if they were buck privates, loving every minute of it. It was a chance to rub noses into the dirt, but if a kid showed something and could take it, then maybe, just maybe, he had it.

Lazo took a deep breath and stepped into the batter's box. Bananas and Shorty had failed miserably and the pitcher was a forty-seven-year-old ex-pro who was now a third-base coach.

The manager, his patience running thin, had no time for excuses.

"I hope ya can hit better than yer two friends," he said. "They sure stunk the joint out din't they?"

He laughed and chewed on the tip of his cigar.

Lazo knew the first pitches would be soft so he didn't smack them too hard. He took light easy strokes and tried to capture the mechanics that let him ravage enemy pitchers back home. The manager watched intently. As the pitches started to come in faster, he swung harder and wasn't doing badly until a low and inside slider caught the corner of the plate. He swung too late and came all the way around with his follow-through.

"Jesus fuckin' Chee-rist!" cried the manager. "Give' im one o' those again."

The pitcher nodded and threw the same pitch. Again Lazo swung and missed.

"You sonofabitch," the manager screamed at Lazo. "I even told ya what he was gonna throw. Whatsa matter with you? Can't ya hit nuthin'?"

Lazo hung his head.

"Let's try'er again!"

This time Lazo was so determined to make contact he brought the bat back farther than normal and began his swing earlier, but all he could muster was a blind stab at the ball and it was even worse than before since now he had lost his swing. His timing was ruined.

"You little cocksucker! Cantcha even hit when ya know what's comin? What's with youse guys? An' ya call yerselves ballplayers? Shit! I should be runnin' a fuckin' tryout fer ballerinas! At least then I'd have some real pussies aroun' here! You guys are a buncha prima donnas! Ev'ry fuckin' one o' ya!"

He ordered the humiliated Lazo out of the batter's box and dispatched him to center field. The older players, the regulars, were mildly amused, but Lazo was crushed. As he scampered into the outfield he caught a wink from the third baseman.

"Don't mind Sarge," he said. "He's harmless."

The pitcher left the mound, grabbed a bat, and started hitting fungoes. He hit them to each and every position, one by one, and whoever played the ball had to direct it to first base. After hitting to all eight players, he did the same thing again, but this time the ball had to go to second. All the infielders and outfielders, including the regulars and newcomers, got into the act and the exercise was more fun for the new hotshots than batting practice had been. Thirty minutes of fielding and the players were joined by the pitchers and catchers. Then the man they called Sarge issued new orders.

"Okay youse assholes, we're gonna have a little game. It's called baseball. We're gonna play the regulars against a team o' Hotshots. Hotshots are up first. Two bucks says the Hotshots don't score a fuckin' run."

One of the Browns' hurlers took to the mound and threw some warm-ups.

"Awright!" hollered the manager a few minutes later. "Let's play ball!"

The first two batters for the team christened Hotshots struck out on straight pitches and with each strikeout the manager exploded into profanity and never once came up for air. Lazo had never seen anyone like him. He was as far from Jackson Wallace as you could get. He was a long-winded, cantankerous old bastard and the new players quietly agreed that they would like nothing more than have one of them power a line drive through his teeth and take his cigar with it.

Bananas was the third batter up and he connected on the first pitch, knocking it into shallow right where it was caught easily to retire the side.

When the Browns came to bat they pummeled the rookies for seven runs – including a grand slam by the eighth hitter. That was all for the Hotshots' starting pitcher. In the next inning, the first two Hotshots were easy outs and then Lazo was up.

"C'mon ya little cocksucker! Let's see whatcha can do in a game!" cried the manager. "Let's see ya swing sumthin' besides those big ears o' yers!"

Lazo tried to settle himself and figured sinking to the same level as the manager was the answer.

"C'mon you asshole, throw me that fuckin' ball!" he shouted, but the pitcher didn't take to him kindly. After all, Lazo was a rookie – even less than a rookie, he was a Hotshot – and the pitcher was a veteran. The first pitch almost parted Lazo's hair. He ducked and fell to the dirt.

"Three more like that and you walk me!" Lazo said dusting off his pants.

The next pitch was high and again Lazo had to duck to avoid being hit. The count was 2-0.

"Whatsa matter?" he yelled to the pitcher. "Afraid I might hit one?"

The pitcher hunched back his shoulders, wound up, and threw a fastball. Lazo swung.

Pffft.

Strike. Lazo dug in. He squeezed the bat and shot a glance to the manager who was half asleep on the bench with his arms crossed. A fastball was next and Lazo read it all the way. At just the right moment he began his swing and smashed it with everything he had.

Gone. A home run.

No one was more surprised than Lazo himself as he scurried around the bases. All the Hotshots were clapping – this was more than a run, it was a victory – and the coaches were busy making mental notes of what they just saw. The crack of the bat meeting the ball awoke the manager and as he watched the ball soar over the center fielder's head the cigar fell out of his mouth.

"Holy fuck, didja see that?" he said to one of his coaches. "Didja see that? The fuckin' kid hit a home run off Jimmy Barnes. Didja see that?"

The game ended mercifully after five innings with the Browns ahead 16-1, the Hotshots doing as expected. The box score in the manager's notes showed seven errors – three by Shorty who was a disaster at second base – and two hits, one of them a single by Bananas. But it was Lazo's home run that made a lasting impression and even when he struck out his next two times it didn't matter.

"Son, see me in my office," the manager said to Lazo when the game broke up.

Lazo looked around. All he saw was an empty playing field with wooden bleachers behind the foul lines. There was no office. Barnes, the pitcher who had almost ripped his head off with a high fastball, was standing next to him.

"That was a helluva hit," he said. "And my best pitch too."

Lazo asked him where the manager's office was and Barnes pointed to center field.

"Out there?" Lazo said.

The manager and his coaches were huddled together talking in the bleachers. After a few minutes the wily old taskmaster asked Lazo to join him for a stroll. They nonchalantly walked out to center field.

"Where'd ya learn to hit like that?" he asked Lazo, who just shrugged. "Ya know, Barnes only gave up six homers last year. Ya hit him pretty good. Ya gotta nice swing. I noticed that right away."

"Thanks."

"I wantcha to come back tomorra. We're gonna weed out some more guys and get down to serious biz'ness."

"That's great, but what about my friends?"

"Oh yeah, yer friends. Well the Gersher kid ain't bad. He's gotta good glove hand and he got himself a hit. He can give it another shot. But the other guy, the midget, he stinks. He's rotten. He's got nuthin'."

"Do you think maybe you could ask them both back. Just for one practice?"

"Why should I do that?"

"Well, we came a long way to be here and Shorty knows he's not the best. He didn't expect to make the team but, well . . ."

"He sure as hell won't make the team. That's for damn sure. Our bat boy can hit better 'n him. Shit. I think my old lady can hit better 'n him."

"I know but . . ."

The manager looked Lazo up and down. He was thinking. It wasn't every Hotshot who hit a home run off Jimmy Barnes and that wasn't just any home run. The kid clubbed the hell out of the ball. He wasn't going to let this one get away. He had to see him again and if letting his little friend come back made him feel good, fine.

"Awright. Bring the midget back. But unless he goes five fer five I don't wanna see 'im again. Y'unnerstan what I'm sayin'?"

"Yessir."

"Six o'clock. You be there."

Lazo held out his hand, expecting the manager to shake it, but he didn't. Not with a Hotshot. It was bad enough just being seen talking to one of them, but at least deep center field was far enough from the crowd. The manager chewed on his cigar, his hands tucked around the ample gut holding up his belt.

"Oh, one more thing," Lazo said.

"Yeah? What's that?"

"The two bucks?"

"What?"

"Didn't you say something about us Hotshots not getting a run?"

The manager, always quick to show irascibility when he got the chance, was incredulous. How could a humble Hotshot have such nerve?

"Why I dunno what yer talkin' about young fella."

"But . . ."

"Lookit Hotshot, lemme give ya a bit of advice. Don't ever bite the hand that feeds ya. Got that?"

"Yeah but . . ."

"But what?"

"Nothing."

The old man they called Sarge – a man with baseball in his blood – smiled. He'd been handling Hotshots for more than twenty years, ever since his playing days were over. He knew what they were made of. The meeting ended, he reminded Lazo about the six o'clock starting time for next practice. Hotshots were prone to forgetting the time.

"That was some hit," he said and then he spit the biggest wad of saliva Lazo ever saw.

◆

Yankee Stadium was a huge, cavernous building that stood with all the invincibility of the Roman Coliseum at the corner of East One Hundred Fifty-Seventh Street and River Avenue. Old Glory flew in the wind from dozens of flagpoles at the top and on any game day, scores of black automobiles encircled the stadium. High above the main entrance was the American League insignia – an eagle with its wings spread.

But playing for the Hoboken Browns and holding down jobs meant it was hard for Lazo and Bananas to get away for Yankee games. Not so with Shorty. He had a job, too, but no baseball career, and went to many games. His last encounter with organized ball was the end for him. The Browns' manager was so uninspired by his o-for-five performance at the plate and two errors at second base in a game against the regulars that he took Shorty aside and told him he was the worst ballplayer he'd ever seen and that he should abandon the sport. Even as a recreational pastime.

"Yer too fuckin' small an' too fuckin' slow. You can't hit for shit. You don't unnerstan' the basics of the game and if that's not enough yer a fuckin' embarrassment to the team. Other than that yer a heckuva ballplayer."

Lazo made the team on the strength of his long-ball prowess and one month into the season – with three home runs to his credit – he found himself starting half of the games. In left field. Bananas was a hanger-on, a utility outfielder, and got into even fewer games than that.

Len, meanwhile, never did show for a tryout and when the others finally caught up with him he told them that baseball was behind him. He was busy working and making money. He was wearing expensive clothes and had bought himself a brand-new Chevy Roadster. The boys wondered how a guy his age, new to the city with not a dollar to his name, could afford a car like that, but soon it was clear. John Barleycorn was indeed his employer.

Len was a bootlegger.

During the month of June baseball had become more than a

game for Lazo and Bananas. It was a job, a way of life, and while they were getting paid it was only a pittance. But playing against semipro competition made them better players and with every home run and every extra-base hit he got Lazo grew more confident. He was really beginning to think he might one day play in The Show. That's what they called it. The Show. The major leagues. The bigs. Making it to The Show was every ballplayer's dream and the biggest show around was the New York Yankees.

Taking in a Yankee game during the week was impossible because of work and on only two weekends through June and July did Lazo get time off from the Browns. The first time the Yankees were out of town, so it was early August before Lazo and Bananas finally got to accompany Shorty to a game.

The Yankees were having a miserable season, stuck in the second division of the American League. It was the first time this had happened since the Babe had joined them from the Red Sox. He had missed the first two months of the season, had only eleven home runs – just eight more than Lazo – and was hitting in the low .260s while Lazo was hitting .284, which wasn't bad for a Hotshot who now deserved to be called rookie.

Something was wrong with the Babe. This year of all years when Lazo was spending the whole summer in New York the big guy was doing nothing. His critics said he was washed up. He was thirty years old, an age when most ballplayers are past their prime, and had lots of injuries. He'd been hospitalized and operated on.

Lazo read every word written about him. He knew that manager Huggins and the Babe had quarreled all season long and that on the last day of June Huggins fined him a thousand dollars, but the next day the man they called the Bambino cracked a pair of home runs and the fine was lifted.

His hitting that summer was sporadic. Sometimes he showed traces of his old self, but usually he was swinging at bad pitches and going down on strikes. He was fat and sloppy and out of shape. Huggins put him down publicly by saying that no team could win with players who weren't in condition. He even said the Babe was dragging the whole team down with him.

The young Lou Gehrig, a bull of a man playing first base, was showing signs of future stardom with twelve home runs to his credit, but he was just a rookie. Earle Combs was a solid center fielder and big Bob Meusel was still a first-rate hitter who played the outfield and backed up at third base. Meusel had twenty-three home runs, which was second best in the league. The Babe and his paltry – for him – eleven homers were tied with a large group of players in fifth place, but apart from those few the Yankees were weak. Hugh Ward, the second baseman, was hitting only .236. Benny Bengough was a less-than-adequate catcher and two aged veterans, Ernie Johnson, who was thirty-seven, and Howard Shanks, who was thirty-five, were being used more than they would have been on a good team.

And there was dissension in the ranks. Some of the players wanted to get rid of Huggins. Every day the *Times* reported an incident involving Whitey Witt, Wally Pipp, Wally Schang, and their leader in rebellion – George Herman Ruth. The Babe was a troublemaker and now he was lashing out at his manager.

"I think it's his wife," said Bananas. "Just last year he had forty-six homers and he hit .378. You don't lose it that fast. She must be driving him nuts. Women can do that."

But Lazo knew he'd been married to the same woman since his Red Sox days.

"That's just it," Bananas said. "He's been married too long. She probably doesn't screw him anymore."

The Babe wasn't the same. Lazo knew about his reputation for womanizing and partying and figured maybe it all caught up with him. But the Babe also had a family – a wife and a daughter. Maybe family pressure got to him. Or a string of bad debts.

"Maybe he's got the clap," said Shorty.

The opposition for Lazo's first-ever Yankee game was the Chicago White Sox and when the big guy came to bat it was 1914 all over again. The awe was still there and so was the magic even though the Babe looked nothing like the Providence Grays' nineteen-year old pitcher. Lazo, Bananas, and Shorty had good seats down the third-base line and Lazo was close enough to recognize that familiar round face and squat nose.

But he looked a lot different. He hadn't just put on some weight since their first encounter. He was huge. Bulging out of his uniform. The image of the Grays' tall slim powerhouse of a pitcher who threw the ball like poetry had stayed with Lazo all these years. He was so smooth and if elegance could describe a ballplayer, he was the epitome. It was the same with his hitting – the great back swing, the clean fluid arc his bat carved through the air, and the enormous follow-through that lifted the ball clear out of the stratosphere.

What happened? Lazo couldn't believe how fat he was. His cheeks were puffy and the skin hung loose under his chin. One look at that big gut and Lazo wondered how he ever got around on his swing.

"Jesus," he said in despair.

He was easily the sloppiest looking player on the field. But this was the man Lazo worshipped. He was the reason Lazo was here, playing semipro ball, getting some seasoning, pointing himself in the direction of The Show. His dream.

The Babe came to bat and the catcalls started immediately. They called him a big jerk, a bum, and booed him relentlessly. They said he couldn't hit anymore. Lazo shook his head. C'mon, Babe, he whispered to himself. Show these creeps what you're made of. Hit one out of here.

Do it.

The first two pitches were balls and he watched them sail by. He always had a good eye. The next one he liked and he swung – all the way around – and missed. He swung at the next one, too, and missed by a country mile. In came the third ball and the count was full.

C'mon, Babe. Hit one for me. I'm pulling for you. I saw you hit your first home run. No one else in Yankee Stadium was there that day, but I was and I'm here now. Hit the damn thing.

Swing and a miss. Strike three.

The booing got worse and they started throwing things on

the field. The hecklers were unmerciful. They said things about the Babe's wife and even his mother and if it was Lazo he would have charged up into the stands after them, but the big guy just took his bat and marched back into the dugout.

The Yankees looked like a beaten team. Passed balls. Wild pitches. Outfielders running into each other. The few times when they did get a hit they couldn't advance the runner. From his seat along the third-base line Lazo could see Huggins screaming his lungs out.

"That guy is goin' nuts," said Bananas.

The White Sox weren't playing well either, but managed to stay ahead in a tight pitcher's duel. At least Yankee pitcher Urban Shocker was tossing a good game to keep the score close. When the Babe came to bat again in the fourth inning the fans wasted no time getting on him and in a game like this when none of the Yankee hitters had it the loudest jeers were saved for him.

He was the fall guy.

Lazo wanted him to do something. Hit it deep, even if it was caught by the wall. At least those few seconds of excitement would get the adrenaline flowing.

The Babe swung at the first pitch and fouled it back. The Yankee players were all screaming at one another. The next pitch was inside and then came two more balls to make the count 3-1. That was ideal for a slugger since the next one had to be good or he'd walk. The Babe was used to walks. He had led the league in walks many times since opposing pitchers would much rather have him sitting on first base than smashing a home run. And most of those walks were intentional. But no one was intentionally walking him this season. Not with eleven homers and a .260-something average.

He dug in. The pitch came in right down the middle. He swung and missed and it was a full count again. Lazo was nervous just watching. There was the windup. The delivery. It looked like a fastball. A big league fastball. The kind that go farthest when you connect with the sweet part of the bat at the right moment. The Babe brought back that enormous bat and started taking it across and up with the little twist of the wrist he was famous for. The twist of the wrist that was responsible for two hundred and ninety-two major league home runs.

Strike three.

The catcalls were even worse than before and got so bad Lazo rose to his feet ready to do battle. Shorty told him to sit down. In the seventh inning the White Sox were leading by a run and the Babe came to bat again. One more chance, Lazo thought. How he'd love to see him shut up these fans with a mighty swing of the bat. But not this time. Huggins was so disgusted with his performance that he did something he had never done before. No one had done it before. Not to the greatest slugger the game had ever seen.

"Now pinch hitting for the Yankees, Bobby Veach."

The Babe was pulled for a pinch hitter. It was the ultimate disgrace. Veach was an old player, a former Tiger star hanging on by his fingertips, here in his final year in the majors. It was more than a disgrace. It was humiliation. Lazo couldn't believe it. Removing the bat of Babe Ruth for a pinch hitter was like keeping football's Red Grange on the bench when it was fourth down and goal to go – which never happened – or seeing Louis Firpo knock heavyweight champion Jack Dempsey clear out of the ring – which he did – but at least Dempsey came back to win the fight.

"Let's get outta here," Lazo said.

They didn't stick around for the outcome, but Lazo read about it in the paper. The game went twelve innings and was decided by a run-scoring single.

The Yankees lost.

◆

Len's Chevy Roadster was a beautiful car that sat two in style and when he took Lazo for a ride, the two of them sitting in the open air with the wind against their faces, it was wonderful. But where did he get the money?

"Mr. Barleycorn," Len said.

"Don't give me that Barleycorn crap again. I know you're a bootlegger. But how'd you make so much?"

Len just smirked.

Lazo knew Prohibition wouldn't quell the drinking habits of six million New Yorkers. Saloons were everywhere and there weren't enough federal agents to make any difference. Lazo knew that. Everyone knew it. Then Len started talking.

"The first night we went out on the town I met some bootleggers," he said. "When I said I was from Canada we talked about all the booze comin' into the States from north of the border. I made like I knew my way around and they asked me if I wanted in. The money they were talkin' was incredible so I said why not. How much you make at that factory job of yours?"

"Twelve fifty a week."

Len laughed.

"Larry, you think only crooks are bootleggers, but you're wrong. Everyone and his brother is doin' it. You either get caught or you make a ton of money, but only the dumb ones get caught. It's easy."

Len said the price of alcohol had jumped because the government extended the three-mile limit off the coast and because the U.S. Coast Guard had a lot of new hardware. The old markup was three dollars a case, but since the feds upped their ante, now it was seven.

"It's supply and demand," he said. "As long as there's enough demand you keep up the supply. The harder it gets to supply the stuff, the more expensive your product becomes. The more expensive it gets, the more you make." He snapped his fingers and patted the dash of his Roadster. "I work for a guy named Owney Madden."

"Owney Madden?" exclaimed Lazo. "The mobster?"

"Well, I don't exactly work for him personally. I never seen the guy or nuthin' like that but he's the one at the top. Sort of the president of the operation. But I did meet Big Bill Dwyer. He's the mastermind behind the Rum Row import business."

Len laughed again.

"Yeah, that's the business I'm in. The import business. I'm an importer. How's that grab you?"

His Roadster came to a red light and two girls waved from the sidewalk. He waved back.

"It's a great life, Larry. Comin' to New York was the best thing that ever happened to me and it all happened so fast. It's like a dream. When I compare this to back home it's unbelievable. I ain't never goin' back. Never."

He inhaled the cool Manhattan air that's appreciated best in the open seat of a car like a Chevy Roadster.

"How's the ball team doin'?"

"Pretty good," said Lazo, his mind thinking how far twelvefifty a week took him. "I'm leading the club in homers."

"That's great. You always had it in you to be a ballplayer. You had more ambition than any of us. You got it in spades. Except for one thing."

"What's that?"

"Money. You have no ambition for money. You think you're gonna make any dough playin' ball?"

"Some guys make a lot of dough playing ball."

Lazo could think of one in particular.

"Yeah, but for every one of 'em there's a hundred guys makin' nuthin'. Listen, Larry, what if I said we got some ballplayers workin' for us?"

"Bootlegging?"

"Sure. I told you everybody does it. These guys are big leaguers but I can't tell you their names. They only make three or four thousand bucks a year in baseball but this way they can triple their incomes and still play ball."

"Triple?"

"And these guys got no brains. But if you're smart you can make some serious money." Len shot Lazo a glance. "How much you wanna make, Larry? How much? Tell me."

Lazo fingered the sleek dash of Len's car.

"Oh, let's say enough to own one of these beauties."

Len flashed his teeth and nodded.

"We could use a guy like you," he said. "You wouldn't have to do much and you could still play ball. You could even hang onto your job at the warehouse but you wouldn't need it. You know these guys who run things can do anything they want. They got money. Women. Fast cars. Big mansions. They got politicians in their pockets. They even got athletes in their pockets."

"What do you mean?"

"I mean these guys can fix the World Series and they did. Remember the Black Sox? That was Arnold Rothstein. Now a guy like him you don't cross. He's into bootleggin', narcotics, you name it. Can't be too careful with a guy like that. Or take Big Bill Dwyer. He can make a heavyweight champ out of a bum like Primo Carnera. Remember Carnera? Shit. I could've knocked him out myself. These guys run the world, Larry. Just think. It's like you got the whole world right in your hand."

"So how much do you make, Len?"

"Enough to own one of these beauties. Lookit this." Len showed Lazo a business card. In the middle was a number. "You know what this is?"

Lazo shook his head.

"It's an admission card to the Club Del Fay, the biggest speakeasy in the city. It's run by a guy named Larry Fay and you wouldn't believe the people who go there. Bank presidents. Movie stars. You can't get in without one of these cards and I got one. I could get you one, too."

"I don't know, Len. You're talking about guys like Madden and . . ."

"Whatsa matter with you, Larry? You think everyone's so clean out there? Jesus. Al Smith, the fuckin' governor of New York, is one of the biggest drunks in the country. So is Jimmy Walker, the mayor. You think these guys wanna close down speakeasies? Where would they go to drink?"

Len took a turn at high speed and stepped on the gas. Lazo liked how his Roadster handled the straightaway. Lazo didn't have a car. A car was out of the question. His father didn't even have one back home. In New York he, Shorty, and Bananas got around by bus and that was only when it was too far to walk and they walked a lot. They lived in a flat. It wasn't bad, but nothing like the place Len had on the west side.

"Know who I once saw at the Club Del Fay? Douglas Fairbanks and Mary Pickford. No kiddin'. It was them. Movie stars are there all the time. Hey. How about you come with me tonight? What d'ya say?"

"Tonight?"

"Sure. I hardly seen you all summer. I'll introduce you to some people. You'll have to get dressed up but I'll take care of that. And you'll need money. If you're short, I'll loan you. What d'ya say?"

Lazo thought about it. Why not? He said okay.

"And I also want you to come with me . . . just once . . . just to get a taste of it . . . on my next run."

"Your next run?"

"On Rum Row. One run and you'll make enough dough to spend a whole month at the Club Del Fay. Then you can kiss that warehouse job good-bye. What d'ya say?"

"I dunno, Len."

"C'mon Larry! You want one of these Roadsters, dontcha? The girls come right off the sidewalk and jump right into yer lap for Chrissake!"

"But it's dangerous. Isn't it?"

"The feds aren't interested in guys like you and me. They want the big boys. Besides, the worst thing that can happen is you get stuck with a fine you can pay off in two seconds. So what d' ya say? Tonight we take in the Club Del Fay and on my next run you tag along."

Lazo thought about it. It was tempting.

"Okay," he said. "I'll go with you. But just once."

Len grabbed his hand and shook it.

"One run is all it'll take," he said. "Then you'll be hooked."

◆

On the way to the Club Del Fay Len told Lazo all about Owney Madden and how he came from England to America with nothing. He was a hard-nosed thug who was immersed in the New York waterfront. He got rich through rum running on the east coast. The Coast Guard put up only token resistance and big-time operators like him ran the blockade with ease. Madden was a director in the city's Big Seven, a corporate-style hierarchy that oversaw organized crime in the eastern United States. He supplied a string of lavish speakeasies in the well-to-do districts of New York where the cream of society went for fun. Len said speakeasies existed wherever there was a market for alcohol.

Which was everywhere.

Bringing rum to the mainland was one thing, but getting it to market was another so ambitious men like Madden built elaborate empires with armies of foot soldiers who manned the contact boats. That's where Len came in. The small but fleet contact boats carried liquor from the big supply ships to couriers on the mainland where the bottles were then loaded onto trucks. From these out-of-the-way rural haunts the goods were transported to the outskirts of the city and from there shipped in the trunks of cars for delivery to nightclubs and private parties. At the parties were businessmen, politicians, and even police officers who would make a cash killing just to keep the main transportation arteries open.

The Club Del Fay at 247 West Fifty-fourth Street was the most popular speakeasy in Manhattan. Its predecessor had been closed down in the spring by federal agents, but its offshoot was running unhindered. Lazo had been to The Mansion and as lavish as it was, it had nothing on this place. The Club Del Fay was extravagant beyond description. Wealth squandered itself from everywhere. Gaining admission meant being dressed to the nines, so Len rented a pair of made-to-measure tuxedos and, just as he said he would, he produced a card for Lazo.

Outside, illegally parked in front, was a big white Packard. It was the biggest car Lazo had ever seen.

"Good evening, Mistah Dixon," said the doorman to Len. He was an English gentleman. After letting them in he stuck his head out the door and noticed the Packard. "My goodness, he's done it again, hasn't he? That automobile must be moved at once. I swear he's about the laziest man I've evah seen."

"You know whose car it is?" Lazo asked him.

"Of course. Mistah Ruth. It's his. Same thing happened last time."

He went inside leaving a white-faced Lazo at the door.

"Did you hear what he said?" Lazo said to Len.

"They say he comes here a lot."

"He does? For what?"

"What do you think? He's rich. He's got money. He's probably on the list. He gets an invitation."

A moment later a waiter burst between them, hurried down the steps, and rushed through the door. Between his thumb and forefinger was a shiny silver dollar. He jumped into the Packard, started the engine, and drove the huge car down the street.

Inside the club a band was playing loudly and a chorus line of girls was showing a lot of leg. Everyone was dancing, drinks in hand. Len walked around like he owned the place and said he wanted to introduce Lazo to Larry Fay. But Lazo had other things on his mind.

"Where is he?" he wanted to know.

"Who?" asked Len.

"The Babe, for Chrissake!"

"How the hell should I know? Probably with some dame."

"Naw."

"What do you mean naw? What d' ya think he comes here for? He has a few drinks and gets laid and he can do it in private. You think Babe Ruth can just walk into any place without attracting a crowd? Here no one bugs him. Oh, Mr. Fay. I want you to meet a buddy of mine. Larry Slack."

"Hello, Len. First time here, Larry?"

Lazo nodded.

"I hope Len shows you a good time."

"Mr. Fay, Larry here's a baseball player with the Hoboken Browns."

"A baseball player? The Hoboken Browns?"

"Semipro team," said Lazo. "They're sort of in the Yankees farm system."

"Well then you'll be right at home here. Some of the Yankees are regular customers of ours."

"I noticed. I saw the Packard out front."

"Yes. Babe Ruth comes here all the time. This must be the only place where he can relax and get away from the fans."

"Larry is a Babe Ruth nut," said Len. "He loves the guy."

"Is that so? Well, if you see him don't hound him for an autograph or anything like that. He doesn't want to be seen. He's had it pretty tough lately. Last time he was here a guy took a shot at him. Shouldn't have done that. Ruth's a big man and he laid him out with one punch."

Lazo was glassy-eyed.

"Poor guy. You really have to feel for him. He's got trouble with his wife. He just got fined a few thousand bucks for breaking curfew. And now Huggins won't even let him play."

"I saw him hit his first home run," Lazo said.

"With Boston?"

"No. In the International League. With the Providence Grays. It was the only minor league homer he ever hit."

"Really? How old was he?"

"Nineteen."

"Nineteen? Jesus Christ. I can't even imagine him at that age. He's thirty now and looks fifty. He must have looked a lot different in those days."

"Best pitcher I ever saw."

"That's right. People forget what a great pitcher he was. He's hit so many home runs for the Yankees the last five years people forget how he used to throw the ball."

With his loud indigo shirt and checkered red tie, Fay stretched out his arm and wheeled it around pretending he was Babe Ruth. Lazo just laughed.

"He never had a losing season," Lazo said. "Not in the minors and not with Boston, either."

"He can do it all, that's for sure," said Fay, pulling his sleeve back into shape. "At least he could. But I don't think he's got it anymore. Nothing's working for him this year. Oh well, no one stays on top forever. Right Len?"

"That's right, Mr. Fay."

"When you got it you go for it and take whatever you can get. Right Len?"

"Absolutely."

Fay jabbed Len in the shoulder.

"Nice meeting you, Larry. Len here will show you around. You boys be sure to have a good time now."

"Yessir," said Lazo.

Not many people at the Club Del Fay were interested in the Yankees. If there was any talk about them at all it was condescending chatter reserved for favorites who don't deliver. The team was in seventh place and looked destined to wind up there. The Babe was warming the bench and hitting a paltry .245. Unknown territory for him. Huggins had slapped him with the suspension after hiring a private detective to follow him around. The Babe was always missing curfews and then a beautiful young widow named Claire Hodgson surfaced. The newspapers cast her as "the other woman."

By one o'clock in the morning, Lazo had had enough. Unlike Len, who slept in every day after his long nights on the sea, Lazo got up at six for his warehouse job. Len said he would drive him home, but there was a huge crowd at the door – this was when things really started to roll – so they edged down a hallway at the back of the club and proceeded to the rear exit. It was there that they saw him. The Babe.

It was him all right. He was being helped down the hall and what a sight. He was hopelessly drunk, his face flushed. Some girl whom Lazo took for one of the club's locals was trying to support him, but failing miserably. She had him up against the wall trying to stop him from falling over.

"Let me give you a hand," Lazo said taking one of his flaccid arms and shoving it over his shoulder. "Is he okay?"

"Thank you, honey," said the girl. "He'll be all right. Just needs to put his head down for a few hours. He wants to go home to his wife. Poor sonofabitch. Couldn't even come. That never happened before."

Lazo was in a dream. Here he was giving the Babe a helping hand and he was sorely crushed. The Babe looked like a down-and-out bum. He smelled so bad Lazo had to hold his breath to avoid inhaling his stink.

"Is he gonna be sick?"

"I don't think so, honey. He can hold his liquor. Just needs some sleep. That's all. He'll be all right."

The Babe was a big man. Huge. Lazo and the girl half dragged his lifeless body through the back door of the Club Del Fay and down the steps to the street where his big white Packard was waiting for him, a driver behind the wheel. The driver, the same waiter who had parked the car earlier, helped Lazo deposit him in the back seat.

"Thanks a lot, bud," the waiter said. "I'll get him home. He'll be okay. Happens sometimes."

"Yeah, sure," said Lazo, on the seat right beside him in the back of the car. It was time to go. But he didn't want to. He checked the Babe's eyes. They were open. Barely.

"Hey Babe! Babe Ruth! You know me. I'm your biggest fan."

His big round head hung limply from his neck. His hair was sopping wet. His mouth was dry and his lips were cracked. Beads of sweat trickled down his cheeks. Lazo took him by the shoulders and held him.

"Babe, I just wanted to tell you I think you're the greatest and I'm gonna be a ballplayer just like you."

The bloodshot eyes opened just a little.

"Whatcha hittin' keed?"

The breath was enough to bowl Lazo over.

"Almost .300."

"Shhhhhit," and the "sh" seemed like it would go on forever.

"That'sh better'n me. I'm hittin' wun-ninety-shicks."

"No, you're not. You're hitting .245 but you'll get better. You'll get back on track. Wait and see."

The Babe's massive head was teetering back and forth like a rock ready to fall off a cliff.

"I am? Shhhhit. I musta got a coupla hits. Is Huggins aroun'?"

"Who? Miller? I don't think so. He's not here."

"Will ya tell 'im sumthin' for me. Will ya keed?"

"Sure, anything you say, Babe. What do you want me to tell him?"

He burped and the odor from it had everything. Liquor. To-bacco. Dried saliva. Even the wind from his stomach.

"Tell the little twirp to go 'n fuck himself. Will ya do that for me?"

"Sure, whatever you say, Babe."

"An' call Helen and tell her I'm comin' right home."

"Sure. Anything else?"

"Yeah . . ."

His head fell to one side and Lazo feared he might snap his neck so he lifted him under the chin and pushed it back to the center. Then the Babe stuck out his hand. Lazo grasped those fingers that had smashed almost three hundred home runs. But now they couldn't hold a match.

"I hope ya make it, keed," he said.

Lazo looked at him and smiled. This was his hero, his reason for being, his motivation for everything he did. This was the greatest ballplayer the world had ever seen and for this one minute in time he was alone with him. It was just like eleven years ago when Lazo was a starstruck boy hankering for an auto-graph he thought he'd never get because he forgot his program.

"Here son."

This was the vision that absorbed his being at the very mo-ment that counted the most. When the Lizzies' city champi-onship was there for the taking. This was the man who gave him the strength and will to do what had to be done.

"Hey keed, that was some poke."

It was him. The Babe. The one and only Babe.

"Thanks," Lazo said. "Thanks a lot."

◆

The small contact boat that Len used to carry liquor from the supply ship to shore was little more than a bare hull. Except for the pilot house with the steering wheel, compass, and navigating equipment, everything had been removed to provide space for the cargo – a hundred cases of rum and whiskey. On the side of each case was the word *Mackerel.*

Len said the two-engine speedboat could do thirty knots and a bit less when full. He and Lazo would work through the night transferring cases from the supply ship to the speedboat before taking them to the mainland for pickup. Then the profits would be shared.

Lazo was surprised at how open business was between the supply ship thirty miles off the mainland and the contact boat. He expected a hush-hush operation, but it wasn't like that at all. The supply ship had thousands of cases of whiskey spread all over the deck – rum, champagne, and ale, all of it piled high, one case on top of the other. The men on the ship bantered constantly, the butt of their jokes the U.S. Coast Guard. Lazo learned that many of the contact boats were built in the same yards as the Coast Guard vessels so everyone knew the top speed of all their new boats.

"Just stay one step ahead and you'll never get caught," Len said.

The bootleggers had well-planned escape routes just in case and though the Coast Guard boasted of its new destroyers most of the liquor run by the big syndicates was getting through. Sometimes aircraft were used at night to help the contact boats locate the supply ships.

The shipment would fetch a profit of five dollars a case, which meant five hundred dollars for a few hours of work. From that Len had to pay Lazo, the cost of running the boat, and a small percentage for an insurance fund should the Coast Guard get lucky and seize the boat. The insurance fund paid for high-priced lawyers who defended the operators in court – and almost always got them off on technicalities – and the cost of buying back the boat at the next government auction.

Len had never been caught.

The only thing left to do was head back to shore and unload the cases for the buyer's courier. Then cash would be exchanged and even that was carefully planned. Len had the top half of a jack of clubs while the courier assigned to the pickup had the bottom half. No money would trade hands until the two pieces, each of them marked with the agreed-upon number of cases, were matched.

When the run was over, Lazo would call in sick since he had no intention of going to work with no sleep. Packing boxes in the warehouse was hard labor and he wouldn't be of any use if he was loading and unloading cases of liquor on the high seas all night long. Besides, twelve-fifty a week didn't go very far.

His take for the evening would be over a hundred dollars – the equivalent of two months at the warehouse – and he realized what Len meant when he said one night on Rum Row and Lazo would never go back to his day job.

It was so easy it was comical. No wonder everyone on the supply ship was in such good humor. Their shipment packed in tight on the speedboat, Lazo and Len would enjoy the clear night sky and take in the bright lights of the city off in the distance. Then they would come to shore, meet the courier, unload the cargo, and go home. The only time Lazo got worried was when Len pointed to the southeast and said that a Coast Guard vessel was out there lurking.

"I don't see anything," said Lazo.

"Neither do I," said Len, "but she's there. You can count on it."

"What if she spots us? Then what?"

"No problem. She probably can't see us since we're too small, but even if she did what could she do? The Coast Guard can't do thirty knots."

"But you said we can't do thirty knots with a full load."

"Pretty darn close though. Besides, if things get really hot, we'll just dump it."

"Dump it?"

"Into the drink. Sometimes you have to do that when the feds are chasing you. You'd be surprised how many cases turn up on shore the next morning."

"You mean you just go back and get them?"

"Sure."

Lazo couldn't believe it. It was ridiculous. Now he knew how Len got that Roadster and that apartment in Manhattan. It was tempting and the best part was that all of it was paid in cash. Every dollar. Maybe it was against the law, but like Len said everyone was doing it and now Lazo was doing it, too. If not him, somebody else.

"Once I thought I was gonna be a pitcher," Len said. "Everybody told me what a great fastball I had. It was better than runnin' numbers on the street and dealin' with bookies all the time. Then I came down here and thought I was gonna try out for the Browns. But I gave up on baseball pretty fast after I tried bootleggin'. This is way more fun. There's a little danger and I like that. You mix with all kinds of people, the kind you see in movies and read about in the paper. Nope. There's no turnin' back for me now. I been doin' this all summer. I got me a car, a fancy place to live, and I meet so many girls at the club I lose count. Shit. If the old man saw me now he'd crap in his pants. So that's what I'm gonna do, Larry. Make a killin' with these runs, screw as many women as I can, and be a happy man. That's not so bad, is it?"

"I guess not."

"It's a helluva lot better than playin' ball in dumpy ballparks. But you're still hangin' onto that dream, aren't you?"

"Yeah and I'm making headway. They say I'm two years away from playing pro, then maybe a couple years in the minors and I could be in the big leagues when I'm twenty-three. I'm gonna do it, Len. I'm really gonna do it. The big time. I'm gonna make The Show if it kills me."

Len didn't say anything. He just shook his head, full of

grudging admiration. Then he stuck up his right thumb in the "go for it" sign. Just like that first night in Hoboken.

"Yeah, Larry, I guess . . ."

"What's that?"

From the corner of his eye Lazo saw two bright lights coming up quickly on the starboard side of the boat. The lights were moving faster than they were. Len took out his eyeglass.

"I dunno know who it is . . . our boats don't go that fast . . . it can't be the Coast Guard. . . ." He kept his eyeglass on the lights while Lazo grabbed the steering wheel. "I dunno who those guys are. But they're gainin' on us awful quick I can tell you that."

Lazo was worried.

"Who are they?" he said.

"I dunno. I never seen no boats that can do that speed. He must be goin' forty knots for Chrissake. I dunno . . . unless . . ."

"Unless what?"

For a moment there was nothing but silence. Len fidgeted with the focus of his eyeglass. Then the boat pursuing them came into view loud and clear.

"Holy shit! Gimme that wheel!"

Len threw his eyeglass on the floor of the pilothouse and grabbed the wheel.

"Start droppin' the booze! Hurry up!"

"Why?"

"Pirates!"

"What?"

"Do what I tell you! Drop those cases! We gotta pick up speed! Hurry up, for Chrissake!"

Lazo didn't know what to do. The cases were piled up everywhere. He couldn't even see the deck.

"Jesus Christ! Start droppin' that stuff! What're you waitin' for?"

Len let go of the wheel, grabbed the nearest case, and dropped it over the side. It fell with a splash. Then he took another. And another. Lazo started doing the same. He dropped them out one side of the boat and Len from the other.

"Keep it up! We gotta dump it! They're gainin' on us!"

No one said anything to Lazo about pirates. He thought the only enemy was the Coast Guard and they didn't seem to be much of an enemy.

"What do you mean pirates?" he said as he kept dropping the cases overboard.

"Pirates for Chrissake! Pirates! Thieves! We do all the work then they raid us and steal our booze! I never seen 'em before but I heard about 'em! C'mon they're still gainin'!"

The little boat picked up some speed and was doing twenty-five knots, twenty-six, twenty-seven, but the other boat was still closing in on them. Then a shot rang out.

"Get down! They're shootin' at us! Get down!"

Lazo hit the deck, his breath short, his heart pounding. Adrenaline was rushing up his spine. Len crawled over to the wheel and took out a compass. His body flat on the deck, he raised his arm and took hold of the wheel, turning the small boat to the north.

"Larry, listen to me! We gotta go for the coast of Long Island or we're done! But it's a long way! We gotta dump more cases!"

Len tried pushing a case off the side, but it wouldn't budge. He tried a second time, but it was no use so Lazo got to his knees. His head down low he wrapped his hands around a case and dumped it. Then he dumped ten more. One by one. Len steered.

"Good! Keep it up! We're up to thirty knots!"

A second shot rang out and Lazo threw himself onto his chest.

Jesus, he thought. What the hell am I doing here? He thought about his mother. She was worried when he said he was going to New York. But he said it would be all right. He was going to play baseball. He'd stay with Bananas and his aunt. It would be all right. Then he noticed the light on top of the pilot-house. It was still on.

"Len, the light! The light! Turn it off! Turn it off!"

The light with a single bulb was on top of the cabin in the middle of the boat. Len reached into his jacket and took out a gun.

"What're you doin'?" screamed Lazo.

"I'm gonna shoot it out so they can't see us!"

"You got a gun?"

Len fired, but missed the light. A shot was returned from the pirates and the bullet whistled close over his head.

Lazo's face was on the floor. The rough surface of the wooden deck was on his lips and on his nose. He had to raise his head to breathe. But where was Len? Lazo turned and saw him lift himself up for another shot at the light. The boat was bouncing along at almost thirty-five knots. The only way to shoot out the light was from close range.

With one hand on the wheel Len got up and steadied himself. He spread his feet apart. Half his body was inside the pilothouse. For a split second he stood in the clear and pointed the gun. There was a shot and Lazo thought he had hit the light. But it stayed on. Len gasped and fell to the floor, gasping.

"Larry!" he cried.

The gun was on the deck by his feet. Lazo crawled over and grabbed it. He stood up, swung around, and took aim at the bulb. With one blast the glass shattered and all was dark. Then Lazo dropped to the deck, still clinging to the gun. It was deathly quiet. The engine was going full throttle and the boat was racing through the water. But it was quiet.

Lazo didn't move. He could hear Len moaning in agony. There were voices. The pirates! They were a ways off, but Lazo could hear them. He couldn't see anything. The light was out. He raised his head over the edge of the boat. The pirate boat was out there.

"Where'd they go?" someone shouted. "Where'd those bastards go?"

Lazo took the wheel and turned it slightly and the boat changed course. The engine was still kicking and the distance between the boats started to widen. They were getting away.

Len was on the floor, his head not far from the wheel. He was breathing quickly and blood was pouring from a hole the size of a dime in the middle of his chest.

"Holy shit, Len," Lazo whispered frantically. "Holy shit."

Len was pale.

"Len, it's okay. They can't see us. I got the light. I got the light."

Len shook his head up and down.

"Good," he said in a weak voice. He tried to say more, but only gagged.

"Len, we're heading for shore. We'll be there soon. I'll get you to a hospital. You'll be all right. You'll be all right."

Soon there was no sign of the pirates.

The blood kept flowing from Len's body and Lazo cried out. He let go of the wheel and knelt beside him. He cradled his head in his hands. He didn't know any first aid and he didn't know what to do for a bullet wound on a boat in the middle of nowhere. He cried out again. He felt useless.

"Len! Len! I'll get you to a hospital! You're gonna be all right! You're gonna be all right!"

The boat started veering away from the course he had set and began turning eastward. That was no good. They had to reach shore. Lazo let go of Len and got behind the wheel. The lights of Long Island were getting closer. He tried to see where he was going, but it was impossible to tell. Then Len's breathing got faster and faster. His eyes began to show their whites.

"Oh my God!" screamed Lazo, dropping to the deck. "Oh my God! No! No!"

Len looked up into his face. He tried to speak, but there were only cracking sounds.

"What Len?" Lazo asked desperately. "What're you tryna say?"

"G . . . g . . .g . . . ood shot . . ."

Lazo held Len's head in his arms and caressed him. His blood was everywhere. But he almost seemed to be smiling.

"Len how'd we ever get into this mess? How'd we ever get into this?"

He dug his fingers through Len's matted hair and held him close. It was almost as if Len were a child and he the mother. Len was so weak and helpless. He couldn't think for himself. Never could. He needed someone to lead him. He had an outer strength, but not an inner one. The one that counts. He needed a beacon and Lazo could have been that beacon. But he got mixed up with bootleggers and pirates and now he got himself shot. In the chest. There was blood. A lot of blood.

"Len?"

Lazo's eyes looked for a sign, any sign.

"Len? Are you there? Are you there? Len?"

His eyes closed and then he went cold. A shiver came over Lazo and he found himself trembling. It started in his feet and worked up through his legs and into his arms and stomach. It was like a steaming hot potion filling his body. But the end was only cold and ice.

"Len? Len?"

He shook him, but Len's head was limp.

"Len! Len! Don't die! You can't die! You can't!"

It was no use. He was gone.

Lazo wrapped his arms around Len's head. The small speed-boat turned completely around and went in circles. Len's blood was all over him, but it didn't matter. Lazo was now alone. There was no life. Nothing. No color. No breeze. Only the black of night and the relentless sound of the boat's engine turning over and over and over.

"Hoodlum," he whispered, "you could've made it. You had a fastball, damn it. You had a fastball. You could've made it."

Seven

"I'm eighty and I feel like a hundred."

Those were his exact words on his eightieth birthday and it wasn't like him. His mind hadn't slowed down a wisp, but he started looking like an old man. When he walked, he walked slowly and methodically. When he sat down he bent his back awkwardly and peered over his shoulder to see where he was going. Everything he did took a little more time and it required some getting used to. Grandpa was never the type of person to slow you down.

But the worst part was his relish for life wasn't the same. He had no energy. I first noticed it the day he tried to hit the ball. He just looked so old.

I must have been blind.

But of course. I was a teenager and busy with myself. Grandpa remained the great advisor he always was and when I did ask him about something he was always there to deliver. But we were both getting older and I knew his day was coming. When someone reaches eighty they must be thinking at least a little about death.

I figured life and death is different for people than it is for birds or hamsters, but I wasn't sure and I wasn't sure because of him. The way he saw it everything that lived – birds, hamsters, tadpoles, and people – were leaves from the same tree. He said we didn't deserve life any more than those other creatures did. Even bugs. We were all in it together. That's what he said.

Sometimes I think Grandpa never gave himself enough credit as a human being – as a man – but that's how he was.

He was the one who taught me about love. The only one, really. My earliest memories were of him holding me and cuddling me. He must have spent so much time with me when I was little and when I got older he was the one who would talk to me and explain things so I might understand more about the world.

We talked about so many different things. Once when he was discussing the rapidly increasing rate of divorce he said that a young couple should pay a lot of money – thousands of dollars – to get a marriage license. That way, he said, they wouldn't rush into it blindly and would show more of a commitment to make it work. But if things didn't work out and they agreed to go their separate ways, then getting a divorce would be easy. Cheap too. Instead of the other way around.

When it came to having children he was of a similar bent. Too many children, he said, were busy having children of their own with no thought to what's involved. It made me think of my own parents and how much they had put into raising me. It wasn't much. They were too concerned about themselves.

He always loved kids and he loved me. He was my saving grace. He made life – especially the early years – worthwhile. He gave them meaning and substance and he taught me what was important. We had stimulating talks on marriage, divorce, child-rearing, and a lot of other things. I was intrigued when I heard about the costly marriage license and asked if he could have afforded it when he got married.

"Never thought of that," he said. "I guess we would have lived in sin."

With my grandmother? I couldn't imagine it. When it came to behavior not acceptable to her way of thinking – and that included a lot of behavior – she just pretended it didn't exist. A man and a woman living together out of wedlock was too disgusting to think about. Only animals did that, she said.

I respected Grandpa. Lots. His influence on me was total, but he didn't abuse it. He wanted me to develop my own ideas and liked to debate with me on any subject as long as I could support my opinion, which I could rarely do. What does a teenage kid who has everything handed to him on a platter know about anything? This was one of Grandpa's greatest gifts to me: my knowing that I knew nothing at all.

He always said the sooner people discover how profoundly ignorant they really are the better off they'll be because that's when they begin to learn. He never came out and said I was an ignoramus or anything. He would never have done that. He let me reach that conclusion for myself.

◆

When I was fifteen, my parents said they would let me spend the summer with Grandpa at his cottage. He said it was his cottage as if he owned it, but he didn't. He and my grandmother borrowed it from a friend who went on a long holiday and they could have it for nothing as long as they maintained the place. But as far as Grandpa was concerned it was *his*.

The cottage was a small, two-bedroom frame structure right on a lake about a three-hour drive from the city. The lake was called Eagle Lake and though the name had its origins in some Indian word for "eagle," I never once saw an eagle there. It was quiet and peaceful. The only problem was I'd miss most of the baseball season and this was by design. My father's design. He was concerned about my growing fascination for the game. Over the three previous summers I had played organized ball. Grandpa, who went to every game – he didn't miss one – even called me the "Bambino" because one season I led the league in home runs. That was one of Babe Ruth's nicknames so I figured I was in select company.

This was a new Grandpa who possessed so much baseball knowledge it was unbelievable. He knew what to do, when to do it, and how to do it. His mind was a baseball encyclopedia and when he wasn't telling me about old players like Babe Ruth, Shoeless Joe Jackson, and Hank Greenberg or those of more recent vintage like Stan Musial or Mickey Mantle, he was telling me how to stand at the plate or how to get a good beeline on my throw from the outfield or when to steal a base from under the nose of the opposing pitcher.

He said an old friend of his was quite a baserunner in his younger days.

I was a city kid and the chance to spend eight weeks with Grandpa at a cottage was too good to pass up. I'd miss much of the baseball season, but we made a pact – Grandpa and me – that he'd spend the whole time there polishing up my baseball skills. And we wouldn't tell my father about it. That was why on the day we drove up we had two gloves, a bat and a ball tucked away in our luggage. At least I thought they were tucked away in our luggage.

Grandpa put a Louisville Slugger – it was our favorite bat and Babe Ruth's too – across the bottom of our biggest piece of luggage, and when my mother asked why he was taking this huge leather suitcase with him he said he was bringing lots of clothes. That got quite a reaction because everyone knew Grandpa to be a light traveler. As the story goes, he would leave for a weeklong sales trip and take one pair of pants, two shirts, and maybe three pairs of socks.

"You're bringing all these clothes?" my mother asked him.

"You're darn tootin I am," he said. "We're going for eight weeks. You think I'm going to wear the same clothes every day?"

The only way the bat fit inside the suitcase was by placing it across the diagonal and even then the suitcase was bulging at the corners. The gloves were a lesser problem since Grandpa stuffed them under his socks and underwear so even a customs agent would have had trouble finding them. Then there was the ball.

On the drive to the cottage I was in the back of the car with my grandparents and I thought the ball was safely deposited in the suitcase when it suddenly appeared at my feet. Grandpa told me later that my father almost caught him with the ball in hand so he hid it in his shirt sleeve – it was an old baggy shirt – just before getting into the car. Then he rolled the ball onto the floor.

That was a mistake.

The ball rolling around on the floor made for a precarious trip. Whenever the car sped up the ball rolled under the driver's seat to the back and when the car slowed down it rolled forward. My father was behind the wheel and a few times the ball almost rolled right into his heels. I figured it was just a matter of time before it rolled into the front and got lodged between the floor and gas pedal, making the car speed up and resulting in a horrendous accident and maybe fatalities for the three people in the back.

My parents would have blamed the deaths on baseball.

When we finally arrived at the cottage, Grandpa had the ball wedged in tight between his two feet, which he had placed directly below my father's seat. I had no idea how long he was in this position, but he was stiff all over by the time we arrived. The problem then was how to get the ball out of the car so no one would see. Slipping it up his sleeve again was a possibility, but if it rolled out our little game would have been over.

Grandpa solved that problem. As soon as we stopped he opened the door and dropped the ball under the car. When my parents drove off they didn't know that a hated baseball was resting below the undercarriage.

Sometimes Grandpa was a real genius.

We weren't worried about my grandmother finding out since she wasn't quick to notice things. Besides, her biggest concern was how to fend off all the bugs she believed were grouping for an attack that night.

The people who cottaged around the lake were just like us, city folk getting away to nature for awhile, but those who actually lived in the nearby town were different. They weren't like city folk at all. Grandpa pointed this out to me on the first day. Old Burt, the man who ran the general store at the marina on Eagle Lake, was typical. He was about seventy and though younger than Grandpa everyone called him Old Burt, everyone but Grandpa who just called him Burt.

When he talked about all the places he'd seen he rattled off a list of towns I had never heard of and when I mentioned Boston, Detroit, New York, Cleveland, Milwaukee, or Baltimore – which were all in the Eastern Division of the American League – he just shook his head.

"Nope, never been there," he said. "If a place is so big there ain't a general store with the name of the place on it then the place is too big for me."

I had never heard of the Philadelphia or Chicago General Store so I didn't bother to ask if he'd been to those cities.

Old Burt and Grandpa got along well. They had a lot in common. For starters, they were both lefties. Southpaws. Grandpa was the only left-hander in our family. It was a trait he had inherited from his father and he was always telling me about famous people of the same bent. In addition to Babe Ruth there were Julius Caesar, Napoleon, Queen Victoria, Michelangelo, Picasso, and Charlie Chaplin. Old Burt knew another one. Jack the Ripper. He also had a theory about left-handers being more creative than the rest of us because he said they used both sides of their brain.

"But some people don't use either side of their brain," said Grandpa to which Old Burt agreed and said that most of them must be from the city.

I took that as a knock against all urban dwellers, but Grandpa didn't think so. He said Old Burt was probably right and that if more city people behaved like country people the world would be a better place, which immediately prompted Old Burt's speech about the total lack of security in town and the fact he never once locked his door or closed his garage when he went out at night.

"Locksmiths don't do too well around here," he said.

Grandpa was a city person, but he didn't act or think like a city person. He didn't approach life as if he was in a race, but took it one day at a time.

So that summer was a real turning point for me. It was time to stop and come up for air and look at who I was, what I was doing and where I was going. It was a chance to ponder what this great mystery called life was all about.

I was damned if I knew.

Grandpa had a lot more experience than me, but he didn't pretend to know the answer either. He could talk all about the glaciers and trilobites and the age of the Canadian Shield and stuff like that, but when it came to life he would just shake his head. But then he'd mention the ball – *that* ball – and conclude it must have something to do with it.

The first few nights we camped out in a two-man tent – just Grandpa and me – while my grandmother slept in the cottage. It was better that way. Those evenings wouldn't have been as meaningful and poignant if she'd been there spraying Raid on every ant that reared its head. There were times when Grandpa and I actually became one with the world just as we had at the Bluffs. I couldn't have done this with anyone but him.

Some nights the sky was so clear it was incredible. You can never see stars like that in the city. We got to talking about things like life and death and God. I asked him if he believed in God and he said he didn't know, that he'd had serious doubts ever since he saw a young life snuffed out.

"Did you see somebody die, Grandpa?"

He got awfully squirmy with that one. I knew he had never been in a war. He was too young for World War I and too old for World War II and if he was ever a soldier I would have known about it.

"It happened a long time ago. He was my friend and he died right in my arms. He wasn't even twenty. It shouldn't have happened."

He was uneasy. This was something he had never talked about. But he could see I was itching to know.

"He was a pitcher. We used to play together on the Lizzies. You know about the Lizzies. He had a hell of a fastball, I can tell you. He just knew what to do. But he was wild. Undisciplined."

He stopped and looked up at the sky. I think he was looking for his dead friend.

"Stephen, I once told you about the time I went down to New York to try out for a semipro ball team. Well he was one of the guys I went with. But I never told you what happened to him. He got into some trouble. He was a good kid really but he didn't think all the time. He just did things."

"What things?"

"He got into some trouble. It was stupid. But he got himself shot . . . and he died."

"You mean with a gun?"

He said he didn't want to talk about it anymore.

"Lookit Stephen, sometimes things are better left alone. All you have to know is that it happened, but it shouldn't have happened. And maybe it was partially my fault, too. I don't know. But for a long time there it made me think about God. So what about you, Stephen? Do you believe in God?"

I said I found the idea complicated.

"What's complicated?" he asked me.

"Life."

"Life is complicated?"

"Sure it is."

"No, it isn't. Life is easy. As easy as pie. All you have to know is that we're here . . . alive. . . ."

"But Grandpa, man isn't around for long. The universe is billions of years old and we're only here for—"

I was going to say sixty or seventy years but suddenly realized how unfair that would have been to him.

"—not too long."

"Nope. We're not here too long at all."

"Then what's the point? Look at your friend. You said he wasn't even twenty and he died. We're just nothing. We're not even a flea."

"Even a flea is alive, Stephen."

"I don't know. The world's such a mess."

Grandpa looked at me in dismay and I know what he was thinking. Cynical. He always said being cynical was the worst thing. Especially for young people. Young people have no reason to be cynical, he would say. They should be so busy learning things that there is no time for being cynical. I knew what cynical meant before any of my friends and I knew because of Grandpa.

Just then he looked older than I had ever seen him before. Even older than the time he tried to hit the baseball. His hair was gray and thinning, his skin tough and dry. He bit hard on his lower lip and the lines on his face crawled from his mouth all the way up to the corners of his eyes. There were lots of lines, new ones, and then he looked straight at me.

"Do you really think things are that bad?"

"Sure they are."

He looked tired and worn out. Even haggard. He'd been around a long time and had done many things and now he was being told what a rotten world it was by his fifteen-year-old grandson who had seen it all.

"Maybe you're right."

He let me stew for a minute to mull that one over. Then he picked up the baseball we had brought along. He had it in his left hand, his throwing hand, and his fingers kept dancing around it. Then he turned the ball and stuck it right in my face.

"But you're not right, Stephen. The world is a wonderful place and you know why? Because there's so much magic in it. That's why. You just have to look for it."

I put my hand over the top of the ball and my fingers went tight around his so both our hands were on it. Grandpa was right. It was a magical moment. There was no one else in the world. Just the two of us and the ball and whatever cynicism was inside me just flowed away.

"Stephen, I think we should take a picture. Of you and me. A good shot of us. What do you think?"

I didn't know what brought that on.

"I don't think we have any pictures of us since you were little.
I'm going to get your grandmother and she's going to take it.
Right now. Okay?"

Before I could say anything he was rushing off to the
cottage. It was a warm night and he was in his summer pajamas.
A few minutes later I could hear my grandmother complaining
about the cold night air even though it was seventy degrees.
Grandpa had an old Polaroid with him. He showed her how to
do it but she was confused so he showed her again.

"Lookit. You look through the little window. You aim. The
flash goes off and presto you've got a picture. The technology is
only forty years old."

When she had it figured out we posed in front of the tent.
The lake was behind us shimmering in the moonlight. Grandpa
put his arm around me, the flash went off and the camera
whirred. In a few seconds the film came out and we had the picture. It wasn't a classic or anything like that and would never be
worthy of a frame. But it was a picture of Grandpa and me and
like he said it was the first one in years.

"Gee, what a good-looking guy," Grandpa said as he examined it.

"Stephen is a good-looking guy," my grandmother replied.

"Who said anything about him? I'm talking about me!"

It was only a Polaroid – and not a good quality one at that – but
still it said a lot about the people in it. I was fifteen, just a kid – or
keed as Grandpa liked to say – and despite my ramblings of despair my whole life was ahead of me. But Grandpa was now
eighty-two and despite his mind being as sharp as a tack he was
ageing and ageing rapidly.

The photograph was proof.

He looked like a man wallowing in the struggle of his ninth
decade. He was old. Really old. And while he joked about the
picture all I saw was a boy and an old man.

We climbed into our sleeping bags and said good night to
each other and soon Grandpa was snoozing like a baby. It only
took him a minute.

◆

Sleeping outside in the wilderness – it wasn't really a wilderness, but it was camping – has a habit of waking you at dawn. The sun just started to blink over the horizon when we began rustling about in our little tent after five hours of sleep. In the *bush* – that's what Grandpa called it – you don't need much sleep. There wasn't much room in there and when he stretched his arms out to the side he almost knocked me in the head. He cleared his throat a few times, unzipped the front of the tent, and spit into the dirt.

"What do you want to do today, Stephen?" he said.

"Let's play some ball."

"Good idea. There's an old diamond a couple miles up the road. We'll go there after breakfast."

My grandmother still asleep, we tiptoed into the kitchen of the cottage where he turned on the gas burner of an old stove. The bacon and eggs, Grandpa's favorite way to start the day, went down nice and easy with a glass of orange juice. Our hunger quenched, we climbed into the beat-up car that had been left by the owner. It was a rusty, late '70s Pontiac and the engine coughed and turned over, but once it got going it worked fine.

The diamond Grandpa mentioned looked like it was abandoned a long time ago. The sagging fence around home plate was old and there wasn't much grass left in the infield. Each base, if you could call it that, was just a circle of hard bare ground. But it was a baseball field.

We started warming up and I was careful throwing to Grandpa. He was more than competent for a man his age and I have no doubt that if they ever put together a team of eighty-year-olds he'd be in the starting lineup. But the image of him swinging that bat was still with me and the last thing I wanted was to hurl a heated hardball his way so I made sure to ease up as we tossed the ball back and forth. I was hoping he might have the energy to trot into the outfield so I could hit a few fly balls his way.

We had heard that games with boys my age took place on the weekends up here in cottage country. Old Burt would know. He knew everything that went on. The last thing Grandpa wanted was for me to lose my edge just because I was spending a few weeks with him. He thought the games were a good idea. The way he figured it we'd be killing two birds with one stone. We could spend all this time together and I'd still get to play some baseball.

I knew there might not be another chance like this. To spend a summer with Grandpa. He was getting old and the Bluffs – where all living creatures go when they die – were beckoning.

We were tossing the ball and got to talking.

"Who was your buddy who stole all those bases?" I asked as we traded light throws between home plate and the pitcher's mound.

"His name was Jack Gershwin. A really good ballplayer. He ran like lightning. He was one of the guys I went to New York with."

"Was he on your school team too? The Lizzies?"

"Sure was. He was the heart of the team."

Grandpa didn't have much on his throws, but he still had enough whip in his wrist so the ball traveled straight and true into my glove.

"We called him Bananas."

"Bananas? What kind of name is that?"

"I don't know but that's what we called him. We had names for everybody. Bronzeman. Pancake. Noser. Holler. Slav . . ."

"What did they call you?"

"Lipsy, but later it was just plain old Larry."

Then it happened. Grandpa had just thrown me the ball when his face went completely white. He grabbed his chest. My first thought was he was having a heart attack.

"Grandpa!"

He tried catching his breath, but couldn't. In between his gasps he kept saying my name.

"Stephen . . . Stephen . . ."

"Grandpa! What is it? What is it?"

He dropped to his knees, still gasping for air. Then he fell all the way down and turned onto his back.

"Stephen . . . I don't . . . feel so good."

"What is it? Your heart?"

"I don't know. . . . I don't think so . . . but I can't breathe. . . . I can't catch my breath."

"Keep still," I said but I had no idea why. He wasn't going anywhere, but "keep still" seemed like the right thing to say. I watched him trying to place his lips around a mouthful of air and take it in. Every time he tried he would get close, but then he lost it and kept gasping. I didn't know what to do. There wasn't a tight collar to loosen around his neck or a pillow to put under his head.

He lay there and for all I knew he could have been lost somewhere. Suspended between life and death. Then he looked at me. He looked right at me.

"Stephen . . . I watched you grow. . . ."

"Grandpa."

He tried raising his hand to touch my face, but couldn't get it up.

"Stephen . . . the ball . . ."

"What?"

"Get the ball."

"What Grandpa?"

"Babe . . . Babe Ruth's ball . . . the one he hit . . . get it. . . ."

It was the first time he had said anything about my retrieving that ball since the day he'd revealed its existence to me. Back then I had agreed that someday I would try to find it. I promised, but that promise was still unfulfilled. I thought about it many times, countless times, and once even flirted with how I might go about getting it, but actually doing it was something else.

"Hey! What's going on here?"

It was a man's voice from across the field. Old Burt. Old Burt from the general store.

"Come on. Quick! Help!" I yelled.

Grandpa was breathing in short strokes and his lips were quivering as if he had no control over them. His hands were shaking and there wasn't fear in his eyes, but a distant look. A look that said he was someplace else. Far away.

"What's wrong? Is he all right?"

Old Burt was out of breath himself from rushing across the field. It was a run I wouldn't have given a second thought to and it made me stop and think. I was in the company of two old men. Their bodies were weak and fragile and they didn't have much energy. It made me realize how much I took for granted. Old Burt was huffing and puffing and his eyes were full of concern for Grandpa.

Grandpa lifted up his arm. His strength was starting to come back.

"I'm okay, Burt," he said still on his back. "I'm okay. What the hell are you doing here?"

"Larry, I owe you sixty-three cents. The last time you were in my store you were in such a hurry you forgot your change. Your wife said you might be up here with your grandson."

Grandpa smiled.

"Sixty-three cents. You came because you owe me sixty-three cents. But I'm glad you did. Can you help me up?"

We lifted Grandpa and when he was sitting up he began to relax a bit. He took two deep breaths and let them out slowly. But he was very pale.

"Lemme get you into my truck and then we're gonna get you to a doctor," Old Burt said. "Doc Ramage's home ain't far away. We'll go there."

"To his home?" said Grandpa. "We just can't go into a man's home."

"Sure we can," said Old Burt as he got under one arm and I got under the other. "Where do you think you are? In the city? C'mon."

We managed to get him to his feet, but he was still shaky. It was a terrifying thing for me. It was an attack of some sort. But I had never known Grandpa to be sick before. Other people got sick. Not him.

We were lucky the doctor was home, but aren't country people always home? He examined Grandpa as best he could right in his living room. Then he wiped his brow with a cold cloth and gave him a glass of water. Grandpa downed it right away.

"I'm okay," he said. "Thanks, Doc. Can I go home now?"

"Not so fast. You have to get to a hospital."

Grandpa wasn't one for hospitals, but the doctor who said he did this kind of thing quite often insisted that he be checked out thoroughly. He could have any number of things wrong with him, he said, and we better be sure before we took any chances.

It was deathly silent in Old Burt's truck as we drove to the nearest hospital which was in a town ten miles away. When we got into the parking lot Old Burt started talking about all his friends who had had similar experiences and who wound up in hospitals with everything from asthma to heart attacks.

"God, but I been goin' to an awful lot of hospitals lately," Old Burt said.

Grandpa spent that night in the hospital and the next day my parents came up. We were allowed to take him home, but when we got back to the city we took him to one of those big general hospitals. Grandpa always said these places think they can solve just about any illness known to man and sometimes they can, he said, but they can never do anything about the simplest things. Like colds. He didn't like hospitals, but he had to spend a whole week in one and it was the first time I ever visited him there. Him of all people.

We got the prognosis on a Friday morning. The whole family was there. My grandmother and I came up by bus. My father came straight from his office and my mother cut short a meeting so she could be there. They were all rallying around Grandpa in a way that seemed odd. He had never been the sort of person who craved attention. The doctor had a clipboard with him and it was full of charts. The sight of him made me think about something Grandpa once said about being wary of doctors in white jackets.

"Mr. Slack?" he said looking around as we gathered in the waiting room.

My father identified himself and the doctor didn't waste any time.

"Your father has a growth and we're going to have to do some more tests. But we have managed to locate it."

"What kind of growth?"

"A tumor."

I could tell from the doctor's tone that it wasn't good. Then he said he wanted to speak alone with my father and the two of them disappeared. They were away so long it seemed like forever, but time always goes by slowly in hospitals. When my father came back he was ashen-faced. He looked at my mother and my grandmother and then at me. He looked at me for the longest time. His eyes didn't blink. Not once. Then he lowered his head and put his hand on my shoulder.

"Stephen . . . Grandpa has cancer."

And for the first time in my life I saw him cry.

Eight

The American Association was professional "AA" ball. In all the cities where it played it was the biggest game in town and it was a good competitive league since any one of the eight clubs could beat any of the others on a given day. But there were only two kinds of players in this loop.

This was the middle rung of the minor leagues and the players to watch were the talented young ones with the muscle, agility, and maybe even the right timing to make it to The Show. Most of them were still lacking the moxie, the know-how, but for a few special ones seasoning here would be enough and then in one year, maybe two, they could make the jump to the International League where a chance to show your stuff in the big leagues was just a phone call away.

The other kind of player was the old-timer, the wily veteran who was past his prime and still on the payroll because he knew when to lay a bunt down the third-base line and catch the infielder napping even if his heart had to outrace his legs to reach first base ahead of the ball.

Lazo was in this group.

He played for Columbus and it wasn't a bad team or a good team. The pundits who gathered in barbershops to discuss the prowess of the local ballplayers and the sportswriters who covered baseball around the circuit figured Columbus would finish in the middle of the pack. Thirty-three games into the 1935 season the team had sixteen wins and seventeen losses. On May 25, 1935, a win at home against Milwaukee would even the record.

Lazo was pushing thirty. It was old for baseball. He found it hard being a pro and not getting a chance to play every day and show what he could do. That was the toughest part. Not showing what he could do.

It had happened in spring training. That was when he'd finally realized this was it. This was as high as he would go. Toiling in the American Association at his age meant nobody in the majors was giving him a second look anymore. They had written him off a few years earlier when during a fourteen-game trial in the International League – one stop below the bigs – he had come to bat thirty-one times and cranked out only four paltry singles. He couldn't hit a low and inside fastball and once word got out it traveled like wildfire and soon the only pitch he ever saw was a low and inside fastball.

Who was to blame? Certainly not Jackson Wallace. The Iceman. His old coach had told him to change his stance more than fifteen years ago when his skills weren't yet locked in place, but Lazo refused. This was the stance that had brought him and this was the stance he would take away, he used to say.

What about Bananas? Lazo had always looked up to Bananas as a hitter. At least when they were boys he did. Chasing him in the batting race was an annual preoccupation. But Bananas didn't fare as well as Lazo once they got the wood out and started playing for keeps. Semipro ball was the farthest he went and he didn't last a year with the Hoboken Browns. Bananas wound up back home working for the railway, but even Bananas said Lazo should change his stance.

But he didn't.

If there was anyone to blame it was the Babe. It was his fault. Where did Lazo get that stance if not from him? It was the Babe who planted his feet eight inches apart, which was much too close for any man over five and a half feet tall, and it was the Babe who stood so far back behind the plate that it was almost impossible to get a good arc on the swing.

It was his fault – the Babe – who spent his life teasing Lazo with his magic, and he had a lot of magic. He was something special. Even with that awkward stance he had enough snap in his wrists, enough power in his arms and more than anything – unbelievable eye-hand coordination and timing – to make it all work.

Oh, how he made it work.

After his sale to the Yankees he spent fifteen momentous seasons on Broadway, leading the team to seven American League pennants and four World Series titles. Twelve of those fifteen years he was the American League home run champion and in 1927 he did what not even Babe Ruth was deemed able to do. He hit sixty home runs, bettering by one that mammoth year of 1921.

Sixty. Count' em. Sixty home runs! It was new ground and immediately became the standard everyone would shoot for. It was one of those records that was owned by the man who did it. The Babe owned it just as if he had put his name, label, and patent on that number. More than any other single feat in all the annals of sport he owned it. The name Babe Ruth and sixty were one and the same.

The 1927 Yankees were the best baseball team in history and the Babe was their biggest star. The middle of the batting order had the kind of power and consistency that no team had ever shown before. Or since. Not only was there the Babe's sixty home runs and .356 average, but the young Lou Gehrig had blossomed into one of the game's most talented players. He hit .373, belted forty-seven home runs, and had 175 runs batted in. The Babe's performance aside, it was enough to earn Gehrig Most Valuable Player honors.

It was something to see these two behemoths sitting side by side on the Yankee bench. A mere glance at baseball's greatest sluggers was usually enough to take the sting out of the opposing pitcher – even before the game began. Gehrig was shorter than the Babe, but more muscular with a wide thick bull-neck, powerful swooping shoulders, and massive arms and legs. His calves were so huge some people thought he wore two or three pairs of thick socks. But he didn't. When Yankee manager Miller Huggins, who was about the size of a flea in comparison, sat between them it was a sight. Even with his Yankee cap on, Huggins didn't come to their shoulders and if the two giants wanted to get a little closer they could have eclipsed him completely.

During the warm-up before the first game of one World Series, the Yankee pitchers made the most of the Ruth-Gehrig spectacle. They eased up in batting practice and everything they tossed – everything – the two hitters smashed clear over the fence while the National League champions watched in dumbfounded silence. That series lasted the minimum four games.

But those 1927 Yankees had more than Ruth and Gehrig. Tony Lazzeri, Earle Combs, and Bob Meusel all hit over .300 as well. The heart of the order was dubbed Murderers' Row and no name was more apt as this contingent tore apart pitching staffs from Boston to St. Louis. If hitting wasn't enough they also had Waite Hoyt, Urban Shocker, and Herb Pennock on the mound, three of the best pitchers in baseball. They had it all and in the 1927 World Series they destroyed the National League's Pittsburgh Pirates.

From 1920 to 1932, the Babe banged out home runs with relentless precision. He was a machine and did it year after year after year. Then, in 1933, the year after the final World Series win of those great Yankee teams, he started to slow down. The next year he slowed down some more and soon it was clear that even Babe Ruth was mortal.

He was almost forty, not old in the common sense, but old for an athlete who has to run, throw, and hit each day, every day,

without fail. He had to do it from late March through those
scorching days of summer to the middle of the fall. He was heavier and slower and watching him lope around the bases on those
few days when he did hit one out was trying for even the most
enthusiastic fan.

But still they came to see him, if not to see a ball break the
laws of physics and gravity, at least to see *him*. He was a legend, a
living legend, the greatest athlete or sportsman of his time or any
other time. He was big and innocent and rough and raw at the
edges; he was a child, an honest one, and sometimes it got him
into trouble since what you saw was exactly what you got. Babe
Ruth never claimed to be anything but a ballplayer and that was
Lazo's dream. To be a ballplayer. To make it to the major leagues
and maybe play for the New York Yankees. And for a while there
it looked like he might.

His first year in Hoboken he hit twenty-seven home runs,
which wasn't league leading by any stretch of the imagination, but
it was enough to raise a few eyebrows. He would have hit more,
too, but a mid-season slump stalled him for a long stretch. The
team manager, whom Lazo would always remember as a coarse
man with little patience for younger players, attributed
his sudden loss of power to an inability to handle pressure. It
was a common ailment for rookies, but Lazo knew that wasn't it.

It was Len.

That terrifying night on the water changed his life. After he
died Lazo couldn't get motivated to do much of anything, least of
all play baseball. He would show up for practice and games, but
his heart wasn't in it. It was numb. They never found out who
had fired the deadly shot that killed Len, but no one had much
sympathy for rum-runners anyway. They were breaking the law
and anyone carrying illegal cargo worth that much was taking a
chance. Len had taken one too many.

After it happened and after the endless hours of police questioning, Lazo was granted a full release – with a fine of twenty
dollars – since they could see he wasn't a bootlegger, just a casual
accomplice out for a good time.

The hard part came later in learning how to cope with the tragedy. Three weeks passed before Lazo collected his next hit and in one game he was even removed from the batting order for a pinch hitter. But soon it began to sink in that Len wasn't coming back. Ever. He was gone and there was nothing Lazo could do about it. Well, almost nothing.

If he was a writer he could have written something for him and if he was an artist he might have created a painting. But Lazo wasn't any of those things. He was just a ballplayer. So he did what he could. He hit for him. He hit for Len. He brought to the plate a rage he had never shown before. A rage rooted in anger, resentment, and even guilt for what had happened. After going zero for fifteen immediately after Len's death, Lazo suddenly broke free and hit ten home runs in six games. He went on a tear that saw his batting average climb fifty points. He was hitting them for Len and Len alone and it carried through to the next year when he upped his home run total to thirty-three and hit an even .300 in the process. That was when the big league scouts started coming around.

"I like that kid with the name I can't pronounce. He's the angriest hitter I've ever seen. Keep him mad and he'll do all right. But his name? What is it? Slack-o-witch? Hell, no ballplayer can be called that. Let's shorten it. How about Slack? Larry Slack. That's better. People can identify with that. The kid has power. Keep your eye on him."

They did and when he was loaned for two games to Harrisburg in the "A" class New York-Pennsylvania League and hit a home run it looked like it was all coming together. They signed him to a contract. He would play pro ball. He was still three leagues away from the big time, but that's how it was. You progress one step at a time. First sandlot ball and a school team in your hometown, then a chance to play regularly with semipros like in Hoboken. He had learned a lot there, more about what not to do. But it wasn't until he got to Harrisburg that he realized there was more to hitting home runs than power alone. Anger wasn't enough to make a pro slugger out of him. He needed technique. Harrisburg was where he first played against men who had actually been in The Show. They were on the way down, their skills pale shadows of what they used to be, but their memories were still sharp. They knew what it took.

Lazo could recognize them instantly. They were a little older, in their late twenties or somewhere in their thirties, but it wasn't age that labeled them as much as that look. The look of a ballplayer who has been there, to the top, to play before tens of thousands of people in Yankee Stadium or Comiskey Park. It was a look that cried out for everyone to hear, "I played in The Show! I made it, damn it, I made it!"

They had stories, these ballplayers who had been there – fabled stories of their ample accomplishments in the majors. Some of them were true and some of them weren't and it was up to the discerning individual to weed out fact from fiction. Every minor league team had at least one player with a collection of baseball history in his hip pocket and in Columbus it was a mediocre relief pitcher. They called him Rabbit because of his teeth that stuck out from his gums so much some players bet they would cut through his upper lip before the season was out. Rabbit was in his mid-thirties and didn't have much anymore, but he had been there in the days when his fastball still had some stuff on it and when his curve could baffle the best of the other team's hitters. He played three seasons for the Detroit Tigers and once won nine games. He played for the Cleveland Indians and for the Chicago Cubs of the National League. And he was part of one most memorable World Series.

Or so he claimed.

Rabbit always told everyone how he faced hitters like Al Simmons and Jimmie Foxx and struck them out on straight pitches. He was a "fireballer" he said, and when he was on a roll he would "mow' em down." They knew he had been to the majors since he knew a lot of older players in the league who had been there too. But the one story he liked to tell was the 1932 World Series between the Yankees and Chicago Cubs. He said he actually saw Babe Ruth's famous called-shot home run in game three.

It was one of those things that immortalized the Babe for all time as he pulled a stunt no one had ever dared. It happened when he came to the plate in the fifth inning – the Yankees had won the first two games easily – and fifty thousand fans at Chicago's Wrigley Field showered him with catcalls and even lemons. During batting practice before the game he had picked up a few lemons that came his way and threw them back into the stands with laughter. He liked to frolic with enemy fans and though baseball addicts the country over called him every name in the book they all loved him.

In the pregame warm-up he and Gehrig had let loose with the full brunt of their monstrous aerial bombardment. As a strong wind blew out to right field he hit nine balls over the fence and Gehrig hit seven. But they saved some for the game, too. His three-run homer and Gehrig's solo shot in the first inning accounted for all the Yankee runs to that point.

When he came up in the fifth inning the score was tied 4-4 and the verbal jousting between the teams had risen to fever pitch. He waited for his turn at bat and another lemon was thrown into the on-deck circle. Finally, he stepped into the batter's box and was greeted with a chorus of boos. The first pitch delivered by Cub starter Charlie Root was a called strike and the fans went wild, but the Babe wasn't deterred. He looked to the Cubs' dugout and extended one finger of his left hand. The next two pitches were balls, but the fourth was another called strike and the fans hit the roof again. Even the Cubs were taunting him. One of them ran onto the field and screamed right in his face.

But the Babe didn't care. He just laughed and waved at the National League champions. He stuck out two fingers of his left hand to show that a batter needed three strikes before he was retired and the message was clear. The next good pitch was going to wind up in the stands.

Whether he actually pointed to the center field fence and hit one out or merely stuck out two fingers of his hand and blasted the next pitch no one knows for sure. Sometimes the Babe and the Babe's legend were so close it was hard to tell where reality ended and myth began. But the sports headline in the paper the next day said: *"Ruth calls shot as he puts homer No. 2 in side pocket."*

The story goes that he did indeed point to the spot where he would hit the next pitch and then proceeded to clout the longest home run ever hit at Wrigley Field. He ran around the bases and was laughing his head off, and so was one of his biggest fans in the VIP box near home plate, Franklin D. Roosevelt.

Pitcher Root was so unnerved with the Babe's antics that his first pitch to the next Yankee hitter – Gehrig – was hit hard and it, too, sailed clear out of the park. Suddenly the score was 6-4 and the Yankees were on their way. They won the game 7-5 and swept the series in game four with a 13-6 rout.

Rabbit said he was on the Chicago bench at the time and saw the whole thing. He said that Ruth stepped out of the batter's box after the second strike, straightened his arm, and pointed to the center field bleachers.

"I was there and I saw it all. It was sumthin' else, I tell ya. The called-shot home run and I was right in the middle of it. And ya know I was supposed to pitch that day? I was the Cubs' fifth starter and if Root got into trouble I was gonna get into the game. I was there. In the World Series."

Lazo wasn't so sure about a pitcher like Rabbit being a fifth starter on a powerhouse team like the 1932 Cubs so he did a little homework. One day, when both of them had been scratched from the Columbus lineup and they were sitting in the dugout, he tried to refresh Rabbit's memory of three years earlier.

"Hey Rabbit, you say you were the number five pitcher for the Cubs in the thirty-two World Series?" Lazo asked.

"That's right."

"So you were pitching behind guys like Lon Warneke, Charlie Root, and Guy Bush?"

"That's right."

"That was a pretty strong pitching staff they had that year. Didn't they also have a guy named Burleigh Grimes?"

"Yeah."

"So you were the fifth starter behind him?" Rabbit just nod-ded. "I see. But as the fifth starter you didn't start too many games?"

"No . . . just a coupla starts . . . that's all."

"You started two games all year? You remember who they were against?"

"Sure. Sure I remember. How could I forget? You don't forget starts in the majors. One was against Cinci and the other was Philly."

"Is that when you struck out Jimmie Foxx?"

"Yeah. That was the time. You shoulda seen it. I mowed 'im down."

"But Jimmie Foxx was with the Athletics. Not the Phillies. He was in the American League."

"Oh, yeah. Well . . . I got traded."

"Okay. Fine. But what about Pat Malone? Wasn't he also a starter with the Cubs that year?"

"Who?"

"Pat Malone. He was one of five starters with the Cubs that year. Lon Warneke. Charlie Root. Guy Bush. Burleigh Grimes. And Pat Malone. That's five starters. Where'd you come in? I never heard of a team with six starters."

"Well . . . I was sort of a relief man."

"But you said you were a starter. That's what you've been say-ing all year."

"Well . . . like I said . . . I started a coupla games. . . ."

"C'mon, Rabbit. Level with me. You were never a starter with the Cubs. You were a starter like Yehudi. Isn't that right? And you weren't there when Babe Ruth called his home run in the World Series either. Were you?"

"Okay, Larry, it's true. So I wasn't. So I made it up. But I pitched for the Tigers and I pitched for the Indians and I pitched a little relief for the Cubs. So what if I wasn't there when it hap-pened? I still made it to the majors which is a helluva lot more than you ever did."

Rabbit was right. Lazo didn't even get close to the majors. When big league scouts see a hitter collect four singles in thirty-one at bats in the International League and only swing at the air when a low inside fastball comes in they forget about him fast. For Lazo the dream was gone. He would never make it. He was too old. He would never play in The Show. And the Yankees? They were for schoolboys – for fourteen-year-olds pretending they're in the Polo Grounds staring Walter Johnson in the face.

It was all for naught. He didn't have it. He just wasn't good enough.

Lazo was almost thirty. Ancient for a ballplayer. He found himself thinking about his life. Did he waste all those years? He looked at a guy like Rabbit. He wasn't even much of a pitcher, but still he'd made it and that made him proud. But did he make it? Really? Making it in the big leagues for a few years didn't change Rabbit's life. This was the Depression and most major leaguers didn't earn much. They were lucky to have jobs at all. Millions of people were on the dole or standing in bread lines every morning. The players even had to take salary cuts. The Babe made more than anybody, but the Depression took its toll on him too. His salary peaked at eighty thousand dollars a year in the early '30s, but then he was asked to take a cut. Times were tough.

But for most of the players in the majors, it wasn't the money that meant they made it. It was that someone who made decisions called and gave them the chance. It was a chance to play first class. That was it. First class. First-class players. First-class parks. None of this "AA" garbage. The majors were first-class, but Lazo never got that chance.

In 1927, the year the Babe stood the baseball world – the entire world – on its ear, Lazo earned a starting position in the Harrisburg outfield. He was twenty-one and teeming with expectation. Thirty-seven home runs later he moved on to the "AA" American Association. The next rung up the ladder.

The low and inside fastball was still a problem, but not all pitchers in the league were pro material and some of them were awful. Lazo remembered his best game when he smacked three home runs and a triple. The pitcher was such a fool he gave him the same pitch every time out. He didn't change a thing. Maybe that was all he could throw. Some hurlers got by on one pitch alone, a curve or screwball. Few of them had a fastball that was destined for the majors.

The next season Lazo joined Louisville in the American Association and cranked out twenty-one home runs, which wasn't bad for a rookie. When you're on the way up, you're a rookie every year until you pass the sophomore jinx in the American League or National League and show that you can stick. But then the dream started to burst. Twenty-one home runs was the most he ever hit in "AA" and soon he would always see that old nemesis of his – low and inside. He settled down to become an average everyday player who got the odd clutch hit and who could hit the leadoff runner with a timely throw. But nothing more.

The adrenaline that filled him after Len's death was gone. With time it just dissipated. It was an aberration. He still thought a lot about Len, but the emotion was no longer ferocious anger. It was sorrow and no one ever hit a home run on that.

When a scout sees an angry young player knocking the skin off the ball, he looks and when he sees thirty-seven home runs – in any league – he takes note. But when a young ballplayer with the potential to be a home run hitter begins to lose it, the scouts start looking elsewhere. Three trades in eight years was par for a journeyman in "AA" ball and while eight years was better than most, eight years as a minor leaguer and you're dead. You were labeled a minor leaguer and wearing a stigma like that was good for life.

"We need to shore up right field with a good arm and someone who can hit. What about this Slack guy up in Scranton? What do you think of him?"

"He's not bad but he's twenty-six. What if he came up and showed something? He'd only be around for a year or two. We'd be better off giving a shot to some young kid who's hungry."

Lazo was a minor leaguer.

He enjoyed those first two years in the league when the dream was still alive. He was the new boy who could hit the long ball and the sportswriters would put whatever he said in the paper. In cities like Harrisburg or Louisville, the local ball team got a lot of ink. Larry Slack was an "up and comer" – that was what one writer said – and when they asked him what ambitions he had in life he said only to play in the majors.

"It's baseball or nothing," Lazo said.

That was his mistake.

Columbus' starting lineup for the Saturday afternoon game against Milwaukee didn't include his name. That wasn't surprising. He'd been removed from the lineup for the past five games anyway and this was an important game. They couldn't chance it on someone like him. It had been eleven years since he left home and had traveled a million miles in old broken-down buses reeking of empty beer bottles with other man-boys who flirted with dreams. While other men his age were married with families and learning a trade, even during these times, he was still playing a boy's game and living that dream. But his body was getting older and he was going nowhere.

He was a bachelor and bachelor life wasn't all it was cracked up to be. Lazo lost count of the number of cold lonely nights in cheap hotel rooms in Toledo, Kansas City, or Williamsport – towns where the only way to while away the time was playing cards and drinking with the other players or investing in one of the local hookers and trying to wrench a few moments of pleasure from an otherwise dreary existence.

It was a dreary existence. If you played too long in one town you wore your welcome out and if you were traded you had to start all over again. Unless you were a rising star destined for the top all you could do was hang in there and soon it didn't even matter if the team won or lost. Once the dream sours, winning isn't important anymore. That's when it becomes a matter of sheer survival. How long can you last? How many years can you say you played pro ball? But even that was embarrassing when strangers approached. Especially kids.

"Hey mister, I hear you play pro. Where do you play? Boston? Philly?"

"I been around."

"St. Louis? New York? Chicago?"

"No. No. Never played there. Just Harrisburg, Columbus, Louisville."

"But you play pro? Well then can I have your autograph?"

"You sure?"

And he gave it. An autograph. Just like the one the Babe gave him, but there was a difference. A big difference. The kid would go home and tell his friends about his good fortune and Lazo could imagine the conversation.

"Who'd ya get? Who'd ya get?"

"Larry Slack."

"Who?"

"Larry Slack. He plays for Columbus."

"Never heard of him."

Maybe somewhere there was a young boy who still hung onto his signature and had it tucked away in a drawer, but what was more likely was that the moment the kid got an autograph from a real major leaguer his name and the slip of paper it was written on would be discarded. Like scrap.

Why he stuck it out for so long he didn't know, but if there was a chance – even a slim chance – that someone would call he was bound to stay. But with each season and each passing year he got a little slower and weaker and then one day the obvious stared him in the face and his heart just wasn't in it anymore.

He climbed out of bed and couldn't even remember the name of the girl he was with. The bad wine they drank had clogged his brain.

"Where you going, Larry?" she said.

He put on his pants, got into his shoes, and drowned his face in some cold water in the bathroom. It felt good, but just for a second and only on the outside. On the inside he still hurt.

"You better leave," he said.

"What do you mean? It's early."

"I have a game today. You gotta go."

He picked her up out of the bed. Her body was limp.

"Get dressed. C'mon. I told you I got a game."

"They gonna play you today?"

When he was sure she could stand on her own he left her in the middle of the room and started to shave.

"Yeah, today's my big chance. The scouts are out. I have to make an impression."

She fell back onto the bed and moaned so he filled a glass full of water and poured it over her head.

"Larry!" she screamed.

"Shhh," he said. "You want to wake up everyone in the building?"

Reluctantly she got dressed. He stuck a coin into her purse and told her to buy a coffee. She said to get a hit for her and then she left.

Ten minutes later Lazo was dressed and had his bag packed. He had made his decision. He wasn't going to hang around and watch a game he couldn't care less about from the dugout. Why should he? He wasn't going to play. Besides, they wanted to see this new kid they just brought up from the Pacific Coast League. Hit .347 and had an arm like a rifle, they said. He deserves a chance. Let him have it, thought Lazo. He had something better to do.

Many of the Columbus ballplayers lived in the same tenement house downtown. It was the type of housing reserved for the working middle class and while it wasn't much, being a member of the working class in the mid-'30s was better than not working at all. The team manager lived two flights down. His bag in hand and his rent paid, Lazo descended the stairs for the last time and rapped on the manager's door. His name was Willie Logger and he was still in bed.

"What time is it, Larry?" he said with a yawn as he answered the door.

"Seven-thirty."

"What're you nuts?"

"I've got to talk to you."

"Now? I was sleepin' for Chrissake."

"It's important."

"What's so important at seven-thirty in the morning? Hey, you got your bag packed. You goin' somewhere?"

"Pittsburgh."

"Pittsburgh? The Pirates need a right fielder?"

"Funny. I've got some business to take care of."

"Oh yeah? Well I just can't let you walk out on the team like that. What if the new kid gets hurt? Who we gonna play in right field?"

"Casey. Let him play. He'll do all right."

"Casey? He can't throw for shit."

"He'll never learn if he doesn't play."

"What's wrong, Larry? What's in Pittsburgh? You got a girl there?"

"Yeah. That's it."

"You gotta go all the way to Pittsburgh for some broad? I don't get it."

Willie was fifty-something. He wasn't married. He used to say he was married to baseball. He retired as a player many years ago and now was managing a .500 ball team in a second-tier minor league. Lazo looked around. It was a dump. Yesterday's clothes were everywhere and the kitchen sink was full of dishes. The place looked like it hadn't been cleaned in months.

"Willie, why don't you hire yourself a cleaning lady?"

"What for?"

"You need a woman, Willie."

But what woman would have a man like him? He'd never done anything but baseball his whole life. He was still doing what he was doing as a kid. He never grew up. It was sad. Willie ate his dinners alone at home and on the road. He was used to being alone and now it just followed him around. After a lifetime in baseball this was what he had to show for it.

"Look, Willie," said Lazo. "I'm quitting. I'm leaving the team. I've had it."

"What? You can't do that. You signed a contract. You're with us for the rest of the year."

"What're you gonna do? Sue me for my contract?" Lazo laughed. "Go ahead. I couldn't care less."

"I don't get it, Larry. The team can still use you. You're good with the young guys. You can still hit. I don't get it."

"Willie, baseball's been using me all my life. I don't want to be used anymore. I've had it."

"But Larry . . ."

"My mind's made up. I'm not even playing anymore so what's the difference?"

"But you'll play again. It's just this weekend that's all."

"It doesn't matter about this weekend, Willie. That new kid will do the job. I'm just making it easier on you by walking out. This way you don't have to tell me to my face so I'm doing you a favor. Besides, even if he doesn't pan out somebody else will. There's always somebody trying to take your job. Well, I'm giving mine away. I'm giving it to anyone who wants it. I'm through."

"Larry. Don't say that."

"I'm not kidding, Willie. This is the end of the line. I'm almost thirty. Be honest with me. For my own good are you for one minute suggesting that I bust my ass for this two-bit team in this two-bit league? Where's it gonna get me? Somebody's gonna call and say some big league club needs a thirty-year old rookie right fielder? C'mon, Willie. It's no good. The call's never gonna come. It never did and it sure as hell ain't gonna come now."

Willie just shook his head.

"It's rough out there, Larry. At least you got a job. You're makin' some money. It might not be much, but it's sumthin'. What're you gonna do if you quit baseball? I don't see no ads lookin' for ex-ballplayers."

"I'll find something."

"No you won't, Larry. I'm tellin' you it's bad. Playin' ball and bein' on the road all the time you dunno how bad it is out there. All you ever see are the people at the park. You don't see no bread lines."

"I know how it is, Willie."

"I don't think so. Look, I tell you what I'm gonna do. Take a week off. Go ahead, take the whole week. Go to Pittsburgh to see your dame. Have a good time. Then call me. We'll be home for a few games. Call me after you have a chance to think it over."

"All right. I will."

Willie put his hand on Lazo's shoulder.

"I'm sorry, Larry. I'm really sorry. You're a good kid. You've always been a good kid."

"But there's just no desire anymore and if there's no desire what have you got? Just a tired worn-out ballplayer."

"The world's full o' tired worn-out ballplayers, Larry. I see 'em every day. Look at me. I had one stinkin' year in The Show warmin' up the bench. Thirty at bats and five fuckin' hits."

Lazo looked once again at Willie's worldly goods.

"How many years you been in baseball, Willie?" he said.

"Thirty-six."

Thirty-six years. And where was he? Now Lazo knew why he was quitting. He had this horrible fear the same thing would happen to him.

"Thirty-six years and five hits," Lazo said.

"Yeah. That's funny, ain't it? But ya know what Larry? I made it. I still made it."

Lazo thought of Rabbit and all the other bush-league players he knew who could say they played out a glimpse of their lives in the big leagues. As if that was enough to make their reason for being worthwhile. Lazo stuck out his hand.

"Thanks, Willie."

"Call me, Larry. Don't forget. You gotta eat. You know, you were one good ballplayer in your day. You were smart. You had power. You could throw."

"But I couldn't hit a low inside fastball."

Willie laughed.

"You couldn't hit a low inside fastball. There's always sumthin'. Sometimes it's only a little thing that keeps a guy from goin' all the way. But you had everything else. If not for that . . ."

"I've had it with ifs, Willie. You take care of yourself."

"You too, Larry. Be sure to call me now. We'll miss you this weekend."

But they wouldn't miss him at all. There were lots of youngsters to choose from and they were a lot more ballplayer than Lazo was. Lazo knew he wasn't going to call and Willie knew it too. This was it. The end. But even if the dream was gone for him there was still something left. His love for the game.

And the Babe.

For the second time in his life, Babe Ruth was unloaded by one team to another as a piece of inventory with some market value to the team moguls. The National League's Boston Braves were owned by Judge Emil Fuchs and consistently poor finishes coupled with the Depression had put the franchise on the verge of bankruptcy. They desperately needed a shot in the arm, something to pick up attendance. They needed a gimmick. The New York Yankees had one very large and very expensive forty-one-year-old right fielder who was making a lot of noise about being the next Yankee manager. But no one wanted him in that capacity so the Yankees' Jacob Ruppert was looking for a way to get rid of him. Fuchs was the opportunity.

Lies were told to the Babe about the role he would play in Boston, the scene of his first triumphs in the majors. They were going to name him assistant manager and if he wanted to play that was fine, too. Fuchs was a money man who talked about everything from stock options in the club to a future executive position in the front office. It sounded good. The salary would be twenty-five thousand with profits on top of that.

A press conference was held at Fuchs' brewery and the Babe wore his best suit. They took pictures of him shaking hands with Ruppert and Fuchs and he became a Boston Brave. That was how professional baseball operated. Give them the sweat off your back and even your blood for fifteen years and when you begin to slip, just a notch, they discard you like old baggage.

Fuchs had no visions of a forty-one-year-old ballplayer lighting up the National League, but he did have visions of more fans coming to see his Braves. And they did. On March 16, 1935, the Yankees and Braves played an exhibition game in St. Petersburg and drew the biggest crowd to ever see a game in Florida. The Babe, all two hundred and forty-five pounds of him, was drawing them in, but he presented a dilemma for Boston manager Bill McKechnie, who wasn't pleased when baseball's all-time home run leader joined the team thinking he'd be manager the next season.

But some of that old magic was still there. On April 4 in Savannah, Georgia, he hit a home run and three days later in Newark, New Jersey, he clubbed two more. But since he was too big and fat to play the outfield, McKechnie tried him at first base where he wouldn't have to run. On opening day, however, he was out in left field and the Braves had their biggest opening day crowd in years. Everyone from Boston society was there. The mayor of the city and the governors of all the New England states. They were all welcoming their Bambino home.

In his first National League regular season game, in his first at-bat, he hit a single and drove in a run. Later he scored and when he came up in the fifth he hit a two-run homer. The Braves won 4-2 and he, the Babe, had been the architect of the victory. He followed that up with two more hits in his second game, but then his bat went dry. The Braves lost game after game and were soon in last place. The Babe wasn't hitting. He couldn't run and when he was missing games because of a cold or the kinds of nagging injuries that plague a forty-one-year-old ballplayer he would act in an official capacity and represent the team at a store opening, which was a long way from being the manager.

Things weren't going well and he and Fuchs quarreled. He was hitting .155. He was in the lineup one day and out the next.

As usual Lazo had his nose plugged into the sports pages and he knew baseball was seeing the last of the Babe. There wasn't much time left. Then, when he read that he was going to be in the lineup for a Saturday afternoon game in Pittsburgh against the Pirates, he decided to go. His own career was over, but now for one last time he would see him play.

The Babe.

With his bag in hand he hitched a ride to the train station. On the way he passed a bread line and it was pathetic. Men, proud men, standing in line for food. They all wanted to work, but there wasn't any work. It was the Depression. People were taking handouts. People who had worked their whole lives and who had never asked for anything were appealing for food because they had no money.

Lazo saw them as he waited for his train to Pittsburgh. The men. The men without work. They stood there by the tracks, their hands hanging onto their belt, or tugging at the ends of their coats. A cigarette would be stuck to their lower lip and a hat would sit slightly askew on their head. They would look straight ahead, right into your eyes to show that they weren't afraid, but they were terrified. Terrified for what the world was doing to them. To their lives. What had happened to America? What had happened to the dream?

Lazo caught the morning train and when he arrived in Pittsburgh there would be just enough time to get to Forbes Field. Then he would watch him play and after that he didn't know what he would do. He knew trains, of course. He always thought them romantic and all those years of riding the rails with ball teams hadn't changed that. You could gaze out the window and see the country going by. You could see the world going by. And it did. Fast.

He had never seen a National League game before. His heart was in the American League with the Yankees, but the Babe's leaving New York changed all that. Now there were no loyalties to speak of. He didn't have any for the Yankees. He didn't have any for the Braves and he didn't even have any for his own Columbus team. That was the saddest part. But he was loyal to the Babe.

Only ten thousand fans were in attendance in Pittsburgh, so it wasn't difficult to edge down to the first row and catch a seat off the third-base line. How the fans hooted and hollered when that big rotund frame emerged from the Boston dugout. The hecklers were doing their thing as expected. Lazo had seen it all before, but that was when he was the home run king. The Sultan of Swat. The Bambino. And now he was just a washed-up old ballplayer.

God he was big. Bigger than ever.

One of the Braves was on base and the big guy at the plate took some swings. It was still smooth as silk. The ball came in just where he liked it and he took a mean cut and smashed it out over the fence for his seven hundred and twelfth home run.

He did it! A shiver went through Lazo's body. It was just like the time he saw him hit one when he was a kid. He jumped up and down in a frenzy. The adrenaline shot up his spine and every ounce of the boy's love for baseball that still remained washed over him. At that moment all was right with the world. There was no bench-warmer in Columbus and there were no hungry people standing in bread lines.

The Babe had hit a homer.

That was enough to make this trip worthwhile for Lazo, but there was more. The next time he came up another pitcher was in. Guy Bush. And another man was on base. He pulled the pitch with the bat handle and when that happens the ball usually goes foul or loops into the infield. But not this time. This wasn't just any hitter at the plate. The ball may have been pulled, but he managed to smash that one out of the park, too. Just barely. The ball cleared the fence by ten feet and almost went foul, but not quite. It was gone.

It wasn't possible. The Babe was forty-one years old and looked like anything but a ballplayer. How different from that innocent afternoon in 1914 when his tall slim frame stood out from all the others. But still the ball carried. He was so big, so awkward and slow that he couldn't even trot around the bases. It was more of a trudging *clomp-clomp-clomp*, but the rules decreed that he only had to touch the bases for the home run to count and it didn't matter how slow he was.

That was seven hundred and thirteen.

Again Lazo clapped his hands and he could feel the energy

oozing through his body. He caught a good look at the Babe from his perch along the third-base line. He was smiling, but breathing hard. Running around the bases was a lot tougher for him than hitting a homer.

Then, with a pair of home runs and four runs batted in to his credit, he came up for his third at-bat in the fifth inning and connected once more. Only this time the ball didn't carry, but went for an infield hit scoring a run. The fans cheered him wildly. Three-for-three. Five runs batted in. A stellar performance.

In the seventh inning he came up for his final at-bat of the game and Bush was still on the mound. The bases were empty. Bush had no intention of going into the record book as the victim of a baseball relic making his last stand so he uncorked a smoking fastball and the Babe watched it sail in for a called strike. That was the way to pitch to an aging Babe Ruth. Usually there was no way to pitch to him because he could hit everything and sometimes you had to walk him, but that wasn't a smart thing to do either because Gehrig was up next and you got burned.

But those days were gone. The Babe was a clumsy old man playing out his career with a rotten team in the NL, so Bush went for muscle and speed. It was the only way. He wound up for another fastball and it arrived one inch, maybe two, off the plate about halfway between his knees and his waist.

Just where he liked it.

He got the fat part of the bat on it. His wrists snapped the way they always did and his body twisted in that familiar motion as the ball assumed a life of its own. It soared like an eagle. Cutting a great arc through the sky. Only once before had Lazo seen a ball fly like that. When the Babe hit his one and only minor league home run twenty-one years earlier. But this was a major league park and the ball went even farther, farther than any ball Lazo had ever seen before. There were three decks of bleachers out in right center field and it cleared the top one. It wasn't supposed to happen. It defied all the laws of averages. How does a left-handed batter – at his age – hit a home run over three decks in right center in a park like Forbes Field?

They said no one had ever hit a ball clear over the roof and they probably hadn't, but just to make sure one of the ushers went after it. It had landed on top of a house, had bounced onto another house, and wound up in a lot where some kid ran off with it. Later, the usher measured the distance from home plate to the first house.

It was six hundred feet.

It had never happened before. Years later, Guy Bush would say it was the longest cockeyed ball he ever saw in his life. He had been stunned by the blaster and when the Babe rounded third base Bush was obliged to tip his cap out of respect. Pitchers don't do that to enemy hitters who take them for the long ball. But the Babe was just days away from his last game. He was the greatest hitter baseball had ever seen and now he was doing what he had always done. For the last time.

As Bush tipped his cap a tear came to Lazo's eyes. The Babe was touched by the pitcher's motion and he returned a salute and smiled. He rounded third and Lazo saw what remained of his famous home run trot. His enormous gut hung so low his shirt looked like it was weighted down with a balloon. He could barely trudge along the base path. When he was halfway between third base and home plate their eyes met. Lazo's and the Babe's. He was running slower now, much slower, just hobbling in to home.

He was coming home.

His feet weren't even touching the ground. They were floating on air. He was flying. He wasn't real anymore. But he was always like that. More than real. Bigger than life. He was a vision. A dream. He was Hope.

Lazo stood up on his feet and waved. He hollered.

"Babe!" he screamed. "Babe! It's me! It's me!"

The Babe looked and saw him. In a blur he raised his left hand and waved back.

"Hey, keed. I chose you, keed. I chose you and you didn't make it, but that's all right. At least you tried. All a man can do is try."

"Babe!"

"See you, keed."

And the vision was gone. His body was still there, but that was all. His feet were back on the dirt and he was so exhausted when he touched the plate they took him out of the game. He had hit three home runs and when it was all over he sat himself in a chair out there on the field. The kids, they couldn't get enough of him. They came from everywhere. There were only ten thousand people in the park and maybe nine thousand of them were kids. He signed autographs until ten o'clock when all the kids had to go home.

He didn't hit any more after that. After twenty-eight games with the Braves he had seven singles, six home runs and a .182 average. There was nothing left and Braves' owner Emil Fuchs knew it. When his manager McKechnie told him the big guy couldn't play anymore, he fired the Babe. Just like that.

It was over.

Nine

When the heart weeps for what it has lost, the
spirit laughs for what it has found.

— Sufi proverb

When doctors say they'll do all they can to try to make the pa-
tient "comfortable," the game is as good as over. At first all they
said was Grandpa had a tumor and it had to be removed. Such
surgery was conducted every day, they said, but once it's out he'll
be all right. He'll be fine. No one said anything about death.
And so a tumor about the size of a pea was removed, but the operation took its toll.

He was back home soon and I thought things would return
to what they were, but I was wrong. It was different. A lot
different. Grandpa slowed down to a crawl. It seemed he was
wearing the same clothes every day and instead of my grandmother asking him for things he was the one making demands.
Still, he maintained a positive outlook.

"Lookit, Stephen," he said. "This is an old body I've got. I can't
expect it to do all the things it used to do. Life just isn't like that. So
at my age some things are bound to go a little wrong and that's
okay. I had a growth in my head and they took it out, but I'll be all
right. You're darn tootin I'll be all right. Just you wait and see."

He was kidding himself and I think he knew it. After a while his condition stabilized, but he couldn't do the things he used to do. Walks to the Bluffs were definitely out. He spent most of his time in the house or on the porch looking out over the street. Then he started getting worse and the doctors became part of our lives. I lived and died with their every word even if I didn't know what they were talking about, even if they were being less than honest with me.

He went back to the hospital for more tests. It was all routine, of course. That was what they said. There was nothing to worry about. Everything to them is routine. Life is routine. Death is routine and it is, I guess, unless it's one of your own. But now the tumors were spreading and there were so many of them nothing could be done. They didn't come right out and say so since that would be admitting defeat. That would be recognition of their own limitations, but they would do all they could. That's what they said.

My father took me aside and laid it all out.

"Stephen, he's not going to come through this so it's up to us to make his last days as worthwhile as we can. Anything he wants . . . anything . . . let him have it."

I don't remember if it was the third or fourth time he was in the hospital since all those visits became a blur. He was there but he wasn't there. His eyes would look straight ahead as he sat in his chair, those horrendous tumors growing and gnawing away at his thinking capacity that had always been as sharp as a knife's edge. It hurt me to see him like that.

I did things for him in the hospital, things he had always done for himself and never thought twice about. I shaved him. I dressed him. I turned him over on the bed and slipped his shoes on so we could take the ten-foot walk to his bathroom.

They were our last walks together.

He once said that people don't realize what they have until they lose it and can never get it back. We take so much for granted, he said, and I didn't think about it much because I had everything. I had all the material things I needed and I had him. He was the one who supplied those things that aren't material.

He was the one who brought value to the trees and the sky and all the creatures of the world with their unique peculiarities and individualities.

On his bad days when he wasn't able to talk – days that came with increasing and frightening regularity – I wanted to give up. I couldn't take it. It was too much so I would drop everything and just wrap my arms around him, thinking of all the things we had done together, relishing all the precious moments we had shared.

How I dreaded going to that hospital every day. But I had to go. And soon it became so routine that I knew every square inch of his room, his ward, the building. It got to the point where I didn't even have to ask the nurses where things were.

At first he was in a regular room, but the last time he was admitted they put him on a different floor. They called it "palliative care," and after learning about its area of specialization I think no two words could be more incongruous than these.

On this particular afternoon I had just finished giving him his dinner like I did every day. He was so helpless. I fed him just the way he had fed me when I was a baby and I don't know why I said something about it then, but I did.

"Grandpa, remember that ball Babe Ruth hit when you were a boy? The one that went into the lake? The one you said I should find? Do you still want me to find it?"

He turned his head slowly and looked out the window of his room. The room that had become his life. His prison. A prison with no reminder of home, except for a three-by-five photograph of the two of us on his night table.

"The ball," he whispered.

They were the first words he said that day.

"The ball . . . the ball . . ."

He turned to me and tears streamed down his face. He gasped, filled his lungs with air, and reached out to me. But his motor ability was failing and I had to guide his hands onto my face. He couldn't do it by himself. His left hand was still stronger than the right. It was always stronger. He pressed it firmly against my cheek and rubbed his fingers against the stubble on my cheeks. He didn't say anything, but there was something about my whiskers that captivated him. I was eighteen and had stubble and shaved every day. Not white stubble, but the kind I once thought only God could grow.

"Stephen," he said slurring my name. "Stephen . . . "

He was trying to talk. He was trying desperately to say something. But it wouldn't come. I wrapped my arms around him with my face next to his. Hugging him. Holding on to him. And then I talked for him. Softly. Right into his ear.

"Grandpa. I know now what that ball means to you. The one Babe Ruth hit. In 1914. The one you saw fall into the lake. I know you want it. You want me to get it for you. Because of what it stands for. About the Babe and the game and the way it used to be. All those things."

Then he got more animated. His arms moved in jerky motions and his head shook as if suffering from great tremors within. Suddenly he was possessed of an energy that just filled him. He found it hard to speak and was frustrated since he couldn't vent his feelings or move his body the way he wanted. But on this subject his thoughts were like a clear sky with no clouds or obstacles to block them.

He looked straight at me and said three words.

"Get the ball."

◆

The Babe was in retirement now and uneasy. When he was too old and too fat to play anymore he desperately wanted to stay in the game in some capacity and being a manager – manager of the Yankees – was his aspiration. Baseball was in his blood and he wanted to be their boss. He even knew what kind of manager he would be, not like Miller Huggins, but then how could he? The Babe, a full head taller and a hundred and forty pounds heavier, was imposing by merely walking into a room, while Huggins walking into a room never generated much of a fuss at all.

The Babe missed that little fellow. He died in 1929 when the

Yankees were still great and even Lou Gehrig – they called him the "Iron Horse" because he never missed a game – was dead, the victim of a crippling disease that took his name. The team would build two monuments to honor the memories of their great little manager and magnificent first baseman and they would be erected in deep center field at Yankee Stadium.

Those two men had something he never had. Respect. Despite all his home run titles, RBI crowns, and World Series feats he knew the Yankees' brass – the managers, the coaches, and especially the owners – didn't respect him as a person. It was the same in Boston with the Red Sox and later with the Braves. They were in awe of the numbers he put up and paid him handsomely for his time. But Babe the man was always treated lightly, like an overgrown kid, and he wanted to be treated like a man.

With respect.

The Yankees were the greatest team in history and he wanted to manage them. He deserved it. After all he had done for them he figured they should come running to his door with the job on a platter. Whatever he wanted, they should give to him. That's what he thought. Hell, they owed it to him.

He was Babe Ruth, for Christ's sake.

He looked at all the players who became managers after retiring. Tris Speaker, Rogers Hornsby, George Sisler, Frank Frisch, Charlie Grimm, and so many others he couldn't keep count of them all. Even Ty Cobb, whom nobody could stand, became a manager. He was the Babe, the most popular, most loved player in history. But it didn't matter. It wasn't meant to be. A manager has to manage an entire team and the Babe, well, he had enough trouble just managing himself and anyone could see that.

Anyone but the Babe.

He spent his time playing golf, going on hunting trips, and doing charity work. A cause, any cause, could always raise more money when his name was attached to it and that was fine, but he was bored. He was a ballplayer and when he couldn't play ball there wasn't much to do. Life became a tedious string of routine tasks with little consequence that called upon him not because of what he could do or even because of who he was. But who he used to be.

After the fiasco with the Boston Braves in 1935 he finally quit playing. The body wouldn't take it anymore, but the next year he came out in public for the ultimate honor. He was one of five players elected to the new Hall of Fame at Cooperstown. The others were Ty Cobb, Honus Wagner, Christy Mathewson, and Walter Johnson. They didn't take only his name, but also his number – the Yankees Number Three, which they retired – as well as the bat he hit his sixtieth home run with in 1927. They took his glove and his shoes too.

Two years later another team, the National League's Brooklyn Dodgers, tried to make a little hay out of his name and signed him on as a coach. Poor Babe. He really thought the Dodgers were going to install him as their manager the following season and he thought maybe he'd even put on the old spikes and get into the lineup for the odd game. It was clear what they were doing, wasn't it? Their present manager didn't plan to stick around, so along comes the Babe as a coach and since two and two make four anyone could see who the next manager was going to be.

Anyone but the Babe.

But after he got into a scuffle with Leo Durocher, the team's veteran shortstop and captain, his Dodger days were numbered. When the season was over Durocher was named the new manager and it all left a bad taste in his mouth. The Dodgers only wanted him to put on their uniform and show the fans he was really there, in the flesh, a human public relations gimmick, and so he retired for good.

The pain over his left eye began in late 1946 and wouldn't go away. He ballooned to two hundred and eighty pounds. Then he had an operation and the doctors knew it was cancer. But they didn't tell him. They couldn't. During his recovery he lost almost half his weight and was so emaciated even he figured he was going to die.

That wasn't the kind of life for the Babe. Not for a man like him. A man like him had to be robust and big – bigger than life. He had to have an enormous appetite that would let him swallow a steak almost whole and then wash it down with a bottle of wine. A man like him needed the energy to stay out all hours of the night, check into his hotel in the morning, and have enough left to sock a pair of home runs over the wall at whatever park he was in that day.

There was no one like him. He was the Babe.

The illness got worse and though he managed to put some weight back on the truth was plain to see. He was withering away. On April 27, in what must have brought back thoughts of the day they had given Gehrig years earlier, the Yankees held a day for him. Babe Ruth Day. Almost sixty thousand people showed up to see him, but he wasn't the Babe they remembered. He was getting X-ray treatment and his hair was gray. His body was frighteningly gaunt and his voice hoarse and weak. They gave him a bat, but instead of walking into the batter's box and show-ing that mighty swing that had captured so much history in this place, he used it to balance himself.

He talked to his fans.

"Thank you very much, ladies and gentlemen. You know how bad my voice sounds. Well, it feels just as bad. You know, this baseball game of ours comes up from the youth. The only real game in the world, I think, is baseball. As a rule some people think if you give them a football or a baseball or something like that, naturally they're athletes right away. But you can't do that in baseball. You've got to start from way down, at the bottom, when you're six or seven years old. You can't wait until you're fifteen or sixteen. You've got to let it grow up with you and if you're successful and you try hard enough, you're bound to come out on top."

It was his standard stuff and he'd given it many times. But this was his last performance.

◆

I had been to the Toronto Islands before, but this time was differ-ent. When I was there as a kid it was on a school trip or with the family or sometimes just with Grandpa. Those were the best times. There were thrilling rides and I was always fascinated by the little pedal boats. They skirted through the canals and water-ways that wound like snakes through the islands. Everything was so manicured it was like a postcard and it hadn't changed much.

But this time my state of mind wasn't that of a six-year-old filling a lazy summer afternoon. This time I had a mission and it was a crazy enough mission. Grandpa wanted that ball and I was determined to get it.

This was exactly where it happened. The home run. The old ballpark on Hanlan's Point had existed somewhere out there on a little runway at the Island Airport. That was what the guide said. He wasn't more than twenty – none of them were more than twenty – and his knowledge of history probably depended on what others told him, but he was sure this was where the ballpark was.

There were only three other passengers with me on the ferry to Hanlan's Point that day. One of them was a boy about my age with bleached hair caked back over his scalp. Two earrings hung from his ear lobes and a bag that said "Carlsberg" was slung over his shoulder. I imagined how my grandmother would have reacted. She would have made a few not-so-indiscreet sneers and then shaken her head in disgust and done it all right in front of him so there was no mistaking her intent. Grandpa would have snickered under his breath and just laughed. More at her than at him.

I thought about him when I went to bed at night and when I got up in the morning. I thought about him at breakfast . . . lunch . . . and dinner. I thought about him at school and when I was out with my friends and even then it was impossible to de-rive any enjoyment from life. He was just with me.

Constantly.

Out in the middle of the bay I recalled the story he told me about his first ball game. He took this same route and it was so long ago. It was even longer than some people lived. But it was no use trying to rationalize what was happening to him. I had tried that many times since he got sick and it didn't help.

He was my grandfather. I loved him dearly and now he was slipping away from me. I was losing him. I would be on my own.

More than ever before. I would be vulnerable. Who would there be to love?

I was eighteen and had my whole life ahead of me, but everything was gray and unyielding. The gulls were crying, but there was even something different about them just as there was something different about the way the water sounded as it smacked against the ferry.

Empty.

There was only one thing left to do. Get that ball that was a guidepost for his whole life and now it was for me as well. But where do you begin searching for a ball that landed in the bay seventy-seven years ago? I saw a photograph of the old park at Hanlan's Point. It was still called Hanlan's Point, but there was no ballpark anymore. It was long gone. I know that a larger and better park called Maple Leaf Stadium – home to the minor league Maple Leafs – once sat on the mainland, but that was gone too. Long before I was born.

I didn't know where to start looking and even if I did I didn't know what I was going to do. I had my swimsuit with me thinking that I might really go in. But I didn't know. There was no plan or strategy. It wasn't like I had a map with a big "X" showing the location of a missing treasure. But still there was no questioning my being there. No questioning my walking on the same hallowed ground that the Providence Grays and their prized pitcher once walked on so many years ago.

I was in the same place. But was it the same place? How could I be sure and was it even the same ground? So much of the islands came from landfill. They say it came from excavations for the last subway line. Maybe some of it came from the Bluffs, which were several miles to the east. The Bluffs, long a victim to water erosion, were protected now by a man-made strip of buffer.

Nothing was the same.

I couldn't come back empty-handed and even though none of it made any sense, I was driven to being there in that place where Grandpa's life was written out with the blow of a bat against a ball.

The first thing you see when stepping off the ferry is a plaque for Ned Hanlan, the great oarsman who once held the world single-sculls championship. That was more than a hundred years ago. The place was named after him, but there was another plaque. More off the beaten path. Not far from the docks where the ferry was resting.

"The plaque over there," one of the guides said pointing to the east. "It's about Babe Ruth and his home run. The old ballpark was over there. Right where the airport is now."

"I heard that the ball landed in the bay and it's been there ever since. Is that right?"

"That's what they say. That it's still out there in the water somewhere. In the old days, a guy used to patrol the bay in a rowboat and he used to pick up the balls that fell in but they never found that one. It's still there. That's what they say."

I should have asked him who exactly *they* were, but I knew. Yehudi.

I thanked him and walked toward the plaque that most people would miss unless they knew about it beforehand and I don't imagine many did. It sat innocent and nondescript on top of a rock just beside the roadway:

Near this site, at the old Hanlan's Point Stadium on 5 September, 1914, baseball's legendary Babe Ruth hit his first home run as a professional – the only home run he ever hit in the minor leagues. The lanky 19-year-old rookie, playing for the Providence Grays in the International League, connected with a pitch off Ellis Johnson of the Toronto Maple Leafs, sending the ball over the fence in right field and scoring three runs for his team. Ruth, as pitcher of the team, allowed only one hit and the Grays shut out Toronto 9-0. His later career made Babe Ruth a monumental figure in baseball history.

I read it again and again. I couldn't get enough of it. Here was living proof of that epic moment other than Grandpa himself. It really happened. Babe Ruth had indeed hit a home run here back in 1914. I stood back and tried to judge how far the plaque was from the water's edge. Then I imagined a great Ruthian clout and thought I could see the ball sailing into the bay.

How far was it to the water?

I paced off ninety-eight steps which was about three hundred feet. But that was just to the water. There was no natural shoreline formed by the elements. A steel barrier that jutted up three or four feet from the surface of the water served as the island's edge now. I looked back at the plaque. Three hundred feet. If it was three hundred feet from home plate to the bay then the ball could have gone another hundred feet out there into the deep.

I could see the city skyline and the new baseball stadium where the Blue Jays played. SkyDome. It was a huge steel trap, a mammoth stadium that could hold more than fifty thousand people with a roof that opened and closed according to the movement of the rain clouds. It stood out like a big white mushroom and brought back all the snide remarks Grandpa used to say about baseball.

"They're not ballplayers today. They used to be ballplayers but not now. They don't work as hard. They're not hungry like they used to be. Hell, they make a million dollars apiece and all they do is stand around waiting for things to happen. They don't love the game, either. That's the worst part."

I wondered.

The pitchers don't work as hard. That's for sure. Today pitching a complete game is rare, but not back then. Grandpa told me about the time Babe Ruth the pitcher, on only three days rest, beat Walter Johnson 1-0 in thirteen innings and both men went the distance. That couldn't happen now. The game is much too specialized. Pitchers are pulled from the mound like pawns in a game of chess. They might come in to pitch to only one batter as the managers second guess each other about who should throw to whom. Laws of averages. Best percentage shots. But they have to do that. A lot of money is at stake. Advertising. Television revenue. A player can make millions of dollars a year as a designated hitter and never wear a glove. How can you be a baseball player and never wear a glove?

I never claimed to believe in spirits, but I felt absorbed by spirits that afternoon. I felt the spirits of the old ballplayers in their old uniforms. I felt the presence of my great grandfather, Josef Slackowicz, long dead, and even of Grandpa himself as an eight-year-old boy named Lazo. There wasn't much time.

I picked up a stone and dropped it into the water, but there was no telling how far down it went before it struck the bottom. Or even if it did. Yet, somewhere on the bottom was that ball and I had to get it.

No one was around. Just me standing alone on the grass between two abandoned lifeguard stations. There was a ladder and a pole and a lifejacket at each one of them and I wondered if this is how they would rescue me. What would I tell them? That I was looking for the home run ball hit by Babe Ruth in 1914? Would they believe that?

Would anyone believe it?

Six tall elm trees were near the water's edge. I didn't know how to tell the age of an elm from sight, but these were old specimens and as I played with the thought of going in I could see them laughing at me, tantalizing me with all the history hidden beneath their dried-up bark. There was a face on one of them. Two big circles where branches had been cut became a giant pair of eyes staring at me, daring me to go back to that time when life was simpler and harder, when the world was on the verge of ripping itself apart with the Great War. When Babe Ruth was all of nineteen, a strapping youth with an amazing fastball.

"How deep is it?" I asked out loud, but the ghosts wouldn't answer. I knew they were there. I could sense them dancing in the mist over the water and feel them breathing down my neck, but they were deathly silent. Then I heard it. The cheering from the airport runway just past the fence. The voices. Celebrating that tremendous home run shot off Ellis Johnson.

A home run, Papa! He got a home run!

I could see a dream building in a boy's mind. About being a ballplayer. And following in the footsteps of his hero. It would be a tragedy, this dream, but the best dreams always are and then I heard him. Crystal clear.

"If you find that ball, Stephen, you can be anything you want to be."

Grandpa. He was talking to me.

"It has a magnetism and it's reaching out to you. You must find it. You have to find it."

I climbed over the wire fence and walked another fifty yards to where some large rocks anchored the east end of the airport grounds against the bay. I took off my shoes and socks and looked up at the six elms that were still laughing at me.

The ghosts were everywhere.

I stripped naked and didn't care if they could see me. I had no shame. I was even proud of what I was doing. I was doing it for Grandpa and for all the hopes and dreams that schoolboys take with them as they toil through the game.

I put on my swimsuit, slid my body along the edges of the rocks and dipped my feet into the water. It was cold. Ice cold. I went in and a shiver ran up my legs. For the first time I felt the stiff breeze against my face.

I surveyed the water before me and visualized a large square with the north part of it open to the bay and mainland. I was near the rocks and looked out across to the ferry dock at Hanlan's Point, but I could only see water. The steel barrier that marked the edge of Hanlan's Point was another line in the square, to the south, so there was an area of about four hundred feet in each direction to cover. Somewhere in this expansive drink was that ball.

I swam out a short way and thought of marathon swimmers who spend thirty hours or more in the water crossing the lake from one country to another. I pushed out in front of the elms and past them to where that ball had splashed.

If that plaque really was near home plate there wouldn't be too much water to cover. The ball went over the right field fence so I swam out to the most likely spot and then went under. I opened my eyes and saw nothing. Only the cold black water of the bay. Deeper and deeper I plunged, all the while counting my strokes, hoping to see the bottom so I could return to the surface and then go in again but this time knowing how long I'd have before coming up.

But no.

I could have been in the middle of the ocean for all I knew.

There was no end to that depth and finally I had to twist my head up and push back to the surface where I filled my lungs with oxygen. This wasn't going to be easy.

I was just off the land, it couldn't have been very deep, and if only man had let things be I would have taken a few strokes and seen the bottom. I would have gone in as many times as it took and then I would have found it, or what was left of it, sitting there on the floor.

Waiting.

But man had stepped in. He had removed the natural shoreline and erected a steel barrier in its place. He had changed the very shape of the land, digging here, adding there, undoing what the ages had done, making it impossible to find a link with the past.

I didn't know how deep the bay was and even if I did I couldn't be sure my ears would stand the pressure. I decided to try again. This time I inhaled as much air as possible before going under. I did ten strokes, eleven, twelve, thirteen, fourteen, fifteen – more than the first time – and still there was no end to it. My lungs were going to burst right then and there so I pushed back to the surface where my mouth exploded open as soon as I broke through the water.

When the sound of my gasping subsided into slow easy breaths, the voices came back. I could hear them. The cheering. I opened my eyes and could even see them standing in the bleachers in that old stadium that faced out to the bay.

There was a boy and a man. His father. They were clapping their hands. Everyone was clapping. A tall solitary figure was jogging around the base paths and as he touched down on first the ball sailed out over the right field fence. I saw it drop into the water with a soft *plop* and when he came home the players mobbed him. Still the spectators cheered. He emerged from the dugout and tipped his cap.

I closed my eyes and it happened again. The boy. The man. The runner. The cheering. The clapping. He touched first base. The ball sailed over the fence and I imagined I was an eagle. In flight. My eyes were fixed on the arc the ball was carving through the sky. It went way over the fence. Easily clearing the tops of the trees near the shoreline.

Once again it fell into the bay and I marked the exact spot in my brain as new strength flowed through my body. I filled my lungs and went in a third time. I did ten strokes before I even opened my eyes and then I looked and wished for the bottom to appear, but there was only blackness. I did ten more strokes, my arms slowing with each one, until there was nothing left and my chest cried for air. The faces were with me and one of them, a big round moon face, motioned down to the left.

"It's just over here, keed. Can't you see it?"

"Where? Where is it?"

"A bit further. Just a bit further. It's right ahead of you. It's always been there. Waiting for you. Go ahead. Take it. Give it to him."

Grandpa was dying and he wanted that ball. There wasn't much time. It was here. I knew it was here. I could feel it pulling me. Through the years. It was his vision. It was a vision we shared. The three of us. It was a dream. We were dealing in dreams. And a dream I had to deliver.

◆

Lazo was bitterly torn the day the Babe died. There wasn't just one but two momentous events occurring in his life, and it was impossible to be in two places at the same time. He had to choose and even though he knew which way his mind would go from the beginning no one understood.

How could they?

The Babe died in his sleep one summer night in 1948. They knew it was close at hand. Four weeks earlier he had received the last rites of the Catholic Church, but then he recovered enough to attend the opening of the film, *The Babe Ruth Story,* and soon it was back to hospital where he stayed. The reporters held a vigil outside as they waited anxiously for the end to come so they could tell the world and when it happened it was almost a relief since his suffering had finally ended.

The tumor that originated in his neck was pressing on the nerves leading from his brain. It was a rotten way for a man like him to die. But Lazo couldn't think of a good way for a man like Babe Ruth to leave the earth. Men like him just don't die. Do they?

He was only fifty-three and had been utterly lost since he had quit playing the game. Thirteen years of pretended pleasures weren't convincing to those who knew him well. As sure as God put man on the earth to multiply, this man was born – he was *meant* – to play baseball. He had a gift, a gift no one could explain. He just had this uncanny ability to hit a ball farther than anyone else and just keep doing it.

The next day all the radio networks interrupted their programming to pay tributes. The flag at the Baseball Hall of Fame in Cooperstown flew at half mast and people from all over – baseball fans and non-fans alike – were moved.

Kids everywhere loved him dearly. They always had. Lazo stood in the rain outside Yankee Stadium where the Babe's body was lying in state and he could see hundreds, maybe thousands, of young boys who had never even seen him play standing in line waiting for a chance to file past the casket and pay their respects. Many of them were with their fathers, their fathers who were young boys themselves once.

The Babe touched them all.

"That's Babe Ruth," the father would tell his son, "the greatest baseball player that ever lived," and the boy would gape in awe at Ruth's lifeless body. Slowly, methodically, the huge queue that surrounded the building moved ahead.

Lazo had stood in line for hours waiting to get in, but there were so many people, many more than there ever were for a game, that things just inched along. But no one left. No one. He heard people tell perfect strangers about their vivid memories of his skills on the field and some of them even said they actually knew him or were friendly with him or at least had an experience of note in his company.

Lazo felt like that. He had a special relationship with him. Maybe there were others who saw his last home run in Pittsburgh.

Maybe there were even a few who saw his first one in Toronto, but no one could have been affected by him the way Lazo was.

It wasn't the Babe's fault Lazo wasn't good enough and maybe it wasn't anybody's fault. But it wasn't the Babe's. What more could he have done? He gave Lazo the dream – he practically handed it to him – and did everything he was supposed to do by racking up all those records and changing the very nature of the game.

Lazo ambled into Yankee Stadium – where he had hoped to play one day – and was compelled to remove his hat. This building was a shrine. Not a church or a temple, but a shrine. It was an institution that would occupy a place in history. This was the House that Ruth Built. He built it just as if he had carried every brick and piece of mortar that went into it and he had emerged at exactly the right time to show how good the game could be.

That was what he did. That was his legacy. To show how good the game could be.

Lazo burst into tears when he thought about being in Yankee Stadium and seeing the great Babe for the last time. And what did he give up to be here? What was his sacrifice? He gave up the birth of his first child, a boy who was born the very night Babe Ruth died.

August 16, 1948.

Nobody understood.

"You can hear about Babe Ruth on the radio," they said.

"You can read about him in the paper. You can even visit one of your rich friends who has a television set and watch an old newsreel of him but going all the way to New York for his funeral is insane."

But Lazo had to go and the fact his son was being born the same night the Babe died convinced him more than anything that some hidden meaning was behind all of this. There was a reason. There had to be. For everything that ever happened to him. And if his life and the Babe's were entwined in some way, then he just had to come.

He had to.

It was touching to see the little children drop the poems they had written as they passed his coffin. Some even said, "Hi Babe" or "Hello Mr. Ruth" before being shuffled along. Men would pause and stare blankly at him and women would leave cards or bend over and kiss him. Then it was his turn. Lazo found himself talking to him when he approached the coffin and there was no thinking about what to say. It just poured out.

"You're really dead, aren't you? I can't believe it. You meant so much to me, Babe. No words can explain it. You were everything. You gave me something to shoot for and I tried to be like you. Oh, how I tried to be like you but I couldn't. I just couldn't. There was only one Babe Ruth. I worshipped you more than any boy could worship a man and to me you were more than a man. You were a dream but you were real. I saw you and I know you remember because of what we meant to each other. It was special. I'll miss you, Babe. God I'll miss you."

Then Lazo touched him on the face, that big round face he had come to love.

"Good-bye, Babe."

He wiped the tears from his eyes and thought of his newborn son who was destined to begin life just when the Babe was ending his. How could this possibly be if not by design?

He had the kind of funeral fitting for a head of state. Only FDR's was larger. And the year after he died they added a third monument next to Gehrig's and Huggins' in deep center field at Yankee Stadium. The words said he was a great ballplayer, a great man, and a great American – and he was. He was all of those things.

He was the Babe.

◆

He was lying on his side facing the window when I arrived. I came to the foot of the bed and called him, but he didn't answer. His eyes were wide open and he stared blankly through the glass. Unblinking.

"Grandpa? It's me. Stephen. Can you see me?"

No response. Not a sign of life in him. His body had withered to ninety pounds and the hospital pajamas they gave him hung loosely from his frame. I was powerless and useless and felt so empty inside. Like I was rotting away with him.

There was a ball in my hands. Its skin was dark, almost soot-blackened, and its surface wasn't smooth, but crusty and rough like the scales of a fish that had been submerged for a great length of time. I held it in front of me and showed it to him.

"Grandpa, look. I've got it. I found it. The ball. Babe Ruth's ball. The one he hit when you were a boy. I've got it. Here."

He moved his head and looked at me. Confused.

"Grandpa. This is the ball. The one you wanted. I found it."

His mouth opened and he tried to speak, but no words would come. His lips touched once, twice, and he desperately fought to put a message together, but his voice was gone. He waved his hand, urging me to raise his bed so he could sit up and I did. I sat there with him. Then I pried open his two hands, put them side by side, and placed the ball into the waiting cradle that they formed.

"That's the ball, Grandpa. Babe Ruth's ball. The one he hit in 1914. His first home run. Remember?"

For a moment he was still. Hauntingly still. Then his eyes lit up like magic and his face became a thing of joy. It was a look I'll never forget as long as I live. It was a look I will always associate with Grandpa.

And dreams.

". . . Stephen . . ."

It was nothing more than a whisper.

"Yes, Grandpa?"

"The . . . ball? The . . . ball?"

"Yes, Grandpa. That's it. I found it."

His fingers shook like an old man's, but they were wrapped around that ball and nothing was going to tear them away from it. Then he began to cry and so did I, but I couldn't let him see. No. My tears were for outside this building. Here in this room where we kept watch over him, I could only show faith, hope, and my deep love for him.

"Grandpa," I said and held his hands in mine.

It was only a baseball and back in 1914 it was only a baseball, but something happened to it. It was touched by a dream and that made it more. Much more.

I stared at his shriveled body and knew instantly there is so much more than the little we see. There is a soul inside crying to come out and in so many people it never does. Maybe in most of us it never does, but not Grandpa. He was always there for the taking and for the giving. Sometimes he was awfully good at hiding it and pretending it didn't exist at all, but he couldn't fool me. He couldn't fool me when I was six and he couldn't fool me now.

He wanted me to lower his bed so he could sleep. I looked into his blue eyes and smiled and when he was flat on his back he whispered some names that I recognized immediately.

"Bananas," he uttered as if it was some tremendous secret.

I couldn't be sure, but I think he smiled back.

"Bananas . . ." he repeated in a whisper. "Bananas . . . Shorty . . . Pancake . . ."

He had the ball in his hands and squeezed it with the little strength he had. Then he said another name.

"Hoodlum . . ." he said shaking his head and I think he was carrying that ball for all of them.

For all of us.

He looked up at me and then I left him there draped in the happiness that eluded him for so long, relishing in the joy that dreams do come true as long as you believe in them. You've got to believe in them. He died that night with all of us around him. My mother and father. My grandmother. Uncle Joe and Auntie Ellen. We were all there. I wasn't even sure just when it happened because he fell asleep clutching that baseball to his breast and never regained consciousness.

His time had come.

Epilogue

It's been a year since Grandpa died, a year to the day, and I know he would have liked a day like this. It is warm, warmer than usual for this time of year. A leisurely breeze is dancing in from the lake, a balance against the hot rays of the sun that are beating upon my head. The soft whispering sounds of this place are just as they've always been, nothing short of a symphony of life, no matter how small or inconsequential the source. Those sounds. I hear them playing so freely. The birds are everywhere. Their music never stops. Not even for a second. Their songs blend into a carefully orchestrated harmony with the rustling of the leaves of the trees in the background. Now and then the sea gulls, who for centuries have hovered here, release their patented cheer as they swoop down from higher altitudes and soar over the exposed clay deposits of the Bluffs.

There is a prominent mound of soft-dried clay that has been savagely worn by the wind and rain. When I was small and used to come here with him it wasn't a mound at all, but a tower. The rampart of an old *great* castle. It rose high above those scarred cliffs like God watching over his domain. But it's gone now.

There isn't even a glimmer of the respect it once commanded. In less than fifteen years it has disappeared and only the memory of how it once was can bring it back for me.

The Bluffs receive many visitors on a day like this. Some of them live nearby and come only to snare a moment from the world and its pace that never abates. They know what to expect but they keep returning just the same. Others are here for the first time and it's easy to spot them as their virgin eyes swallow the magnificent timelessness of the peace that is captured here.

I still feel that way. The tranquility of this place is enough to stop the pendulum from swinging. If only for an instant. It gives me a chance to begin exploring my reason for being and for everything that happens.

Why does the shoreline curve the way it does and why are the Bluffs so much higher here where I stand than they are just off to the west? Why does this oxygen replenish my lungs with renewed vigor while every other planet known to man would squeeze the very life from me? Why do these trees grow as they do into long twisting pretzels of wood and bark? How did all these insects of such spectacular shapes and sizes that defy imagination come about? Where is the blueprint for all this fine work and who is its craftsman?

Far out on the lake a sailboat is sitting on the water like a speck of dust on a smooth undulating windowpane. It is vulnerable to the elements as it rocks and sways with the waves and the air currents that catch its white canvas with ease. Now and then a strong gust blows in and gently pushes it along to wherever it's headed. But just as mysteriously the current suddenly dies, there is only stillness in the air and the little sailboat rests without going anywhere at all.

There is no answer as to why it happens. It just does.

I am lost in such thoughts until the buzzing of a bee brings me back to reality. The bee makes me uneasy since I know the power of its sting. It lands on the ground near my feet and I could step on it and kill it so easily if I wanted and might have if I was five or six and didn't understand that its reason is every bit as valid as my own.

I think that is one of Grandpa's greatest gifts to me. Respect for life. He showed me that the world is greater than mere immediate surroundings and that everything capable of movement, everything that's placed upon the earth for some small tangible reason, is worthy of some measure of respect. That is one of his greatest gifts and the knowledge that what we see isn't all there is.

There is always something more.

We can ask questions and beat ourselves to death with mind games if we choose and fancy that we are the center of the universe. But who consults us when it rains or snows? Do we wield some omniscient mastery over earthquakes and droughts? What role do we play when the skies finally clear and the great ball of gases in our sun gives light and warmth to everything below? Humans think they have accomplished so much, but they are in no more command of things than that little sailboat out on the lake or that single pebble that sits alone on the sandy beach at the bottom of the Bluffs.

The local authorities, who for years grappled with how to preserve the majestic raw beauty of the Bluffs, finally came up with their solution. Thousands of tons of landfill piled end over end down there at the base. A sprawling waterfront park and marina with long grassy tentacles and spits of sand reaching out in hideous man-made ugliness. And for what purpose? To protect those edges from further erosion. The marina, home to hundreds of private boats, looks like high-density housing from the city, and what view isn't spoiled by that parking lot of outboards is tarnished by a long road running down the center and by a concrete parking lot jammed with cars, minivans, and pickup trucks.

How Grandpa would have laughed and sneered had he seen this travesty. He would have laughed out loud. I can see and hear him doing it just as if he was standing by me this very minute.

"Those idiots. They think they saved the Bluffs with this monstrosity they created but they haven't. Why don't they just leave it all alone? Nature formed the Bluffs and nature will just as surely change them. That's how it goes. They should let it be. The only thing they did was destroy a beautiful view of the lake and if they don't dig it up themselves and change it back the day will come when another Ice Age will roll over that thing like it's nothing. Mark my words, Stephen. It'll happen. You're darn tootin it'll happen."

He is buried not far away in an old and quaint – if I can use such a word – cemetery. It is the only cemetery near the Bluffs and some of the gravestones go back to the early 1800s. Somehow I always knew he would wind up here.

A whole year has passed and it's just like yesterday that I was walking with him. Asking him about the glaciers and the mountains of ice. But I believe what he is saying. That the Ice Age will return. It will. Even the scientists say it will return.

The night he died he held that ball in his hands, that magical ball I had purchased two days earlier. The box said "Official American League Baseball" and on the inside it was wrapped. Just like a gift. In tissue paper. It was everything a modern baseball should be with a cushioned cork center, the name "Rawling's" in blue, the bright red stitching, and the signature of the league president added as a stamp of approval. The outside of the ball was clean and white since it was brand new and had never been used. Not even for a bunt.

After taking it home and soaking it for hours in the sink, I waited for the rains to come and then went to the ravine where he had first explained about the tadpoles and metamorphosis. It was there that I dug a hole, planted it in the soft muck, and left it overnight where it miraculously aged three-quarters of a century.

It was a treasure, a diamond, a piece of gold. It gave off an energy that escaped time and place and that changed grown men into little boys and back again.

That ball had a power. Just the way he always said. What did it matter that the real thing was lost forever in the deep dark waters of the bay? To Grandpa this was the symbol of his dreams. It was the symbol of a game and a man whose skill could only be described as *awesome* and who played the game so well he became a living and breathing God to all who worshipped him.

That was the only kind of God Grandpa could hang onto.

One he could see and touch and read about.

One that was a man.

That was the kind of God I always worshiped. A man. He was a ballplayer too, and a ballplayer I had never known until it was almost too late. But that was just a small part of him. A tiny almost insignificant part. The truest dimension of Grandpa was his heart, his huge magnificent heart that reached out and touched me in a way no one else could.

His funeral was a day of black and flowers. Of crowded limousines rented by the hour. Of distant cousins I barely knew. It was a day of open graves and caskets being lowered into the ground. It was a day of quiet reflection. A day to observe a man who lived his life as it was meant to be and it would have been worse if not for that ball.

The night he died they found it still in his grasp and when they asked what it was doing there and how it got there I just told them to give it to me. Later when the brief service was finished and I stood over him and planted a kiss on his forehead – it had so many lines I couldn't count them all – I tucked the ball under his throwing hand, his left hand, wrapped his fingers around it and placed his other hand on top so no one could see. A moment later they closed the coffin and that ball is still with him today.

It will stay with him long after I'm gone and long after my children are gone. It will stay with him after the last man has departed from this earth and even after the next ice age comes to carry everything away. It will stay with him when his remains are but another granule in an earlier layer of life not far above those of the ancient trilobites and sea turtles. It will stay with him.

Forever.

Acknowledgments

I would like to thank some special people who helped me along the way in writing *Gift of the Bambino.*

John Robert Colombo was the first editor who reviewed the manuscript in its original, longer form, and his thoughtful insights and knowledge of what goes into a story were of great help and inspiration. He hung on with me through thick and thin and I am forever grateful.

I would also like to thank all those wonderful people I met at Hofstra University who accepted me into their Babe Ruth fraternity at the conference "Baseball and the Sultan of Swat." This was a chance to learn more about the man from sportswriters, announcers, and people who knew him. It was also an opportunity to meet Robert Creamer, former baseball editor at *Sports Illustrated,* whose excellent biography *Babe: The Legend Comes to Life* helped point me in the right direction when there were many forks in the road.

I would like to thank the Lizzies organization and, in particular, one very special reunion where I was able to meet many gentlemen who played baseball in the old days.

I cannot ignore the City of New York, which has suffered so much, and which has shown such courage and resilience in its recovery, for providing the stage for baseball's greatest star and, most important, for never forgetting him.

Special thanks must also go to Paul Quarrington, whom I first met at the Humber School of Writers in 1992 and who is as fine a gentleman as he is a writer; editor Lori McLellan who helped clean up my grammar, and Max Maccari of Boheme Press for seeing promise in the *Bambino*.

To my wife, Dorothy, and to Michael and Michelle: Thank you for your understanding during all those hours when I while away at my keyboard.

And last, but certainly not least, I would like to thank my father – the original southpaw – who in his kindness to my children was able to show me what being a grandfather is all about.

About the Author

Jerry Amernic started his career as a newspaper reporter, but eventually went out on his own as a public relations consultant, specializing in the media. Over the years he has been a newspaper columnist, feature writer for magazines, editor, and adviser to many organizations. He was a member of the inaugural class of the Humber School of Writers at Humber College of Applied Arts and Technology in Toronto, where he later taught writing in the School of Media Studies. *Gift of the Bambino* is his first novel, and he is currently at work on another. He lives with his wife and family in Toronto.